"A beautiful, comforting, and wildly satisfying end to our [...] Rebel Blue! This book is as tender as it gets while also serving up the hottest, down bad cowboy I've ever read!"
—Sarah Adams, *New York Times* bestselling author of *The Rule Book*

"*Wild and Wrangled* is as sweet, achy, and sexy as we've come to expect from Lyla Sage. Dusty and Cam make my heart hurt and my skin tingle. This is absolutely my favorite of the Rebel Blue Ranch series!"
—Julie Soto, *USA Today* bestselling author

"*Wild and Wrangled* is the romance genre at its finest! Cam and Dusty's chemistry leaps off the page, and their second-chance romance melted my heart. I am so sad to say goodbye to the Ryder family, but I could not think of a more fitting end to the Rebel Blue Ranch series!'"
—Falon Ballard, author of *Right on Cue*

"*Wild and Wrangled* is a swoon-worthy, show-stopping conclusion to the Rebel Blue series. Sage truly shines with Dusty and Cam's story, flawlessly weaving fun flirtation with aching tenderness. I never want to say goodbye to the Rebel Blue series, but Sage knocks it out of the park. Tattoo this book on my body like Dusty's ink, please."
—BK Borison, *USA Today* bestselling author of *Business Casual*

"*Wild and Wrangled* is the perfect farewell to the Rebel Blue Ranch series. Dusty and Cam's story shines with what I love so much about Lyla Sage's world: it's comforting and soft, filled with hot cowboys (important), and it serves as a reminder that home will always be there waiting for you when you're ready to go back. I dare you to get to the last page without turning right back around to walk through the gates of Rebel Blue all over again. I'll see you there."
—Jessica Joyce, *USA Today* bestselling author of *The Ex Vows*

By Lyla Sage

Done and Dusted
Swift and Saddled
Lost and Lassoed
Wild and Wrangled

WILD AND WRANGLED

WILD AND WRANGLED

A Rebel Blue Ranch Novel

LYLA SAGE

The Dial Press

New York

A Dial Press Trade Paperback Original

Published in the United States by The Dial Press, an imprint of
Random House, a division of Penguin Random House LLC,
1745 Broadway, New York, NY 10019.

THE DIAL PRESS is a registered trademark and the colophon is a trademark
of Penguin Random House LLC.

DIAL DELIGHTS and colophon are trademarks of
Penguin Random House LLC.

LIBRARY OF CONGRESS CATALOGING-IN-PUBLICATION DATA
Names: Sage, Lyla, author.
Title: Wild and wrangled / Lyla Sage.
Description: New York, NY: The Dial Press, 2025.
Identifiers: LCCN 2024040662 (print) | LCCN 2024040663 (ebook) |
ISBN 9780593732472 (paperback; acid-free paper) |
ISBN 9780593732489 (ebook)
Subjects: LCGFT: Romance fiction. | Novels.
Classification: LCC PS3619.A384 W55 2025 (print) | LCC PS3619.A384 (ebook) |
DDC 813/.6—dc23/eng/20240830
LC record available at https://lccn.loc.gov/2024040662
LC ebook record available at https://lccn.loc.gov/2024040663

Printed in the United States of America on acid-free paper

randomhousebooks.com
penguinrandomhouse.com

2 4 6 8 9 7 5 3 1

Book design by Virginia Norey
Mountain: nura/ stock.adobe.com
Cowboy hat: DELstudio/ stock.adobe.com

The authorized representative in the EU for product safety and compliance
is Penguin Random House Ireland, Morrison Chambers, 32 Nassau Street,
Dublin D02 YH68, Ireland, https://eucontact.penguin.ie.

This one is for me—for the girl who had a dream
and for the woman who made it come true.

And for my mom, who taught me how to dream
in the first place.

Author's Note

Dear Reader,

I am not a good enough writer to even begin to describe the feelings and emotions that are swirling around in my head, heart, and soul as I share the last book in the Rebel Blue Ranch series with you. But I'm not sure if I'm ready to talk about this being the end, so instead, I'll go back to the beginning.

Rebel Blue Ranch started as a place of refuge for me— a place I could go in my head when I was longing for sunshine and big blue skies. When I decided to share this wonderful place with others, nothing could've prepared me for what was about to happen: all of you.

From the bottom of my heart, thank you for coming on this journey with me—for running alongside me, cheering me on, and making my dreams come true. The past two years have been the absolute best of my life.

Because of that, it's equal parts bitter, sweet, thrilling, and terrifying to share the last novel of the Rebel Blue Ranch series with you. Cam and Dusty's love story is one that I've held close to my chest since I first started kicking around the idea for this series. They challenged me and pushed me. They made me cry, and they made me laugh. I wrote this book with my heart in my throat and a hand on my heart.

I've always said that Rebel Blue Ranch is a love letter to the people and places that built me. That's still true, but *Wild and*

Wrangled is more than that. It's a love letter to Rebel Blue Ranch itself—to the family that was found, the love stories that were told, and the community that has shown up for every part of it.

This book, just like the sunrise on its cover, is also a tribute to new beginnings. It's an evergreen reminder that even though this series is coming to an end, the horizon remains vast, beautiful, and ours for the taking.

And who knows, maybe I'll meet you at the Rebel Blue Ranch headgate again someday. Because nothing lasts forever, you know. Not even goodbyes.

Welcome home.

Lyla

WILD AND WRANGLED

Chapter 1

Cam

In my opinion, there was almost nothing better than a good checklist. Crossing things off was probably the best feeling in the world. Today, my checklist was supposed to be easy—mindless, even—because, for the first time in who knows how long, there was only one thing on it: get married.

I'd done everything else. I got the marriage license, showed up to the chapel, and wore the ballgown my mother picked out. It should've been simple—walk down the aisle, listen to the generic vows the officiant was told to use, and plant one on my fiancé.

So why was I sitting in the diviest dive bar in all of Wyoming, wearing my wedding dress, drinking straight vodka?

As with nearly every large project, getting married required more than one person. But group projects had never been my strong suit. I didn't like putting my fate in the hands of others, but today I thought I'd be fine. How much harm can one other person do to something so easy?

A lot, actually. Because if just one person doesn't show up, everything goes to shit.

Well, my groom didn't show up, and everything went to shit.

I thought about the note he'd left—noble of him—as I picked up my glass of vodka and took a healthy swig.

Camille,
I'm sorry. I couldn't do it.
Graham

I ignored the eyes of the other Devil's Boot patrons that were burning into the back of my skull, wondering why poor Camille was sitting at the bar in her wedding dress when she was supposed to be getting married.

I felt the alcohol burn all the way down my throat. I took another sip. And another. *He* couldn't do it? This whole thing was *his* idea. He was the one who said it was going to be okay, that we would be as happy as we could be.

And then *he* didn't show up.

He didn't even warn me, just left me the note on the dressing room table. As I was reading it, Amos Ryder knocked on the door. Amos was my daughter, Riley's, grandfather, but he was also the closest thing I had to a loving and steady father figure. I'd originally asked him to walk me down the aisle today, but my actual father wasn't very pleased with that and did what he normally did: threatened to cause a scene, take away my and my daughter's inheritance, revoke her trust fund—that sort of thing.

So I gave in. I always give in.

But when I needed someone, my dad was nowhere near

the scene. Amos, however, was always there when it mattered. Ever since the day Gus, his son, told him I was pregnant, Amos has treated me like another daughter.

He had spent the morning of the wedding with me because I asked him to. Amos was a good person to have around when you were worried that nerves might get the best of you. He was calm and strong and steady—like a river, Gus had always said. I always wished he could've sat next to me when I took the bar exam—no doubt I would've passed on the first try.

"Come in," I croaked, and as soon as I saw his black-and-gray hair and soft green eyes, tears bubbled up in my own. I wasn't sad because Graham wasn't here and wasn't coming but because I'd already given up so much of myself for this wedding, and now it wasn't going to happen. I was sad about the complete waste of time and effort.

"Cam?" he'd said as he closed the door behind him and rushed toward me. "What's wrong?" His eyes zeroed in on the note in my hand, and I watched his face fall. He knew.

Instead of answering, I let out a shaky breath and hugged him. He hugged me back. Riley, who had followed her grandpa into the room, jumped in the hug, too, even though she didn't know what was going on. That girl just loves a snuggle.

"Let's go see if your dad is here, Sunshine," he said to her. She nodded excitedly and twirled in her flower girl dress. She was so damn excited to throw petals and walk down the aisle before me. My chest constricted. How could I even tell her what had happened?

"Can you . . . can you send him back here?" I asked quietly.

Amos brought Gus back less than a minute later. I told him Graham wasn't coming and that I needed him and his fiancée, Teddy, to take Riley for the rest of the day. Since I'd had a second to compose myself, my voice was professional—unfeeling, even—but the look Gus was giving me was anything but. His nostrils flared, and I could almost see him biting his tongue—trying not to let his anger get the best of him.

"I need to get out of here," I said as I ripped the veil out of the low chignon it had been secured in just a few minutes earlier.

"Go," Gus and Amos said at the same time. "We'll take care of it," Gus followed up. I trusted them to do that. I ran out the back of the church—not in a runaway bride on her way to freedom sort of way, but in a jilted bride who needed to keep moving so she didn't crumble type of way.

Well, that was depressing as hell.

And now I was here mainlining vodka at three in the afternoon. I was sufficiently buzzed—the tension in my neck and shoulders loosened by the alcohol. Maybe I'd stay here all day—listen to Hank Williams wax poetic about tears and beers from the jukebox until the sun went down. Then, maybe I'd ride the mechanical bull in my wedding dress and give the town even more to talk about.

I picked my drink up again and was deeply disappointed when the only thing that met my lips was ice. I wanted vodka. And chocolate. And jalapeño cheddar Cheetos.

Right as the front door opened, my eyes locked on the bottle of vodka that was on the other side of the bar. I saw Gus, his brother Wes, and the man who owned that bottle of vodka, Luke Brooks, ramble through it.

I knew they were looking for me, that they wanted to make sure I was okay, but I couldn't deal with it yet. I didn't want to know what happened at the church or how my parents reacted or what people were saying.

So I pushed myself up and over the bar, grabbed the bottle of vodka, and slid out of my stool as quickly and quietly as possible. I headed for the bathroom, but I saw Wes notice me and, sure enough, a second later—

"Cam!" Gus called, but I kept moving.

Damn it.

"Are you really stealing from my bar right now?" Brooks asked.

"You look great, though!" Wes followed up.

I only had a few more steps to the bathroom. I could make it before they got to me. "Cam," Gus said again. "Let's talk!"

"I'm good," I called back without looking. "Is Riley okay?" I asked, even though I knew the answer. Gus wouldn't have come here before Riley was taken care of. He was a good dad—the best dad.

"Yes," he said right as I reached the bathroom door. I opened it.

"Then we're good!" I said as I stepped into the bathroom and shut the door behind me, making sure to lock it before I pressed my back against the old wood. I stared at the yellow tiles on the floor before I sank down to it—bottle in hand.

There was a knock. "Cam?" It was Gus. "C'mon, let's get you out of here and talk." I didn't want to talk. I wanted to drink. And eat.

"I'm fine here," I called through the door. I listened to him continue to try to cajole me out, but I didn't budge. I sat on the floor of the Devil's Boot bathroom—the place where probably half of Meadowlark's population had been conceived—

and I didn't even care. My gaze was unfocused and my eyes heavy.

I tried to cry—really I did—but nothing came out. I *wanted* to cry. I would have loved to feel *something* about the fact that my life just got turned upside down.

Instead, I was numb. Blissfully and comfortably numb. Maybe this was a good thing—that I didn't feel anything. My feelings had always gotten me in trouble.

I don't know how long I stayed there, my wedding dress puddled around me, or how long Gus knocked at the door. He was persistent, but after a while the knocking stopped.

All I could hear was the music from the jukebox—it slid its way under the door, and I welcomed it into my fortress. It felt nice, being wrapped in it. I didn't get wrapped in things—music, arms, embraces—very often.

I didn't register that the music was the only thing I could hear—no talking, no bar patrons, or stools skating across the floor—until there was another knock at the bathroom door.

It was softer this time—like the person doing it didn't want to disturb me or something. Three taps. They were on beat with the music.

"Ash?" a voice said. I straightened my spine. I'd know that voice anywhere. If I had slipped into a coma, it would wake me up. If I was six feet under, I'd dig myself out of the grave just to be closer to it, which was dramatic and startling and tragic and stupid.

But it was true.

"It's just me out here," he said. "The bar's cleared out." *I'll love you until we're dust in the wind, Camille Ashwood.* "I'm here, Cam."

For some reason, I reached up and unlocked the door—the

click was unmistakable. "I'm going to open the door, okay?" he said, and I scooted away from it. When the door opened, my eyes found his without even trying.

Dusty Tucker.

His blond and light brown hair fell just past his chin, and his face had only gotten sharper and more angular as he got older. The silver ring that went through his right nostril was almost the same color as his eyes, but they were more slate than silver. He was beautiful. He always had been, but beautiful things can be dangerous, too.

Silence and the weight of the years past hung between us. Finally, I was the one who broke it.

"Take me somewhere." That's what I said. Dusty squatted in front of me so his gray eyes were level with my brown ones and stretched out a tattooed hand. I took it without thinking.

Chapter 2

Dusty

I'm not normally a drown-my-sorrows type of guy. I don't really have a lot of sorrows. Honestly, I probably have one single sorrow, so I've never really had much to drown. But that one sorrow packed a hell of a punch—especially today.

Because, today, she was getting married.

She had invited me. Well, she invited my mom. "Aggie Tucker and family" is what the invitation said. The "and family" probably meant my little sister, Greer, even though she didn't live around here anymore. It for damn sure didn't mean me, which was probably a good thing.

I didn't think I could do it—sit in the church and watch her walk toward her future with another man. Actually, I knew I couldn't do it. So I was here, in the corner of the bar, drinking bourbon and drowning sorrows.

It was dark in the Devil's Boot. There weren't any big windows, and most of the light came from the neon signs throughout the bar. I'd talked Joe, the bartender, into giving me my own bottle and a glass, so I wouldn't have to get up from my spot in the corner. It actually didn't take that much convincing. He knew why I was here. Everyone knew Cam and I had history. There were no secrets in Meadowlark.

Pathetic. I was pathetic. With the way I was feeling, you'd think that Camille Ashwood had broken my heart this morning—not more than a decade ago. Well, for the first time. She broke my heart a million times after that, too, and time never did what it was supposed to do: heal or whatever.

Cam was an open wound, and time was salt.

I lifted my glass to my lips and took a sip of my drink. It was only my second or third sip. I was shit at drowning my sorrows, apparently.

I needed to get better at it, because my stupid head would not quiet down. It was shouting at me to *go*, to *do* something—to run to the church or to run away. I didn't know which, so I didn't do either.

It could've been a minute or an hour when I heard the front door to the bar open. My eyes swung to it because it hadn't opened once since I got here. Probably because it was three o'clock on a Saturday afternoon.

I saw a white dress and dark hair. It couldn't be her. I blinked a few times—thinking this weird fucking apparition of her would go away. I shook my head—trying to shake her right out the door, but she didn't go. She was still there, in her white dress.

What the hell was she doing here?

I looked down at my watch. She should be married by now—was she married by now? Were they coming here after the wedding? I couldn't imagine Rutherford and Lillian Ashwood would be too pleased about that. And if they were coming here, Teddy would've told me—she knew all about the drowning-sorrows plan and where those plans were taking place.

Cam looked . . . beautiful. Like she always did. But her curly hair was straightened and the dress looked like it was drowning her—there were a lot of layers. The look on her face made me want to track down Greg or Graham or whatever the fuck his name was and kick the shit out of him. What the hell happened?

I waited for her eyes to scan the bar and inevitably land on me, but they didn't. She went straight to the bar and sat down. She dropped the long, white veil she was dragging behind her on the floor.

Joe looked at her with wide eyes as she sat down, but he knew better than to say anything. She spoke to him, and he filled a glass with ice and clear liquid. I couldn't see what it was—vodka, probably—and slid it across the counter. Her fingers gripped the glass as she picked it up and drank nearly half of it in one go.

She didn't even flinch.

It took effort to turn away from her, but I needed a second. Plus, I was probably the last person she wanted to see. Judging by the presence of the vodka and wedding dress and the absence of the groom, I was starting to think the wedding hadn't happened.

Or maybe it happened, and it was shit?

But what if it hadn't?

I looked down at my hands resting on the table. They started to shake, and I balled them into fists to make them stop.

My phone lit up on the table, and I quickly picked it up. I

saw a message from Teddy, and more were coming. She could never send just one text. I'd always seen Teddy as another sister; now that my mom and her dad were together, that was truer than ever.

TEDDY: Dusty fuckin' Tucker
TEDDY: WE'RE GOING TO HAVE A LOT TO TALK ABOUT LATER
TEDDY: SOMETHING DRAMATIC HAPPENED
TEDDY: Are you at DB?
TEDDY: Has a beautiful woman wearing a very expensive white dress showed up? We can't find her.

Shit. Cam was a runaway bride. But why did she come here? I typed out a quick response to Teddy.

DUSTY: She's here.
TEDDY: Gus is coming.
TEDDY: DON'T INVADE HER SPACE.
TEDDY: SHE'S HAD A ROUGH DAY.
TEDDY: (but I have so much to tell you)
DUSTY: Haven't talked to her. She hasn't seen me.

What would she do if she did? Run in the other direction? She'd been damn good at avoiding me for the past year since I came home, and in a town like Meadowlark, that took a lot of effort.

My thoughts flashed back to when I saw her last year—for the first time in years. Emmy, Teddy, Ada, and Cam were having some girls' night. I walked in on it, and there she was.

And she was wearing *my* Margaritaville T-shirt. I'd given it to her the summer after high school. It had been in the back of my truck after we went swimming, and she'd needed something to wear. I had completely forgotten about it until I saw her wearing it that night.

It put ideas in my head—about what coming home meant for me. And then, I looked down and saw the giant rock on her ring finger.

Hopes: dashed.

Whatever. It was fine. I was fine. It was stupid to think that the girl I'd loved would be a woman waiting for me—I knew that, but it didn't hurt any less.

The door to the bar swung open a while later. This time, three men came through the door. Gus and Wes Ryder and Luke Brooks.

Gus called out for Cam, and her head shot up to him. She looked like she'd just been caught doing something she shouldn't have, which made more sense when I saw the bottle of vodka clutched in one of her hands.

I smiled.

She made her way through the bar while Gus tried to stop her. She stumbled over her dress a few times before making it to the bathroom, where she slammed the door.

Brooks looked up, and his eyes scanned the bar. When he saw me, he turned to say something to Gus before making his way over to where I was sitting.

"Hey, man," he said with a nod. Brooks cleaned up nice in a pair of black slacks and a white button-down.

"Hey," I said. My voice cracked a little—nice. "What's going on there?" I gestured toward the bathroom door, where both Gus and Wes were knocking. I tried to be nonchalant about it but knew I probably failed.

Brooks shook his head. "Groom didn't show." My mouth fell open. At his words, I felt my ears get hot.

"Seriously?" I asked. Who the hell doesn't show up when they're getting married to a woman like that? What a fucking idiot, I thought—talk about fumbling the bag.

"Seriously," Brooks said. "It's safe to say the wedding is off." My heart kicked at my rib cage. "Gus and Amos handled almost everything, but Cam's parents are pieces of work." I already knew that. Rutherford and Lillian sucked—they always had. They probably always would.

"Where's Riley?"

"With Teddy and Emmy. Leaving her with them was the only way we could guarantee that they wouldn't hunt Graham down and kick his teeth in." They would, too. Emmy and Teddy weren't a duo that you wanted to mess with—especially if they had a common goal. If they had their heart set on ruining that guy's life, it'd be done by tomorrow.

"Shit," I breathed.

"Shit." Brooks nodded. I looked over at the bathroom door again. Gus was still knocking, but Wes was making his way over to us.

"I don't think she's coming out," he said.

"She's not," I said. Cam was stubborn, and she didn't like to be at the center of everything. She liked the outskirts. The way people would rally around her now would probably make her uncomfortable—even though she deserved people showing up for her. That didn't matter, though. Cam would prefer to disappear.

She probably wouldn't leave the bathroom until the bar was empty, like totally empty.

"I know how to get her out," I said to Brooks. "But we've

gotta clear this place. She won't come out with all these people around. Can we do that?"

Brooks nodded and called over to Gus and Wes, who started walking toward us. "Dusty has an idea," he said as they approached.

Gus narrowed his eyes at me—always the protector. Gus Ryder was a good man. I idolized him growing up and still looked up to him more than he knew. "What's your plan?"

"She doesn't want to face any of these people here," I said. "And she definitely doesn't want to see any of you." Wes deflated a little bit at that.

"But she'll want to see you?" Gus asked, folding his arms across his chest.

"Probably not," I said. "But I'm the only one out of the four of us who wasn't at the, uh, wedding." I stumbled out that word but hoped they didn't notice.

"Why does that matter?" Gus asked.

"It just does." I shrugged. Because in Cam's mind, it meant that I was the only one who hadn't witnessed her embarrassment. Cam was a prideful woman—not in a bad way. She just cared what other people thought of her—she wanted to be perfect. I blame her mother.

"I think we should let Dusty try," Wes piped up.

"Me too," Brooks said.

"Is that because you care about Cam or because you want her out of your bathroom?" Gus asked with a glare in his direction.

"Both." Brooks shrugged.

Gus rolled his shoulders back and down. "Fine," he said and then pointed a finger at me. "But you keep your hands to yourself."

I rolled my eyes. He and Teddy really were perfect for each other, weren't they? "Cam is my friend," I said. Well, she used to be. I didn't know what we were now. Maybe once we got everybody out of the Devil's Boot, I'd be able to find out.

Chapter 3

Cam

Fifteen Years Ago

Meadowlark High School was already my favorite place, and I'd only been here for a few hours. It was my first day—my first day here, my first day of public school after years of private schools—and the first time I'd ever seen a boy with a nose ring. I could see it—up close and personal—because I'd run straight into him while leaving the main office. My books and class schedule were now scattered all over the floor.

Great.

"Whoa there," he said. His hands were on my upper arms, which were covered by a navy blue cardigan.

"I—I'm sorry," I stammered out before looking up at the human wall I'd just hit. Gray eyes stared down at me. Oh.

"It's okay," he said with a devilish smile. "I'm used to girls throwing themselves at me." A smile tugged at the corners of my mouth, but I didn't know how to respond to that, so I didn't. Instead, I looked down at the mess of my belongings.

As I bent to pick them up, the boy with the gray eyes did, too. "Let me help," he said, and I stayed quiet. While he started gathering papers and books, I got a better look at him. A mop of blond hair that my mother would say was too long, but I liked it. I think.

He had a sharp jawline and a cleft chin and eyebrows that matched the darker parts of his hair. My gaze snagged on the silver ring through his nostril. I must've stared at it for a second too long because he said, "Like it?" while gesturing to his nose with one hand—the other was full of my books. I hadn't picked up a thing. Distracted, I guess. "Lost a bet with my buddy Wes a few months ago, but it's grown on me."

This boy kept talking to me, and I stayed silent. I didn't know what to say. Did I like it? Yes. Did I want to tell him that? Absolutely not. I also noticed a tattoo on his forearm. I couldn't tell what it was, and I didn't want to be caught staring again. Could seventeen-year-olds even have tattoos? Was that legal?

"You're new here, right?" he asked. This time, I nodded. He stood up, with my books and papers still in one of his hands, and I rose with him. My class schedule was on top of the pile, and I watched him take it in.

"Camille Ashwood," he read out loud. "Good name." I wanted to ask what his was, but my stupid tongue still wasn't working. "Do you know where you're going for chemistry?"

"How do you know I'm going to chemistry?" I asked.

"She speaks," he said with a tilted smile. I felt a blush creep up my neck. I wasn't really a shy girl. I mean, I wasn't a chatterbox, but I normally knew how to respond to questions. But this guy was just so . . . pretty. It was intimidating. "It's on your class schedule, Camille."

There was something about the way he moved his mouth when he talked that had my attention—the way his top and bottom teeth *were always slightly parted no matter what he said—that was kind of hypnotizing.*

"Right," I said.

"So," he said as he handed my books and schedule back to me, "do you know where you're going?"

I gave him a quick nod and turned in the other direction.

"Wrong way, Camille," he called after me. Damn. My face heated as I turned around and walked past him again. When I did, he reached his hand out and said, "I'm Dusty, by the way."

I kept walking.

Chapter 4

Cam

I both hated and loved how easy it was for me to take Dusty's hand and run out of the Devil's Boot—into its dirt parking lot with my wedding dress floating and rustling around me. It was cold as shit, but I didn't really notice.

When Dusty looked back at me as we ran toward his Bronco, he had a lopsided smile on his face, and it reminded me so much of the boy I used to know, how much I missed him when I let myself think about him.

I pushed the thought down as we made it to his truck. He opened the door for me and asked, "You're sure?" I wasn't. But instead of answering, I grabbed on to the front of the door and hoisted myself up into the cab—like I'd done a million times before. Dusty helped me gather my dress and make sure all of it was inside the truck. "No offense, but this dress is fucking ridiculous," he said.

"I know," I said with a breath that turned into a laugh. After Dusty shut the door, he made his way to the driver's side and hopped in.

"Any requests?" he asked as the Bronco roared to life.

I shook my head. "Just drive."

Dusty gave me that tilted smile again, and I couldn't help but smile back. My heart was beating in my ears; I could feel the blood pumping through my veins. My whole body felt alive, as if it had been dormant before.

He started driving and flipped on the radio. Charlie Rich started flowing through the speakers. We didn't talk, but it wasn't uncomfortable. Normally, when faced with silence, my head felt loud. It had felt loud all day.

But right now, it was blissfully quiet.

I looked over at Dusty one more time—one of his wrists was hanging over the steering wheel and the other was tapping along to the music—before I leaned my head against the cool glass of the window and watched Wyoming roll by.

"Ash," Dusty said softly a little while later. I lifted my head from the window, slightly disoriented. The landscape around me was no longer moving—we were parked somewhere. "You fell asleep. Feel okay?"

"Yeah," I said groggily. "Where are we?"

"I thought you might like a change of clothes," he said. "We're at a gas station about an hour outside of Meadowlark."

"Clothes from a gas station?" I said, arching a brow at him. My voice didn't hold much weight, though, because my dress was starting to dig at me in all the wrong places.

Dusty looked amused. "Sorry. Nordstroms are in short supply around here."

I sighed and pushed my door open. The full skirt of my dress started to tumble out of the truck. God, this thing was big and gaudy and awful. My mother picked it out—she had chosen every detail about today. The church (not for me), the florals (expensive), the food (I hate fish), the music (boring), and of course, the groom—well, I mostly picked that, but it was my parents who influenced the choice. I thought that if I married someone in their circle, I'd get some validation from them. Being their daughter didn't get me any, but I thought Graham Rawlins might.

Rutherford Ashwood (or Ford, if you were his friend—I wasn't) was the heir to the oldest and largest bank west of the Missouri River. His grandparents—old money, like Vanderbilt and Rothschild adjacent—came out west with the gold rush and established Basin Bank. If you lived in the West and had any sort of money, it was at Basin.

Enter Sherman Rawlins, owner of Rawlins Associates—one of the largest hedge funds in the country—and Graham's father. Yeah, *that* Graham. The one who left me at the altar a few hours ago because he just "couldn't do it."

I shook all the thoughts about my family and Graham and my failed wedding out of my head. Not now.

Once I was out of the truck and on the ground, I went to pull my dress up, worried it might get dirty, but then I remembered I wasn't walking down the aisle. I was walking into a random gas station off the side of a Wyoming highway that looked like it was the same age as the mountains surrounding it.

I let the dress drop and drag through the mud, slush, and gravel as I walked. Well, stumbled. The heels my mother had picked out to go with this dress were stilettos that probably cost as much as some cars and were not making this journey easy.

The gas station was small. It looked like it had been painted mint green a few decades ago. Out front, there were handwritten signs for homemade beef jerky and five-dollar cigarettes. There were only two fuel pumps, and I wasn't convinced that they worked.

Dusty fell into step beside me—not too close, not too far away. Silence hung between us again, but this time, there wasn't music to fill it—just ten years of space and time. Good thing I was an expert at pushing down my feelings or else the weight of this moment—any moment or memory with Dusty—could crush me.

A bell rang on the rickety door as Dusty opened it for me. The middle-aged man at the checkout counter did a double take at the two of us—me in my wedding dress and Dusty in his normal attire—faded jeans, black T-shirt that was cropped a little, just enough to give me a glimpse of his abdomen every time he moved, black cowboy boots, black leather jacket. I looked over at him just as he pushed a hand through his blond waves.

I looked away immediately.

"Hey, Stan," Dusty said. How did he know this guy? We were far out of town.

"You got something to tell me, kid?" the presumed Stan responded. He was still eyeing me and my wedding dress.

Dusty chuckled. "Nah, but do you still have T-shirts?"

Stan nodded and jerked his chin. "In the back."

"Thanks, man. If you have any new jerky flavors, leave them up here for me," Dusty said as he put his hand on the small of my back and softly guided me farther inside.

Don't think about it.

As soon as we were headed in the right direction, his hand moved. I missed the comfort of it immediately, or maybe I just missed his hand on me—like I had for the past decade.

Not thinking about it.

At the back corner of the store, there were two clothing racks—one of them held together at the corner by duct tape—full of mismatched T-shirts. There were folded sweatpants and shorts on a cardboard box next to them.

I started looking through the shirts on the racks. There were lots of wildlife options, a few generic Wyoming ones, one with a jackalope, and . . .

"If you get this one," Dusty said as he reached for the dark green shirt I was currently looking at and pulled it off the rack, "we can match."

"'Show me your Tetons'?" I asked, reading the white text on the shirt, and a smile tugged at the corners of my mouth.

Dusty grinned back at me. "Only if you show me yours."

"In your dreams, Dusty Tucker," I said on an eye roll, trying to stifle a giggle. He'd always been able to make me laugh, even when I didn't want to.

He gave me an exaggerated wink. "You have no idea, Ash."

"Stop flirting with me while I'm still in my wedding dress." Leave it to Dusty to make me feel comfortable enough to make a joke about something that should not be remotely funny yet.

"We better get you out of it then."

I huffed in mock exasperation. "You are ridiculous," I said and then shoved the shirt into his arms. "Hold this for me. I need to find some pants."

"Do you?"

"*Yes,* Dusty," I said. "Or should I call you by your legal name?" Dusty's gray eyes widened, but he was smiling, like he was thrilled I was playing with him.

"You wouldn't," he said.

"Try me, Tuck," I responded, the nickname rolling off my tongue for the first time since he came home last year. His eyes glittered.

He took the shirt from me, and I stepped toward the shoddily folded piles of sweatpants. They were all basic drawstring sweatpants. My color choices were gray, navy blue, and hot pink.

I went with the navy blue that had the Wyoming Bucking Horse on the hip. My eyes scanned the rest of the clothing—looking for a sweatshirt or jacket or something, but the only one I found was an extra small that looked like it would fit Riley.

"I have an extra coat and a pair of boots in my truck," Dusty said, reading my mind. "The bathroom is out the back door"—he pointed down a hallway to our left—"but we have to go get the key from Stan."

Changing out of my wedding dress in a backwoods gas station bathroom felt like a step too far. "Can I just change in your truck?"

Dusty looked down at the floor, suddenly bashful. "Oh . . . uh. Sure," he said. I watched his Adam's apple bob, and it made my cheeks heat.

"Great," I said quickly. This space suddenly felt too small for both of us, so I started walking back toward the front. I tripped over one of the uneven floorboards. In my periphery, I saw Dusty reach for me, but I righted myself before he could touch me again.

Once we reached the counter, I set my sweatpants near the register, and Dusty put my shirt next to it, along with three plastic water bottles that he must've picked up on the way. There were also clear plastic bags of beef jerky there, too.

"There's honey jalapeño, brown sugar bourbon, and dill pickle," Stan said as he pointed at each bag before scanning the rest of our items. Dill pickle beef jerky? I could get into that. "Forty-two seventy-three. Do you need a bag?"

"We're good," Dusty said. He pulled his wallet out of his back pocket and dropped three twenties on the counter. "Thanks, Stan. Appreciate it." I waited for a second for Stan to get Dusty's change, but Dusty had already gathered up the items and was waiting for me to lead the way toward the door.

"See ya, Dusty and . . ." He looked at me, waiting for my name.

"Cam," I said with a smile.

"Dusty and Cam." Stan rolled our names around in his mouth, and I rolled them around in my head. I forgot how . . . easy they sounded together. "Thanks for stopping by."

"And, Stan, I'll come back up as soon as I can, and we'll get that fallen tree out front taken care of, all right?"

"Appreciate it, kid," Stan said, and Dusty gave him a nod before we went out the door.

"How often do you come here?" I asked.

"Once a month, probably." Dusty shrugged. "Stan's a good guy—gas station has been in his family for generations." When we got to the Bronco, Dusty leaned up against the side of it, arms folded across his chest. "He actually retired a few years ago, and his son took over, but his son passed away last year, so he had to come back. He's the only person left in his family."

"Oh," I said. I wasn't expecting all of this information, but I guess I should've. Dusty liked people. He could talk to anyone.

"He has a hard time managing this place, so I help when I can."

"What happens to it when he's gone?" I asked.

Dusty looked sad as he shrugged. "Places like this—the ones that are tucked away and outdated—usually die with the people who love them." He said it like he'd watched it happen before.

"That's . . . depressing," I said.

"Better enjoy them while we can, eh?" I loved that grin. That mischievous and devilish grin. I nodded. "I'll start the truck and get the heater going, and then the dressing room is all yours."

"Thank you," I said, realizing then how freezing I was. I got in the passenger seat right as the Bronco roared to life. God, this thing was so loud.

"I'll get your boots and coat out of the back."

He opened the driver's-side door and was about to get out when I said, "Wait." I couldn't believe I was going to have to ask this, but I couldn't do it myself. The back of the dress was too high. "Can you . . ." I paused, stumbling over my words a bit. "Can you, um, unzip me?"

I didn't look at him, but I heard him swallow.

"You know what," I said. "Never mind, I can figure it out." Even though I knew I couldn't. It had taken three people to get me into this dress, so it was going to take at least one other person to get me out of it.

"It's fine, Cam," Dusty said. His voice was strained. "It's just a dress."

Just a dress. Right. If you would've told me ten years ago that Dusty Tucker would be unzipping my wedding dress, I would've probably said, "Duh." I never could have imagined it would be a wedding dress I was wearing to marry another man who didn't show up to the altar.

Back then, the future I saw for myself was intertwined with his. Now, we were basically strangers. I always thought it would hurt less over time.

It hadn't.

"Okay," I whispered. "Thank you." I turned my back toward him. When his fingers came to the clasp between my shoulder blades, goosebumps rose on my skin. I felt him grip the fabric on each side of the hook-and-eye closure to undo it. I closed my eyes, telling myself it was because I didn't want to think about Dusty touching me, but really, I was basking in it.

His fingers moved to the zipper, and I heard him take a deep breath before he started pulling it down—achingly slowly.

A noise came from Dusty's throat when he saw what I had on under my dress—a powder blue lace bustier. It was the only thing I'd picked out myself for today. I had thought that if I could just make this one choice, maybe I'd feel more confident as I walked down the aisle and married a man I didn't love. Now, it felt stupid.

My wedding dress started to loosen around my ribs and waist as Dusty dragged the zipper down until it stopped. One of the straps slipped off my shoulder.

"A-all good," Dusty said. His voice was shaky and low. "Knock on the window when you're done, and I'll grab the boots and coat out of the back."

"Thank you." The inside of his truck was completely devoid of air, and my heart was beating in my ears again. Suddenly, I felt one of his knuckles dragging up my spine and stopping at the nape of my neck. I wanted to turn to him, see his face, but I didn't. I stayed where I was and kept my eyes closed.

I felt his breath on the back of my neck, so he must've leaned in, and before I could give in and let my head fall back on his shoulder, he said, "I'm sorry," got out of the truck, and shut the driver's-side door.

Chapter 5

Dusty

Dusty Tucker, get your shit together. You are supposed to be getting her out of her head. That's it. That's all.

Holding her hand while we ran to my car? Harmless. Touching the small of her back to guide her to the back of Stan's store? Necessary. She didn't know where she was going. Unzipping her wedding dress? That's fine—she asked me to.

Dragging my fingers over whatever blue lace contraption she had on underneath it? Dangerously reckless.

Fuck.

I stood outside of my truck, letting the cold air outside bite at my cheeks and nose. I could hear my truck wobbling and creaking on its shocks—a reminder that Cam was in there taking her clothes—her *wedding dress*—off. It wasn't the first time she'd stripped down in my car, but it was the first time I wasn't in there while it was happening.

Take a breath, Dusty.

I dragged a hand down my face. *She doesn't need this from you right now, dumbass.* She needs a friend. To help her escape for a few hours before both of us have to go back to real life—

the place where Cam and I weren't even friends, at least I didn't think so.

While we were driving, I did my best to keep my eyes on the road and mountains ahead of me. There weren't a lot of cars on this two-lane. It wasn't the main highway—it twisted and turned around the mountains instead of going through them, so it took a lot longer to get where you were going. But it was my favorite road—the only one I took in and out of Meadow-lark.

Now, I was looking at the mountains again—trying to think about anything but the woman who was undressing in the front seat of my truck, but I couldn't. An image of her with her forehead pressed up against the window flashed in my brain, and I closed my eyes. The fact that she felt comfortable enough to fall asleep in my passenger seat had my insides doing a full gymnastics routine—twists, flips, jumps and all.

After what felt like forever, I heard two knocks on the window. My jaw unclenched, and I felt my shoulders drop slightly. I turned back to the truck and went straight to the back, opening the hatch to pull out a big Carhartt coat, a clean towel I'd just put in there, a pair of boots, and a pair of thick socks. I had to dig for those, but I was glad I found them.

I always made sure I had supplies in my truck—especially in the winter. You never knew when a canyon would close due to snow, and you'd be stuck in your car for at least one night, sometimes more.

Then I went to Cam's door and pulled it open. I took her in, just for a second—she was drowning in that ridiculous T-shirt with her hair and makeup all done. God, she'd just gotten more beautiful with time.

"Coat," I said and draped it across her lap with the towel.

"Socks." I looked down at her feet. She'd taken her heels off, and her feet looked red and painful. There were indents where her shoe straps had been, as if they'd been crushing her something fierce. I hated thinking that she'd been in pain this whole time.

I set the socks on top of the coat and the boots on the ground next to me before gently grabbing one of her ankles. "What are you doing?" Cam asked.

"I just thought . . ." I mumbled as I started to rub one of them with both of my hands. It was so damn cold. "Your feet look like they hurt."

"I guess they do a little," she said quietly.

"Does this feel okay?" She nodded—a woman of few words. I kept rubbing for a few minutes before putting one of the socks on, switching to the other foot, and starting over.

"What's the towel for?" she asked after a second.

"In case you wanted to get your hair wet," I said. Cam tilted her head in question. "Your hair . . . you don't like it when it's straight." I shrugged. "I know you'll say it'll be frizzy or whatever, but the extra water and towel are there—if you want them."

Her brown eyes were soft as she looked at me. Too soft. I couldn't handle it, so I put the other sock on her foot and said, "We've got a thirty-minute drive to our destination, so you don't need to put these on yet." I put the boots on the floor of the truck.

"Where are you taking me?"

I shook my head. "I'm not telling, but I promise, you're going to love it."

Almost exactly thirty minutes later, we rolled into a parking lot. "You brought me to a fucking Chili's?" Cam said with a shocked laugh.

I smiled over at her as I cut the engine. "Sure did." While we were driving, she took her hair out of its bun and ran water through the strands with her hands. Curls started to form almost immediately. She seemed so much lighter than she did a few hours ago.

"This is so ridiculous," she said.

"You know," I said, "there are very few things that a mid-range chain restaurant can't fix—especially one with chips and salsa and a sizzling fajita situation."

Cam's stomach growled. "All right," she said. "I could do some damage to an order of chips and salsa." She leaned down and slid the boots on.

"Ready to rock and roll?" I asked.

"Let's do it."

We got out of the car, and I had the urge to grab her hand as we walked toward the door, but I didn't, of course. It was weird—before this morning, I hadn't held her hand in nearly fifteen years, but reaching for it felt like the most natural thing in the world.

I looked over at her. She looked fucking adorable right now with her messy hair and how she was absolutely swimming in my coat and her new outfit from the gas station.

When we got inside, we were greeted by a hostess and a very bright "Hi, welcome to Chili's. How many?"

"Two," I said.

"Table or booth?"

"Booth," Cam and I said at the same time.

The hostess nodded. "Right this way." She led us to a four-person booth near the back of the restaurant. I waited for Cam to sit before I did, then I slid into the bench across from her. When we sat down, I watched Cam's eyes latch on to the tattoo on my neck for a second, but when I caught her looking, she looked away quickly.

"Here are some menus, and your server will be right with you." The hostess laid a menu in front of each of us.

"Thank you," I said, and she nodded and walked away.

Cam picked her menu up. I watched her eyes track back and forth as she read. I liked watching her. I had spent so long not seeing her or only seeing pictures, so now, when I had the opportunity to look at her—which didn't come as often as I'd like—I did it.

Her dark brown hair was longer now—and maybe darker, too. When it was curly, it fell to the middle of her biceps. Her face was less round than it used to be, and she didn't tweeze her eyebrows as thin as she used to. They looked good on her face. She'd always been stunning. Now, she was . . . almost regal, too.

"Are you going to look at the menu, or . . . ?" Cam said without looking up.

"Don't need to," I said. "Ultimate fajita platter."

"Are you a Chili's regular?" She sounded amused.

"I fucking love Chili's," I said. "Sometimes the craving strikes for that middle-class fancy shit, you know?"

"Like Applebee's?"

"Meh." I shrugged. "Not my favorite, but I like all the iterations of Applebee's."

"What do you mean?"

"Well," I said, "right now, we're at Southwest Applebee's. Texas Roadhouse is like Cowboy Applebee's, and Olive Garden is Italian Applebee's."

"Red Lobster?" Cam chimed in.

"Seafood Applebee's. We should go there next," I said.

"I could fuck up a Cheddar Bay biscuit any day." She nodded, and I laughed. She was loosening up.

Just then, our server came to the table. "Hi y'all," she said with a perfect customer service tone. "My name is Cara, and I'll be your server today. Can I start you with anything to drink?"

I nodded at Cam, waiting for her to go first. I watched our server Cara take in her appearance. "I'll just have a water, please." The server nodded and looked at me. I didn't miss the smile she gave me.

"Water, please, and also can we get a Tiki Beach Party Margarita." I flashed Cara a smile and held up two fingers. "With two straws."

Cara's eyes flitted to Cam again as she wrote everything down, and then said, "Are you ready to order food, or do you need a minute?" She was only talking to me.

I looked at Cam, waiting for her. "Margarita grilled chicken, please," she said, setting her menu down and looking over at me. I gave my order, too, grabbed Cam's menu, and handed both to Cara. "Thank you," I said before she walked away.

"The server is into you," Cam said once she was out of earshot. I shrugged. "She's probably wondering what the hell someone who looks like you is doing here with me."

"Someone who looks like me?" I smirked. "What do I look like?"

"You know exactly what you look like," Cam said pointedly. "You always have."

"What if I want you to tell me, though?" I couldn't help playing with her. It came so easy.

"Too bad. Women who got left at the altar don't have to do anything they don't want to do for at least a few hours afterward."

"Does that mean you're ready to talk about it, then?" I asked. We had avoided the subject until now. Cam didn't like to be pushed, and I didn't like to be reminded that she was engaged to someone else, or at least, she used to be, so it had been a win-win.

She shifted her eyes away from mine and started drawing mindless circles on the table with her pointer finger. "There's not much to talk about," Cam said. That was a lie. There was everything to talk about. "I showed up. He didn't. It's pretty cut and dried."

It didn't sound "cut and dried" to me. It sounded messy, but Cam didn't like messy things.

"Hey," I said. "Look at me." She didn't. "Ash," I said more firmly. Her eyes flicked up to mine like they couldn't help it. "You didn't deserve that." Cam always thought everything was her fault. I knew the way she was probably talking to herself in her head, and it made my teeth clench. "I need to know that you know you didn't deserve that."

"I think I did deserve it," she said quietly. I wanted to throw the table. I wanted to get it out of my way, so I could hold her, but before I could even think about doing anything, Cara brought our waters and our drink.

"Your food will be right out," she said again only to me and walked away. I looked at Cam, whose face had gone blank. No more talking, I guess—at least about the wedding. I opened both of the straws and put them in the giant glass of blue margarita.

"This is massive," she said, eyeing the glass. She was wearing a small smile now. "And looks disgusting."

"It is both of those things," I said. "You're going to hate it, but you're also going to love it."

"What does it even taste like?" she asked.

I leaned over toward the middle of the table to take a sip. "Artificial blue," I said afterward.

"Well," she sighed. "Blue *is* my favorite color."

I know.

Chapter 6

Cam

G us called Dusty to check in while we were eating dinner. Dusty handed the phone to me. "Hello?"

"You doing okay?" Gus's voice was low and concerned.

"I'm fine," I said. "How's Riley?"

"Good. She was wiped out from today." That made two of us. "Fell asleep on the couch about an hour ago."

"Thank you for taking care of everything," I said quietly.

"Always, Cam. We'll talk about everything tomorrow, okay? I just wanted to check and see how you were."

"I'm fine," I said again. "All things considered."

"Okay. Well, I've got Riley, and my dad has a bed for you. I figured . . ." Gus trailed off. And that's when I realized: I couldn't go to my house because it was technically Graham's. That was a hill to climb another day—today, I was too tired to even think about it.

"You figured right," I said, grateful that he didn't try to elaborate further. "Thank you. I'll talk to you tomorrow."

"Be safe, Cam. Good night."

"Night," I said before hanging up and handing the phone back to Dusty. I didn't even know where my phone was. It was with my stuff in my dressing room last time I saw it. I wasn't ready to face the music yet, but that phone call from Gus was essentially the orchestra warming up.

So, after dinner, Dusty and I drove back to Rebel Blue Ranch—the Ryder family's home and one of the largest cattle ranches in Wyoming—mostly in silence. Our day was coming to an end. My sense of self-preservation, which was always so fleeting around him, kicked in as we drove, and I retreated back into my head.

He pulled up to the Big House just after midnight. He didn't cut the engine when his Bronco came to a stop—it would be too loud to start up again at this time of night. It reminded me of all the times I would sneak out with him, and he'd have to park three streets away to pick me up and drop me off.

Dusty's hands dropped from the steering wheel, and he looked over at me. He almost glowed in the moonlight. "Are you going to be okay?" he asked.

I nodded once and swallowed. Today sucked, but it didn't really hurt—but I knew what I was about to say would.

"Thank you for being there for me," I said. "I'm happy you were at the bar—that you got me out of there." Dusty tilted his head, waiting for me to keep going. "I just, um—" I stumbled over my words when I met his gaze, so I looked away. "—I think today should just be . . . today. And after tonight we should . . . just go back to how it had been before . . . with us."

Dusty was quiet for a second. I kept my eyes focused on the dashboard. I didn't want to know what his expression was—

didn't want it to threaten the resolve I'd spent the entire drive back to Meadowlark building.

"If that's what you want," he finally said.

"It is." I nodded. "I have a lot to figure out—a lot of things to focus on."

"You don't have to explain yourself to me, Ash," he said. "If you want to forget about it, we'll forget about it."

I told him that's what I wanted—what I needed, so why did I feel disappointed in his response? "Okay," I whispered.

"Okay," he responded.

After a few more beats of silence, I pushed the passenger door open. I waited for him to say goodbye, but I was relieved when he didn't. We were never good at saying goodbyes.

"Ash?" he called right before I was about to shut the door. I couldn't stop myself from looking at him. He ran one of his hands through his hair and then rubbed at the back of his neck. "Sleep good."

"You too," I said, and then I shut the door. He didn't drive off right away—not until I was inside and had closed the front door behind me.

The Big House was dark. I slipped off Dusty's boots and hung his coat by the door. I'd have Gus give them back—he saw Dusty almost every day because he worked at Rebel Blue. The socks Dusty had given me made my steps almost silent, but I couldn't think about the socks because if I thought about the socks, I would think about my feet. And if I thought about my feet, I would think about how Dusty had noticed they were red and swollen, and his first instinct was to make me feel better.

Just like it had always been.

When it came to Dusty, I understood what people meant when they said the more things change, the more they stay the same. Or that old habits die hard. Dusty was a habit—thinking about him, missing him, or at least the idea of him: It was a cycle that I'd always struggled to break. Especially because I also found myself missing who I had been when he was in my life.

I meant what I said. I was glad he had been at the bar today. Gus and everybody else would've treated me like I was covered in fragile stickers. Dusty acted like it was just another day—even though it wasn't. It was the first time we'd spent more than five minutes together in years. We talked, we laughed, we had fun.

And now it was over.

There was a soft glow coming from the living room, so I went that way. I hoped no one was waiting up for me. When I made it to the living room, I found Emmy and Ada asleep—their heads on opposite sides of the couch with their feet tangled together in the middle under the same blanket.

I took another step into the living room and hit a creaky floorboard. I froze. In the dead of night, it was the loudest sound in the world.

Emmy's eyelids fluttered open. "Cam?" she said on a yawn.

"Hey," I said softly. "I didn't mean to wake you."

She sat up and pushed the blanket off her. When she stood, I knew what she was coming for. The Ryders were huggers—even Gus.

I let Emmy wrap her arms around me, and I let myself hug her back. "I'm so sorry, Cam," she said. "Today must've really sucked."

"It actually wasn't so bad," I said. "After, you know, the

whole groom disappearing thing, everything else was pretty good."

Emmy pulled back and raised a brow at me. "So . . . everything with Dusty was . . . okay?"

"Yeah," I said honestly. I didn't have a reason to hide anything from Emmy. "It was comforting, you know? Like going back in time . . . back to when I had less worries . . . and didn't just get left at the altar. I'm happy he was there."

"Then so am I." Emmy pulled me toward the other couch, and I sat down next to her.

"You didn't have to wait up for me," I said.

"I know. Ada and I wanted to. I know you're like the leader of the 'I can take care of myself' movement, but we were worried about you. Wes is asleep in his old room, and Luke is in mine. My dad made up Gus's old bed for you."

My throat closed again. I didn't know what I did in a past life to make these people care about me so much, but it must've been really damn good.

"Thank you," I said, and Emmy laid her head on my shoulder.

"Are you going to be okay, Cam?"

"I don't really have a choice, do I?" I said dryly.

"You do, actually," Emmy said. "You can cry and scream and fall apart. You can do whatever you want. You don't have to be okay right now. It's just us . . . and Ada, I guess. But she's conked out."

I let out a half laugh. Much to my surprise, tears welled up in my eyes at Emmy's words. Ever since I found out I was pregnant with Riley, Emmy has been the closest thing I've ever had to a sister, which is saying something considering that I actually *do* have a sister. But Violet couldn't even be bothered to show up to my wedding, let alone help me pick up the pieces afterward.

"I don't know what to do next, Emmy."

"Well, I think you can start by getting some sleep. Everything looks different in the light of day."

"And after that?"

"You start over," Emmy said softly. "And you lean on the people around you who love you and your daughter. You let us help."

The Ryders had never been anything but kind and loving to me, but sometimes I couldn't help but wonder if they would have shown me love like this if I hadn't gotten pregnant. I was a necessary part of their family because I was Riley's mom, but would they have ever really wanted me on my own? I put walls up with everyone, but even my highest and strongest walls crumbled around the Ryders. You couldn't help but love them, and love had always scared me a little.

"I don't know if I can do that, Em," I whispered.

"Why not?"

"I don't even know if I can start over because I don't know if I ever actually started in the first place."

Chapter 7

Cam

Fifteen Years Ago

"Camille." *Dusty's voice came from the seat behind me. Since the bell hadn't rung yet, I turned around to face him with an eye roll.*

"What do you want, Dusty?"

He flashed me a smile that I felt in my stomach. He did it all the time. I didn't have a lot of experience with boys. All the ones I'd ever known were trust fund kids who had never been denied anything and loved to flaunt their dad's money. They didn't interest me, and I didn't interest them.

But Dusty interested me—at least as a friend. I hadn't really made a lot of friends yet. Just Wes Ryder, but he was nice to everyone. I knew some of the other girls on the soccer team, but I was a late addition, so the cliques had already formed. But since my first day, I could almost always count on Dusty stopping by my locker to say good morning, and he carried my books when we were going the same direction. It was nice.

Being at Meadowlark High was so different from being at any of my other schools. I knew it would be. That's why I wanted to come here.

My dad bought a house here a few years ago. A house and a lot of land. There were rumors of oil in Meadowlark, and my dad had money to spare, so he tried to get ahead of it. The first time we came here, I was enamored by all of it—the way the main street felt, how everyone waved at one another without a second thought. It seemed welcoming, like anyone could find their place here, and I had never really felt like I had found a place anywhere. I wanted to feel that sort of connection, that sense of belonging. I wanted to immerse myself in every part of this town—including the high school.

My parents said no at first—I knew they would. And usually, I'd let it go, because I always did when it came to the things that I wanted that didn't mesh with their desires. I knew that's what they expected me to do.

But I didn't. I didn't push hard, but I pushed. I gave them lists of pros—a decent number of AP classes, good athletics, and free (because the only thing they loved more than making money? Holding on to it). Plus, I already had as many college credits as a junior as Violet had when she graduated. With the AP classes available at Meadowlark High, I'd technically be ahead of her. After a few months, they said yes and told me to stop talking about it. I don't think they were used to me using my voice.

That's how I learned that the only thing my parents wanted more than control was quiet.

"Can I borrow a pencil?" Dusty asked.

"Do you need me to buy you some pencils?" I asked. He asked me to borrow one every time we had English or history together—so basically every day.

"*But then I couldn't borrow yours,*" he said with a wink.

I sighed and pulled a pencil out of my pouch and handed it to him. "*You better give that back,*" I said. "*I just got those.*" I loved this new pack of mechanical pencils, and I had color-coordinated them to my notebooks for each class.

"*Cross my heart,*" Dusty said, dragging his pointer finger over his chest to draw an invisible X. "*Can I have a piece of paper, too?*"

"*Oh my god, Dusty,*" I said with faux annoyance. "*Do you even go to school here?*"

"*Occasionally,*" he said. "*But I promise, I just need the paper for today—after this I'll only ever ask for pencils.*"

I huffed and opened my notebook, carefully tore out a page along the perforated edges, and handed it back to him with more force than necessary.

"*Ooooh, college-ruled,*" he remarked. "*Fancy girl.*" Yeah, because wide-ruled paper sucked, and I was about to tell him as much when the bell rang, and Mr. Watson—our English teacher—walked to the front of the room and called for the class's attention, which I gave him immediately.

I heard a pencil scratching on paper behind me, even though Mr. Watson had barely started teaching. We were just reviewing the general feedback on the papers we turned in last week before we got them back. What could Dusty possibly be writing back there?

After Mr. Watson had returned all of our papers—I got an A— and handed out a grammar worksheet on sentence structure, which was apparently something we all needed to work on, Dusty threw a folded piece of paper—the piece of paper I gave him—onto my desk.

My heart fluttered, but I didn't want to get in trouble. I turned around slyly and gave him a questioning look.

"Open it," he mouthed. I shook my head. He pouted a little before mouthing, "Please." My stomach flipped. I rolled my eyes and turned around. I kept the folded note under my grammar work-sheet, but I couldn't stop thinking about it.

So, after I finished my assignment, I finally unfolded it.

> *Camille,*
>
> *I feel like I need a nickname for you. I like Camille. It's pretty. You're pretty, too, by the way. I just feel like Camille is too formal for our relationship. You know? Do people always call you Cam? If they do, I need to think of another one. I want mine to be special.*
>
> *Anyway, I have some questions for you. So, if you could kindly write your answers below and return this back to me, I would appreciate it.*
>
> *What's your favorite color?*
>
> *What's your favorite food?*
>
> *What's the last TV show that made you laugh?*
>
> *Do you have any siblings?*
>
> *When is the soccer team's next home game? What's your jersey number?*
>
> *Do you like MHS so far? What's your favorite part about it? Me? ;)*
>
> *When's your birthday?*
>
> *Favorite class? English or History? Just kidding. Kind of.*
>
> *What do you like to do for fun? Do you like hiking? Because I know a good spot.*
>
> *That's a good start on the getting-to-know-you questions. Plus, you should have plenty of time to answer them be-*

cause I know you'll finish this stupid worksheet way before the rest of us.

Dusty

I was grinning like an idiot. I quickly looked around me to make sure no one noticed. Everyone was still working on the assignment or was on their phone under their desk.

I picked my pencil up off my desk and started writing.

Chapter 8

Dusty

CAM: Thanks again for today. Or yesterday, I guess.
DUSTY: Anytime.

I'd been staring at that text exchange for the past week. Every spare moment I had—in the middle of the night when I couldn't sleep, in the early morning while I was getting ready for work—I looked at those two lines.

I hadn't heard anything from her since. I didn't really expect to. I'd been back in Meadowlark for a year, and before Saturday, the most I'd seen of her was the day I got home and accidentally intruded on girls' night. Occasionally, I'd get a text from her, but that had been happening for ten years.

First, when my dad died, then on my birthday, and a few times a year after that. They were always short and to the point, sometimes just pictures of Meadowlark or Rebel Blue or things she thought were funny. I responded most of the time, but not all of the time, because it hurt when she didn't keep the conversation going, which she never did.

She had Gus give me back my boots and my coat, but she kept the socks. I liked that, but I couldn't exactly explain why.

Cam's fancy car—a black Audi SUV—was outside of Gus's when I rode past on Saturday morning. It had been there all week. I figured she had started staying there instead of at the Big House.

It was nice that she had people she could lean on. I wished I could be one of those people.

Normally, I worked a lot on Saturdays—dropped hay by myself, checked cattle—which I usually used as an excuse for a nice long ride and pulled pastures, but today I had plans with my mom, so I only stayed at Rebel Blue for a few hours.

I told myself that I had chosen to ride the trail that went by Gus's because it was the fastest way to cut through the middle of the ranch, which was true, but that didn't mean I wasn't hoping for at least a glimpse of Cam. But no luck.

When I got back to my truck, I immediately put the heater on full blast and blew hot air into my hands. I pulled my phone out—a few texts from my mom making sure we were still on for today, a couple from ranch hands, and some other random notifications.

I texted my mom and told her I was on my way and cleared the rest. I'd worry about everyone else later.

Before I could set my phone down, it lit up with Greer's name and picture. I answered immediately.

"Talk to me," I said. It was how my dad used to answer the phone, and without realizing it, Greer and I started using it but only when we called each other.

"Hey," she said. "Are you on your way to Mom's?"

"You are way too aware of my schedule for someone who lives in Alaska," I said.

"I just got off the phone with her," Greer responded. "She told me that Cam's wedding didn't happen." Of course she did.

"Have you ever thought about easing into a topic, rather than throwing it all out there?"

"Nope. So?"

"So what?"

"Does that mean you're staying in Meadowlark?" Greer understood the restlessness I felt, how easy it became to move from place to place, season to season.

"Who wants to know?" I asked.

"There's this cattle ranch like a hundred miles from me that is looking for workers for summer—including like a ranch manager. Apparently, someone died." Greer was always a blunt person. "Some of the guys were talking about it."

I swallowed. Normally, this time of the year would be when I'd start looking for something new—prepping for the seasonal shift. This also wasn't the first job someone had put on my radar recently.

"I don't know, G," I said. "I'll have to see how things shake out."

"Right," Greer responded. I could hear her eye roll. "Things."

"Yeah, things," I said. "And I think Mom likes having one of us around. How would she feel if I ditched her to come hang out with you in Alaska?" I missed my sister, and it would be nice to be close to her, but I wasn't looking for something new—I didn't think.

"Okay, cheap shot," Greer said. "But do you want me to send you the info? In case things shake the wrong way?"

"Sure," I said. "I'll look at it."

"Coming your way. I gotta go, though. I'll call you later this week?"

"Sounds good," I said. "Love you."

"Love you." Greer hung up, and I continued my drive.

The drive from Rebel Blue to my mom's house was about twenty-five minutes—maybe a little more since coming down from Rebel Blue was a little more precarious in the winter. The already skinny roads were even skinnier because they were lined with snow, and you had to watch for ice. Once you got to the bottom of the hill, though, it got better.

Aggie Tucker lived on a five-acre plot of land on the other side of town—only about ten minutes from Hank, Teddy's dad. It was the same house I had grown up in—a small farmhouse with three bedrooms, one for my parents, one for Greer, and one for me—and two bathrooms, which meant that I shared a bathroom with my sister. I was still traumatized by it. Girls were messy as hell. And there was always hair everywhere.

When I made it to my mom's, I wanted to get out of my car and into the house as quickly as I could, but first I grabbed a small pile of firewood from the side of the house before opening the door.

The floorboards creaked, and there was always a draft blowing through from somewhere, but it was still home. It smelled like cinnamon and coffee; my mom had been putting cinnamon in her coffee grounds for as long as I could remember. She also made coffee strong enough that it tasted vaguely like motor oil. But it always did the trick.

I found her in the kitchen, washing out her coffeepot and getting it ready for the next morning.

"Knock, knock," I said, tapping my knuckles on the open doorframe that led into the kitchen.

"You think I didn't hear that squeaky as hell door hinge when you came in?" my mom said without looking up from her task. Her long, gray hair was in a braid down her back, and she was wearing a pair of dark brown coveralls. Her stack of silver bracelets on each wrist jingled as she moved.

"Is that your way of telling me I need to fix it?"

My mom looked up and gave me a smile. "Thank you so much for offering, sweetie. How was work today?"

"Good," I said. "Cold." Working at Rebel Blue in the winter was a lot different from any other season—most of the cattle were moved to a lower ground, winter pasture, but it was a good time for indoor and outdoor maintenance, which was what I was doing today. Winter was all about preparation, and Gus was a hardass for preparation. Well, a hardass in general, but he knew what he was doing.

This was my first time in a long time working an actual winter in the mountains. Usually, after whatever job or ranch I was on in the summer, I would head to Arizona, New Mexico, or South America and work someplace warm. I was like a bird: I preferred to fly south for the winter. I was still getting used to staying put.

"This winter hasn't been too bad," my mom said as she poured water into the back of her coffeepot, which had seen better days. "Just as cold as usual but not that much snow."

"Should I buy you a new coffeepot?" I asked, nodding toward hers.

"Don't you dare," my mom said. "I want to be buried with this one."

"Morbid, Mom," I murmured.

"No." She shook her head. She was scooping in the ground coffee now. "What's morbid is knowing the only people at my funeral will be you and Greer—no significant others, no grandkids."

Again? She'd really been on this lately. "Mo-ther," I said, enunciating and dragging out each syllable.

"I'm just saying is all." My mom shrugged as she threw a dash of cinnamon in the ground coffee. "How's Cam?"

My mom was as subtle as a gunshot. That's where Greer got it from. "I thought we were building shit today," I said. "Having some good ol' fashioned bonding time."

"We are," she said.

"Can we do it without the interrogation?" I asked.

"Afraid not, kiddo," she said. "But we can wait until we get in the workshop." My mom handed me a thermos of coffee and picked up one for herself—she must have poured them from her batch of coffee this morning. She never made less than a full pot.

I sighed and followed her out the back door toward the barn with my coffee and the firewood. When my mom and dad had bought the house, it had been a functional barn, but they quickly converted it to a workshop for her. She had been working out of it for as long as I could remember.

She unlocked the door and slid it open. In the summer, she worked with the barn door open to let the mountain breezes in, but it was too cold now. I headed toward the back and pushed open a window for ventilation before I got the fire going nearby. There was a small chimney, but ventilation was important in a small space—especially in a small space full of wood. And sawdust. So much sawdust.

"So," I said, rubbing my hands together, "what are we building today?"

"Mid-century-style credenza and a couple of custom bookshelves," my mom said. "And if we get through that, you can help me place wood for a butcher block countertop."

My mom was ridiculously talented. She made beautiful things that withstood generations—like the Ryders' kitchen table and the bar at the Devil's Boot.

"Good stuff," I said, taking off my coat but leaving my jacket on. Once we got working, it would get a little warmer—especially with the fire going. My mom handed me a piece of paper that had on it her sketches and a detailed breakdown of every piece of wood she needed cut and its size, which was my job today.

I loved her sketches. She always did them on a legal notepad, and when she was done with the job, I tried to keep as many of them as I could before she'd throw them away. She would say I was too sentimental, but I just liked collecting the things that showcased her work. Some people got written recipes or sewing patterns from their moms; I got these. I started saving them after my dad died. I wished I had more from him.

There was a stack of wood planks next to the saw, ready for cutting. I walked over to it and started getting everything ready.

"So," my mom said, "how is Cam?"

"I don't know, Mom." I sighed. "It's not like we talk."

"But you do play shotgun rider to her runaway bride after her non-wedding?" I rolled my eyes. Of course she knew about that. If I had to guess, that gossip Luke Brooks was probably to blame.

Technically speaking, Cam was the shotgun rider, not me. "That was nothing," I said. "Just me helping out a friend."

"So you two are friends?"

"No." Maybe? I ran a hand through my hair, a little

frustrated—not at my mom, but at the whole situation. I didn't like the questioning.

"But you just said that you were helping out a friend."

"Cam is my friend," I said, which was true—at least to me. "But I don't know if I'm hers."

"That doesn't make any sense." I knew my mom was giving me a pointed look, but I didn't look up at her.

"You're telling me," I muttered.

"So what are you going to do?" she asked.

"Nothing, Mom," I said. "I know that you love Cam, and I know you think she's the reason I came home, but she isn't. Just because she's technically 'available' now, or whatever, doesn't mean that anything is going to happen between us." I swallowed, trying to smother the hope ember that burned in my chest whenever I thought about Cam. "I feel bad that she got hurt, and I wanted to help her feel better . . . by being her friend."

"But you still feel something for her," my mom said.

"How could I not?" I asked. "But I don't even know her anymore." My feelings for Cam were like an earthquake and its aftershocks. When they started, they were big and overwhelming, and once the main event had passed—once we'd gone our separate ways—I'd learned to live with the way they still shook me up at unexpected times.

And when I saw her now, I still felt that small tremor in my bones. But I didn't know if the feelings were real or if they were the ghosts of something I hadn't felt in a long time.

"But isn't there an opportunity to get to know her again now?"

"I don't know if I can," I said, even though I really wanted to. "Without everything else getting in the way." Cam and I had baggage—baggage that I didn't know if I was ready to open.

"You drive your mother crazy, Ter—"

I cut my mom off immediately. "All right, no need to bring the full name into this. You made your point."

My mom gave me a smug smile. "Think I could pull off blackmail? What if I take out an ad in the paper with your full name unless you ask Cam on a date—once the appropriate waiting period after her wedding has passed, of course."

"I think you could," I said. "But I don't think you would."

My mom shook a finger at me. "God damn the fact that I love you so much, Dusty. Let's build shit."

Chapter 9

Cam

When I woke up on Saturday morning, I found Ada, Emmy, and Teddy waiting for me in Gus's kitchen. It smelled like they had made coffee and breakfast.

"Morning!" Emmy said cheerfully. She was holding a coffee cup with both hands, soaking in its warmth. Emmy was never this cheery in the morning, a legendary grumpy riser.

"Are you hungry?" Teddy asked. She was at the stove piling a plate high with pancakes. Ada just smiled at me and went back to what she was doing on her iPad.

"What's going on?" I asked suspiciously, taking a seat at the kitchen table.

Emmy bit her lip and was quiet for a second. "It's time, Cam," she said. "You've been staying at your baby daddy's house for a week—we think it might be time to start thinking about what's next." Emmy's voice was soft—thoughtful. I had only stayed at the Big House with Amos for two nights before I migrated over here. I knew Gus had been worried about me.

"Not that we don't love having you," Teddy chimed in as

she slid a plate of pancakes toward me. "We'd all do anything for you, but it might be time to re-establish some routine here. Maybe some normal boundaries, you know?"

Oh god. Teddy Andersen was telling me about routine? And boundaries?

She took the seat next to me and bumped my shoulder with hers. "I am a saint, but a week is where I have to draw the line," she said with a laugh. "I need to get laid."

Ada snorted at that, and Emmy made a gagging noise.

"Oh, grow up, Clementine," Teddy teased. "I'm just saying—things have taken a little bit of a hit in that department lately. But I don't want Cam to be subjected to all of the sounds coming from our bedroom across the hall when the dam finally breaks."

"Oh god." Emmy put her hands over her ears. "Make it stop."

"Understandable." I sighed. Both she and Gus had been so kind to me this week—too kind, almost—especially for two people who were better known for their tough love.

"But only if you're ready," Emmy said, and Teddy and Ada nodded in agreement.

"It's understandable if you aren't," Ada said. "You can also come stay with me and Wes to give Gus and Teddy some . . . um . . . alone time."

"I can't just bounce between all of your houses for the foreseeable future." I sighed. "Teddy's right. It's time to get some routine back—for me and Riley."

Teddy smiled. "I was hoping you'd say that. Not in a 'I want you out of my house' way but in a 'we have a plan' way."

"What did you have in mind?" I asked.

"Well," Ada said from across the table, "I've put together a list of every home in Meadowlark that's for sale or for rent, which is not that many, but it's enough for us to work with." She slid her iPad across the table to me.

"The ones highlighted in green are the ones that I think are the most promising based on size, cost, and location. I figured at least three bedrooms and at least close-ish to Rebel Blue."

Ada's love of organization spoke to my soul. I slowly scrolled through her list, thankful that she'd included pictures. I got to a blue Craftsman-style cottage and stopped.

"Is this the Wilson house?" I asked and looked up, even though I already knew the answer.

Emmy nodded excitedly. "Just went up for rent yesterday. Apparently, Mrs. Wilson moved into a care facility."

Anne Wilson was a kind, elderly woman who was as much a part of Meadowlark as the diner or the Devil's Boot. I met her when I was in high school. Dusty and I used to park at her house before we went hiking, and she would leave treats on her porch for when we were done. Like everyone I knew, Anne loved Dusty. I remember him weeding her yard in the summer and shoveling snow for her in the winter, but most of all, I remember him talking to her and listening to her stories.

I thought back to the gas station and how Dusty was so at ease with Stan. He'd always had a knack for people and loved building and maintaining relationships. There were probably hundreds of Annes and Stans in the world now, since Dusty had been all around it.

"According to the clerk at the post office," Ada said, "there's already been a lot of interest in it." My shoulders sagged a little. Of course there was—it was a beautiful home.

"But," Teddy said, holding a finger up, "we have an advantage."

"How so?" I asked.

"Well, you obviously get pity points because you got left at the altar," Teddy said with a wave of her hand. "And the real estate agent in charge of vetting tenants is Ed Wyatt."

I didn't know Ed. "How does that give me an advantage?" I asked.

"Because Ed's little brother still has a soft spot for his high school homecoming date." Teddy's gaze moved to Emmy. "The one and only Clementine Ryder."

Emmy rolled her eyes and held up her left hand and wiggled her ring finger, which was adorned with a simple diamond-encrusted gold band. "I don't think that advantage applies anymore, Ted."

"Only one way to find out," Teddy said before looking back at me. "Is this the house you want, Cam?" That didn't even cover it. This is the house I had *always* wanted. I slowly nodded. "All right then. Let's get it for you."

Teddy stood up, walked over to Emmy, and pulled Emmy's phone out of her back pocket. Emmy immediately tried to snatch it back, but Teddy was already on the move.

"I can't believe your password is 'brooks,'" she called back to Emmy as Emmy chased her around the table. "You two are so predictable."

"Give me the phone, Teddy!"

"Kenny Wyatt, where are you?" Teddy was focused on scrolling but was still managing to evade Emmy. "There you are, you cheating bastard."

"You really need to get over that," Emmy said. "He kissed another girl at *junior homecoming*." Emmy emphasized the last two words of her sentence. "As in *high school*!"

"As your best friend, I will never be getting over that,"

Teddy said before she tapped Emmy's phone screen a few times. The ring tone of an outgoing call filled the room, and Teddy finally gave the phone back to Emmy.

"What do I even say?" Emmy whisper-yelled, but Teddy didn't have time to answer because a man's voice picked up the phone.

"Emmy?" Kenny Wyatt's voice was on the other end.

"Hey, Kenny," Emmy said calmly. If I couldn't see her, I would never know that she was giving Teddy the world's dirtiest looks. "How are you?"

"Uh . . . good?" I'd never heard a man sound more confused than right now.

"That's good," Emmy said, and Teddy gestured for her to keep going. "So, um, I don't know if you heard about Cam . . ." Emmy trailed off, and I flinched.

"Oh, yeah," Kenny said. "I'm really sorry. That really sucks." Kenny did not even sound a little bit sorry.

"Yeah, so Cam needs a new place to live—we're trying to keep her in Meadowlark because of Riley, you know . . ."—nice, use the kid—"and I saw that your brother is vetting renters for Anne Wilson's place."

"Yeah, he is. His phone has been ringing off the hook, apparently."

"I'm sure," Emmy said, getting a little more confident in her delivery. "Cam loves the house, and it would be so perfect for her and Riley. I was wondering if you might be able to put in a good word for Cam?"

"Oh, Emmy, I don't—" Emmy cut him off.

"Please, Kenny. It would mean a lot to me." If she were face-to-face with Kenny right now, I am a thousand percent certain she would've batted her eyelashes at him.

The phone was silent, and I held my breath.

"Okay," Kenny finally said. "I'll call him now. I'll text you when I hear from him."

"Okay! Thanks, Kenny."

"Anytime." Emmy cringed as she said goodbye and hung up the phone. She immediately pointed a finger at Teddy.

"You are the most annoying person that has ever walked the planet," she said.

Teddy just smiled. "All right, now that that's taken care of"—she shifted her gaze to me—"let's talk about how we're going to get your shit out of dickwad's house."

"Don't I need to like . . . send an email or something? Make sure Ed knows that I'm interested in touring the property?"

"Already sent on your behalf while Emmy was on the phone," Ada chimed in. These women were unstoppable.

Emmy and Teddy both sat down at the table. "So," Teddy said, "have you talked to Graham at all?" I shook my head. I hadn't talked to anyone. I'd even ignored every call from my parents, which I would no doubt pay for very soon. When I was here, at Rebel Blue, surrounded by my daughter's family, I felt braver than I normally did—not brave enough to deal with Graham on my own, though.

"Do you want one of us to do it?" Emmy asked thoughtfully.

"I can," Ada said, and I nodded. I trusted Ada with this. I trusted Teddy and Emmy, too, but I could depend on Ada to do this gently and quietly and in a way that allowed me to get in and out with minimal damage. She would let me avoid what I wanted to avoid. I wasn't like Emmy or Teddy, who never backed down from a fight. I didn't have it in me to get mad at Graham or tell him all the ways in which what he did was wrong. Sometimes, I wished I wasn't so comfortable with going quietly, but I would just rather things be easy.

"Thank you," I said.

"No problem," she said with a kind smile. I met Ada when she came to Meadowlark last year to help Wes renovate one of Rebel Blue's buildings into a guest ranch. I liked her immediately. She and I were similar. We were both a little quieter and tended to live inside of our own heads. Sometimes, we both felt a little outside of everything, which wasn't a bad thing— being in the center of the action was never really my thing; I preferred to watch from the outside, and so did Ada. We did it together. I handed my phone to her, and she nodded.

"Kenny texted!" Emmy said excitedly. "We can look at the house today at four."

"Seems like that soft spot is still as soft as a marshmallow," Teddy said with a mischievous smile. "Kind of a bummer that he never stood a chance."

Chapter 10

Cam

Fifteen Years Ago

Cam,

Thanks for letting me borrow another piece of paper. You've turned me into a college-ruled snob. There's so much more room to talk to you on this. I've been thinking about the answers to all of your questions. We have the same favorite color, which is kind of a big deal—could be a sign, I think. And you've got some weird favorite foods, but I kind of like it. I don't know if I have a favorite food. My mom says I'm a bottomless pit, though.

Good luck at your soccer game today. I hope you kick all the ass.

Dusty

P.S. I'm still working on a nickname for you, but don't worry, I'll figure something out.

I triple-checked my ponytail before I left the locker room. I did the same thing for every game—high ponytail, braided, so my curls wouldn't show as much when I started to sweat, and a pre-wrap headband. I smoothed out the wrinkles in my crimson-and-white uniform for what felt like the ninth time.

Today was my first game as a Meadowlark Mustang. I wasn't nervous about playing; I loved soccer, and I was good at it. I was nervous about playing here. I wanted to prove to my team that I was an essential part of it, that I had found my place at Meadowlark High. I was so used to caring about my parents' expectations of me; it felt good to care about my own expectations for myself. But it was scary, too.

"Ready, Cam?" one of my teammates, Chloe, called. Most of the team had taken to calling me that. I liked it. I'd never had a nickname before. It made me feel like I was part of something.

"Yeah," I said as I hoisted my duffel onto my shoulders. "Let's do this."

Walking out onto the field was incredible. There were so many people in the stands—or maybe the stands were just tiny. Either way, it felt electric and buzzing.

Chloe waved to someone in the stands, and I followed her gaze. "My parents," she said. "Are yours here?"

I swallowed. "Not this time," I said. Not ever. My parents never come to my games. They never would. They would much rather I row or play field hockey or even tennis or some other sport that was rich people coded. They definitely wouldn't come for soccer.

They wouldn't come for me.

My parents weren't really the supportive kind—at least not in the being involved in the things I liked sort of way. They supported *me in other ways, though—the material ways. I'd never really wanted for anything that could be bought, which I was grateful for, but I wanted plenty for the stuff that couldn't.*

I scanned the stands and spotted a familiar mop of blond hair near the middle. Dusty. Did he usually come to soccer games? He was talking to a couple of cheerleaders. They didn't have to dress in their uniforms for girls' soccer because they weren't cheering, but they still wore their glittery scrunchies in their ponytails and matching T-shirts.

One of the girls was gripping Dusty's face by his chin, and it looked like she was . . . drawing on him?

A knot formed in my stomach at the sight of them, and I felt my brows knit together. I didn't know what this feeling was, but I really didn't like it.

So I did what I always do with my feelings: I ignored them and prepared to go out onto the field.

After the game, Chloe pulled me into a side hug as we walked off the field. "Hell of a game, Cam!" she said. I was awkward about it—didn't quite know what to do, but she didn't seem to notice.

"Thanks, Chloe. You too!"

"But I didn't score two goals," she said with a smile. I felt my cheeks heat a little, and I tried not to smile. I did have a great game. Maybe it was because I was extra focused; I didn't want to look over at Dusty and the cheerleaders.

Before I could respond to Chloe, a pair of arms wrapped around me, lifting me, and whipping me around. "Holy shit, Cam." Dusty's voice. Dusty's arms. Dusty's smell. "You were incredible out there!"

A surprised laugh escaped me as he spun me around one more time before lowering me to the ground. His gray eyes met mine. They were bright and excited—they matched his smile.

"*You were like a machine,*" *he continued excitedly.* "*And when you knocked that girl down?*" *Dusty winked at me.* "*Hot.*"

I blushed a deep red as I looked up at Dusty. His right cheek caught my eye. In black eyeliner, someone—the cheerleader, apparently—had written the number 33. My number.

"*You have something on your face,*" *I said—not acknowledging the "hot" thing. No one had ever called me that before.*

Dusty's smile widened. "*Like it?*" *he said, holding one of his hands under his cheek.* "*I did it for you.*"

Chloe cleared her throat before I could respond. I forgot she was standing by me. When I looked over at her, she had a knowing smirk on her face. "*You good?*" *she asked.*

"*Yeah,*" *I said.* "*I'm good.*"

She nodded. "*I'll see you tomorrow.*" *She turned to Dusty.* "*Bye, Dusty.*"

"*See you, Chloe. I'm weeding your grandma's yard this weekend if you want to help,*" *he said with a grin.*

"*Unlike you, I can park there to hike without feeling like I need to do manual labor, so I'll pass,*" *Chloe called back as she walked away.*

Dusty brought his attention back to me. "*So,*" *he said,* "*are your parents here or anything?*"

I shook my head. "*They don't really come to my games,*" *I said.* "*My dad, um, works a lot, and my mom doesn't like soccer.*"

"*Oh,*" *Dusty said. He looked confused by that.* "*But they'll be happy that you won, right? And that you scored a goal?*"

"*Yeah,*" *I said.* "*I'll, um, tell them later.*"

"*So, if they're not here, can I give you a ride home?*"

"*Um,*" *I said. I had a driver's license—I just didn't have a car. Usually, my parents had my driver—Matthew—drive me to and from school and everything else. I didn't know how they'd react to a boy dropping me off. Maybe they wouldn't notice? I pulled out my phone, flipped it open, and sent a quick text to Matthew, letting him know that I didn't need a ride home.*

"Sure," I said. "Yeah. Just let me get my bag." Dusty walked over to the sidelines with me, and when he saw my number on my duffel, he picked it up and slung it over his shoulder.

Before we started walking, he looked at me, and his eyes narrowed a little bit. "Is your hair naturally curly?" he asked. I normally straightened it for school, so Dusty hadn't seen it before. I frantically tried to smooth my ponytail and tuck the stray ringlets behind my ears. "No, don't," he said as he grabbed my wrist softly. "I like it."

Chapter 11

Cam

Emmy came with me to see the house. Gus had taken Riley on a snowy trail ride through Rebel Blue this morning and had planned for them to eat dinner with his dad, so I was officially off mom duty for the afternoon and evening. Though I guess finding a place to live for my child and me is still mom duty.

I had been worried about how Riley would deal with the move and the absence of Graham, but so far, it has been okay. I think going between my place and Gus's house throughout her life made her a little more adaptable. She was a curious kid and asked a lot of questions about why Graham wasn't coming with us or why I wasn't married when I said I was going to be. Both Gus and I went with the "sometimes things don't work out" explanation, which, thankfully, seemed to work.

The Wilson house was only ten minutes from the entrance of Rebel Blue. It was placed perfectly between there and town. It had neighbors but not close ones. Also, if you walked through the trees in the backyard, you'd end up at one of Meadowlark's best trailheads that led to so many trail systems, you'd never run out of things to explore. Riley would love it. But I couldn't get ahead of myself.

Emmy drove her truck down the long gravel driveway—the house was tucked back in an alcove. You'd never see it if you didn't know it was there. The driveway was framed by evergreens, which were currently dusted with snow.

After a few minutes, a powder blue house came into view. It was a classic craftsman with gorgeous lines and a large front porch—complete with a swing. The yard around it was covered in more than a foot of snow, but I knew it was big, and in the summer, teeming with greenery and flowers and buzzing with bumblebees.

The truck rolled to a stop in front of the house, right next to a flashy Mercedes SUV, which was probably Ed's. Emmy cut the engine, and quiet filled the cab in place of Chris Stapleton.

I sat with the quiet, grateful that Emmy did, too. I used to long for quiet, but lately, I had felt afraid of it. There were so many things waiting inside of it that I had to face. But I was happy to stay here—just for a second.

"Ready?" Emmy asked softly. Instead of answering, I pushed open the passenger door and let the cold bite at the exposed skin on my face, neck, and hands. I hated winter, but I loved the way that the air hit my lungs with a jolting refresh. I needed that right now.

My feet hit the gravel as Emmy walked around the front of her truck and looped her arm through mine as we walked toward the stairs, steadying me.

"You feel okay?" she asked.

"Yeah," I said. "Just don't want to get my hopes up, you know?"

"Let's manifest the Teddy Andersen approach to life: Only have a Plan A and trust everything works out," she said with a light laugh.

We walked up the stairs, and Emmy knocked on the door. I heard footsteps approach from inside.

A few seconds later, Ed Wyatt opened the door. He had dark brown hair and was wearing a suit that didn't quite fit right. That was one skill being an Ashwood gave me—I could spot a bad suit from a mile away.

"Ed, hi!" Emmy said. "How are you?"

"Good to see you, Emmy," he said with an outstretched hand, which Emmy took. He looked at me, then, and said, "You're Camille?"

"That's me," I said, trying to keep my voice light.

"Nice to meet you," he said as he moved his hand from Emmy's to mine. "Anne was excited to hear that you were interested in the house."

"She was?" I asked, touched that Anne even remembered who I was.

Ed nodded. "She said you spent a lot of time here in high school." "A lot" was generous, but this house and I were definitely familiar. "She said not to even show it to anyone else unless you decide you don't want it."

Emmy squeezed my arm. "Oh my god, that's great news!" she exclaimed. "I didn't know you and Anne were that close, Cam." I laughed sheepishly. Me either.

"So let me walk you through," Ed said, turning to start walking deeper into the house. "The house was built in 1929. Anne and her husband, Arnold, bought it in the fifties. They raised three children here, and it was well loved by their grandkids and their neighborhood, too.

"Over here we have the formal living room," Ed said. There were two cream-colored love seats and a pink velvet chair. "Kind of a relic, but with bay windows like that, you'll definitely be spending some time in here, I'm sure. Formal dining is on the other side, but Anne currently has that set up as a library."

"Is she hoping to rent the house furnished?" Emmy asked.

"So only the common areas are furnished currently, and Anne is happy to leave them that way. The bedrooms, though, are a clean slate." That was good. Riley loved her canopy bed.

"Partially furnished is great," I chimed in. The only furniture that I owned was Riley's. Graham had bought everything else for the house—it was all his. I'd have to figure out a bed and stuff for myself, but that didn't matter.

"Great," Ed said. "Let's keep going." We walked down a short hallway toward an open space. "Kitchen and living room. There is a fully functioning wood-burning fireplace there." Ed pointed at the north side of the room. The fireplace was outlined by gorgeous red brick and a dark wood mantel.

"Kitchen appliances were updated about five years ago. All stainless steel, and the stove is gas," Ed said. "And a dishwasher was added, which wasn't there before."

"It's beautiful," I said as I looked around. It was so close to how I remembered it—warm and inviting. A mishmash of colors and styles, maybe one too many for me, but the way they came together made it feel unique and classic all at once. Plus I thought Ada could help me with design to make it feel more cohesive. A little simpler, which was just the way I liked things.

"The primary bedroom is behind the living room, and the two other bedrooms are behind the kitchen," Ed said.

I nodded. "En suite bath in the primary and a shared bathroom for the other bedrooms, right?"

"That's right. Laundry is in the basement—it's unfinished, so it's a little scary down there, but nothing too crazy."

"This is great," I said. "Really great." I could see Riley and me here. We'd be close to her dad—to her family.

"So you're feeling good about it then?" Ed asked. "Any questions?"

"Loads," I said, "but I think we're going to want this no matter what."

Ed clapped his hands together. "Perfect! There are a few housekeeping items that Anne wanted me to go over with you. Is that okay?" I nodded, waiting for him to continue. "Right now, she'll have you sign a twelve-month lease. The lease can be renewed if—this part is a little bit of a bummer, sorry—Anne is still with us. If she passes on during the tenure of your lease, it's contracted that you'll be able to finish it out, but it's up to the new owner's discretion on whether or not you can renew."

Christ, that was a downer. "Okay," I said. "Does she already know whose hands the house will fall into if that happens?"

"She does, and they've agreed to these terms."

"That's fine with me," I said. A year was plenty of time to figure my shit out—I hoped.

"The other stuff is less intense. She asks that you don't make any structural changes to the home, but you're welcome to hang things and do renter-friendly projects. The fireplace requires a lot of care, so she asks that you only use it if the groundskeeper gets it going and has permission to put it out."

"Groundskeeper?" I asked. That was new.

"Oh, yeah," Ed said with a "not a big deal" hand motion. "There's a smaller house on the edge of the property—basically a studio apartment but in house form. It's about two hundred square feet. Anne started renting it to a tenant last year. In exchange, he takes care of snow removal, yard work in the summer, and a lot of maintenance that Anne could no longer do. He's been a godsend to her."

"Who is it?" I asked, still wrapping my head around the fact that there was someone else on this property. That could be a game-changer.

"Maybe you know him," Ed said, pulling out his phone. "He's local. It's Dusty Tucker."

Chapter 12

Dusty

Cam,

I think I'm going to start writing you more notes. You kind of make me nervous, so it's easier to write things down. Don't tell anyone about the nervous thing, though. I have a reputation to uphold, ya know?

Can I give you a ride home from your soccer game again today? I'd like to make that a habit I think.

Also, my mom wants to know if you want to come to dinner sometime. Don't worry, she's nice and so is my dad. My little sister will probably be kind of annoying, but just because she'll be obsessed with you.

Say yes.

(please)

Dusty

I walked through the automatic doors of the Meadowlark Assisted Living Facility with flowers in one hand and a small bag of groceries in the other. The bag only had two things in it: tapioca pudding and canned peaches—Anne's favorites.

The assisted living facility in Meadowlark was small. It was less than a mile away from the hospital and had stunning views of the mountains out the back windows. Anne had been here for a few months, and I tried to come see her once a week to give her updates on what was going on at the house as well as some company. She didn't have any kids or grandkids who had stayed in Meadowlark, and even though I don't think she was lonely—she made friends fast—I liked coming here.

I found her in the sunroom with her e-reader. Anne had her reading glasses on, and the text on the screen was so large that only a paragraph fit on the screen at a time. I could read it from where I stood, but I didn't. I knew better than to read over a woman's shoulder. I had manners. She looked up before I said anything.

"I had a feeling that was you," she said with a smile. Anne's hair was short, white, and permed. She exclusively wore worn-out crewnecks in the winter and gingham button-downs in the summer.

"How'd you know?" I asked as I bent at the waist to hug her.

"You make a lot of noise," she said. "All those rings and buckles clinking around."

"New flowers for your room," I said, handing over the small baby's breath bouquet. "And some snacks."

"Just in time," Anne said with a soft smile. "I just threw out the old flowers yesterday. Thank you."

I nodded. "How are you?" I asked.

Anne's blue eyes gleamed. "I'm great," she said. "Apparently, one of the nurses started dating the son of one of the residents a few weeks ago, and they just had a big blowout breakup because the son was flirting with one of the nursing assistants."

I huffed a laugh and shook my head. "As much as I appreciate the gossip, I asked how you were."

"So you don't want to hear about the fact that I'm pretty sure Donald has two girlfriends, but neither of them know about the other because they're in different activity groups?" Donald was Anne's neighbor.

"I didn't say that," I said, smiling. "But I always want to know about you first."

Anne took off her reading glasses and let out a contented sigh. "I like it here more than I thought I would," she said. "Sometimes, I miss the house, but I don't miss feeling so isolated." She had a hard time getting around, and she didn't like to drive anymore. Her kids had been worried that her house was too secluded for her to get help if she needed it, so she didn't fight them when they brought up the move. "It's nice being so close to people, and there's always something going on. It's like living at the post office," she said with a grin. It was well known that the Meadowlark Post Office was a gossip hot spot.

"I'm glad," I said. "What did you do this week?"

Anne thought about it for a moment. "The service dogs came," she said. "And there was a painting class, too. I'm a shit painter."

"What did you paint?" I asked on a chuckle.

"One of the service dogs," she said. "I was going to give it to the owner next time they came, but I'm afraid they would think it's an insult." I shook my head on a laugh. "How's the house?" Anne asked after a second.

"Good," I said. "I probably need to replace the HVAC system before next winter. The heat has gone out a few times, but so far, it's been a quick fix every time."

"I should have Ed tell Cam about that," Anne said, looking back down at her e-reader. "She's looking at the house today."

I felt my eyes widen, but I tried to control my expression as I swallowed hard. I knew the house had been put up for rent, obviously. I knew Cam loved the house as much as I did. And I also knew that due to recent changes, Cam would be looking for a new place. But I'm not sure I ever could have really been prepared for the possibility that Cam and I could end up in such close proximity. "That's good," I said. I tried not to sound ruffled by it—to stay cool, calm, and steady.

"Does she know you live on the property?" Anne asked pointedly.

I rubbed at the back of my neck. "I don't know," I said. "But I'm sure she will soon if she doesn't already."

"It's a shame what happened to her. Poor girl," Anne said with a sigh. "I hope she's able to find some happiness. She's always been a good egg."

I nodded, not really sure what to say.

"Are you two still friends?" Anne asked.

"Kind of," I said. "We didn't really keep in touch while I was gone, but I've seen her a few times since I've been home." I was giving Anne the quick and easy version of events.

"Ah." Anne nodded. "Sounds like there's a story there." I felt it then, the hope ember starting to burn and glow in my chest again. That motherfucker refused to be smothered, and it was nearly impossible to ignore. Honestly, I didn't know if I wanted to smother it—didn't know if I could see the world without it being lit by the glow, but I knew my life would probably be a hell of a lot easier if it just went out.

I rolled my eyes. "You're worse than my mom," I said.

"She came to see me this week, too." That meant they probably spent a lot of time talking about me.

"Well, don't you have a packed social calendar," I responded.

Anne nodded. "That I do." On the small table next to her chair, her phone chimed and lit up with a message. I could read who it was from. Ed Wyatt.

Anne picked up her phone and unlocked it using her pointer finger. She smiled. "I've got a packed social calendar, and it looks like you're about to have a new neighbor."

I swallowed hard. *Here we go.*

Chapter 13

Cam

On Monday morning, I finally decided it was time to call my mother. Now that I had a plan—well, a place to live, at least—I felt that I could finally face her. I sat on the edge of the sofa bed in Gus's guest room and stared down at my phone. It was early, but she would be up.

And then I could move on with my day. It was moving day, after all.

I had made a pro and con list after finding out Dusty would basically be my neighbor. Ultimately, it wasn't ideal, but the Wilson house had been my dream home since I first laid eyes on it, and it had many things going for it, despite its closeness to a certain nose ring.

Everything about it was perfect—including the rent I could afford without access to my trust fund, the furniture, unique lease terms, and Gus being close, for Riley's sake. And from what Ed said, everything Dusty did for Anne was outside, except for the fireplace, which I had already decided I would never use.

But how was it that Dusty was *everywhere*? I didn't even know how he had time to do things for Anne while working at Rebel Blue and apparently visiting out-of-the-way gas stations to buy beef jerky once a month.

Luckily for me, I was an expert avoider—a gold medalist in avoidance.

I took a deep breath. *Let's get this over with.*

I scrolled through my contacts for Lillian Ashwood. Not Mom—Lillian. I clicked on her name before I could talk myself out of it and brought the phone up to my ear.

It only rang once.

"Camille," Lillian said. Her voice was dripping with disdain and disappointment. One word from her, and I already felt like I was two feet tall. "I was wondering when I'd hear from you."

"I'm sorry," I said quietly.

"Do you know how embarrassing it was for your father and me to be told that you'd left your own wedding? That the groom didn't even show up?" I stayed quiet. She didn't need me for this lecture. "And then, you spend over a week ignoring our calls—using that man"—Gus—"to give us updates on your whereabouts. And what about your daughter? How do you think she feels?"

I shut my eyes tight. "I'm sorry," I said again.

"It's not enough," she said. "Your father is beside himself. Graham's parents are blaming you, you know—saying you were the one that made this difficult." Interesting conclusion, considering I was the one who showed up. "And now, two years of planning and airtight contracts that would benefit both of our families are just gone."

"I know," I said. It didn't start this way—with the contracts or whatever. It started with me and Graham realizing we had a lot in common when it came to our parents—mostly that we wanted them to leave us alone. But both pairs of parents saw us getting married as a fortuitous opportunity, and everything just spiraled from there. Our fathers saw a partnership between our family businesses. It would be mutually beneficial—my father's bank would raise the capital of Graham's father's hedge fund and in turn, they would be in a good position to provide their clients an excellent return on investment, and all parties involved would make money. Which, of course, was always the most important thing. By the time I realized what was happening, I couldn't make them stop, so I decided to try to make the best of it by making sure Riley could benefit.

"And everything we agreed on for your daughter is gone with it," my mother said, as if she could read my mind. Riley was my mother's favorite weapon. This marriage was supposed to guarantee security for Riley. I had wanted to make sure she would never be forced to choose a specific degree or career . . . unlike me. When I was growing up, my parents had looked at me like an investment, so they incentivized the access to my trust to make sure they were getting the most for their money. I had to pick from a specific set of colleges and from there, a specific list of degrees that would lead to an approved career path. And, don't get me wrong, there were some things about their agreement that I appreciated—like I couldn't get married until I was twenty-five, but my parents had some stake in who I would end up marrying, obviously. But what had always made me most anxious about my own arrangement was that, if I didn't follow their guidelines, my trust fund could get revoked at any point. I know that makes me sound entitled and spoiled—maybe I am—but I've been taught my whole life that money matters. And, yeah, I know that money doesn't solve every problem, but for most people, I think it would solve most of them.

But I didn't want Riley to ever feel as if she was under anybody's thumb, not even mine. So I did what I'd watched my father do with his business my whole life: I seized the opportunity. I told my parents I wanted something out of this marriage, too—something tangible and airtight. A substantial trust fund for her, and her alone, and the cost of college covered to study wherever and whatever she wanted. When I came to them with my plans and a proposal for an agreement, I swear it was the first time my dad seemed proud of me. The contract was crafted carefully and meticulously by me and several senior attorneys at my firm in Jackson Hole. Once I got married, the trust would be put in Riley's name, and it couldn't be accessed by my parents or me. Amos would be the custodian—I trusted him. It was an irrevocable trust. There were no take-backs.

And I spent every piece of capital I had with my parents to make it that way. Capital that I'd been working on since I was eighteen—after I'd dug myself into the world's deepest hole with them because of Dusty.

But my marriage to Graham was the trigger, and it didn't happen, so everything I'd done for Riley and for this money and her future was for naught. Anger bubbled underneath my skin.

"Graham was the one who didn't hold up his end of the bargain, Mother," I said without thinking.

"Excuse me?" Lillian sounded shocked that I would talk back to her.

"Never mind," I said.

"This was a good thing for you, Camille. Who knows if you'll ever get an opportunity like that again. You come with a lot of . . . baggage." Did she just call Riley my "baggage"?

"I'm sorry," I said again through gritted teeth. Lillian was the reason I slept with a mouth guard.

My mother continued to ignore my apology. I wasn't even sure what I was apologizing for. "Your father and I need to do some damage control. I'll be in touch with updates about how we can possibly salvage your future. I expect you to answer your phone when I call."

"Yes, Mother," I said with a sigh that she could definitely hear.

And then she hung up.

Well, that wasn't so bad. It could've been a million times worse—it had been before. Maybe I was right to give both of my parents a cooling-off period. I looked around the room. I'd packed everything last night and cleaned it the best I could. I didn't have much—just what I'd packed for what was supposed to be my very glamourous honeymoon to a ski cabin in Park City, Utah. I'd brought the bag to the church with me, which in hindsight was a very good call.

I let out a breath as I reflected on the past week. I thought about how weird it was that I was staying in my baby daddy's guest room and yet, how it didn't feel weird at all that he and his fiancée had been there for me. I'd known since Gus and Teddy got together that she was good for my daughter, but it was a special thing to witness—how attentive Teddy was to Riley and her needs, how she brought out the best side of Gus, which he preferred to hide, and how when he told her I was staying here for a little while, she didn't bat an eye.

I knew why Gus offered up his guest room instead of letting me stay at the Big House with Amos. It wasn't just that he was worried. He knew that it would take a lot longer for me to leave the Big House than it would for me to leave his. I'd feel too safe, get too comfortable. I'd let Amos cook me breakfast and make me green smoothies for the rest of forever. But Gus knew that I'd start feeling weird if I stayed at his house for too long. It blurred the few boundaries that Gus's and my co-parenting relationship was built on. We parented together, but we were also our own people with our own lives—no matter how much they overlapped. He knew that if I stayed here, I'd eventually realize that I had to get up and stand on my own two feet again.

With one last look around the room, making sure I didn't forget anything, I wheeled my suitcase out to the kitchen, where Gus was drinking his coffee at the kitchen table.

"Morning," I said as I got closer to him.

"Morning," he said. "How are you feeling about today?"

"Good," I said. "Ada should be here soon. We'll take my car to Graham's, take everything we can fit. Wes and Brooks will follow with a truck and do the heavy lifting of Riley's furniture."

"Will Graham be there?" Gus asked.

I nodded. "Just to make sure I get inside."

"Have you talked to him at all?"

"No," I said. "Ada set this up. Plus, there's nothing for us to talk about." He went back on his word and on our agreement. He knew what that would cost me, and he didn't care. I didn't blame him, but I didn't need to talk to him about it.

Gus's dark eyebrows furrowed. "I feel like there's probably a lot for you guys to talk about," he said.

"There isn't." I shrugged. "Thank you for this week. You and Teddy have been incredible. I'm happy our daughter has you." My throat tightened. "I'm happy you're her dad—that she has a good one."

"She has a good mom, too, you know." *Does she?* I didn't feel that way—especially after my mother had just reminded me of everything that Riley had lost. I hoped she wouldn't miss something she never knew she was supposed to have.

"And tell your dad thank you for watching her today," I said. "I'll come pick her up tomorrow, and we'll get back to our regularly scheduled programming."

"Cam," Gus said. "Are you, you know—are you okay?"

"Fine," I said with a shrug. Always fine. "Ada and Wes are here," I said, looking down at my phone. "I'm just going to peek in Riley's room, and then I'm going to head out."

Gus looked like he wanted to say more but didn't. I walked past the table and headed up the stairs to Riley's room. Her door was open—Gus liked to peek in when he woke up. I didn't want to risk waking her, so I stood in the doorway.

She moved so much when she slept. Her comforter and sheets were chaotic—the fitted sheet was even pulled off the mattress in the corner. Her curly hair was just as crazy. The legs of her pajama pants had ridden up and were bunched around her thighs. Her mouth was wide open as she slept.

Every time I looked at my daughter, I got overwhelmed. I couldn't believe she existed and that she was mine. I couldn't believe something so smart and tenacious and clever came from me. And I wanted to make sure I could give her everything.

I wanted to stand in this doorway and watch her forever,

but I knew I had to get our new home ready. I blew her sleeping form a kiss and quietly descended back down the stairs.

Gus wasn't at the table anymore—probably went to say goodbye to Teddy—so I grabbed my suitcase and walked out the front door, where I found Wes and Ada parked and making out in the cab of Wes's truck.

Sometimes it was exhausting to be surrounded by people who were in love. I hit the hood of the truck with my palm, and the two of them jumped apart.

Wes had the decency to blush and look embarrassed, but Ada looked pleased as hell as she got out of the truck and gave me a hug.

"Disgusting," I said as she pulled me into a hug.

"Shut up," she said. "I told him to give us a fifteen-minute head start and then he's going to pick up Brooks—that way we can make sure Graham is gone before he gets there. Wes is the world's sweetest man, but I'm scared he might punch Graham in the face if given the opportunity. And Brooks is a wild card, honestly."

"Good call," I said, sending Wes a wave. He got out of the truck and immediately came for my suitcase.

"I'll put this in your trunk for you," he said. Always the gentleman.

"Thank you," I said. "And thank you for your help today. I appreciate it."

"Anywhere, anytime," he said with a smile.

"Do you want me to drive?" Ada asked, and I nodded as I handed her the keys. I was grateful she offered.

We got into my car and waved goodbye to Wes and started making our way out of Rebel Blue.

"So," Ada said, "I've been thinking."

"Dangerous," I responded.

"Since I'm coming to your rescue today, I think it's time you tell me what went down with you and Dusty." I froze. That was not what I was expecting.

"What do you mean?" I asked.

"I mean, I just think it's kind of weird that I've never really seen you guys interact, at least not if you can avoid it, yet he was the one you chose to spend the day of your almost-wedding with.

"You pretend like he doesn't exist, you don't talk about him at all, but you're okay with him living on the same property as you. I just want to know what the hell happened between you two that created this weird . . . thing . . . you guys have going on."

"We dated in high school," I said with a shrug. When I said that, it made it sound like that's all it was. Young love.

It was more than that, but when you fall in love that young, a lot of people spend a lot of time trying to convince you that it isn't real, and there's no way it will last.

I guess they were right about the latter part.

Dusty was my first everything, but not in just a first love way. He was my first real friend. He was the first person who cared enough to get to know me, who peeled back the layers I had drawn around myself and liked what they saw. He made me want to like myself, too.

"Well, duh," Ada said. "I know that, but everything about you two screams a whole lot more details than high school fling or sweethearts—especially in a town where those things are common."

I shrugged. "I don't really want to talk about it."

"Why?"

Because it hurts. "Because I don't."

"Cam," Ada said firmly. "I'm sorry, but you have to give me something. As your friend, I'm worried about you, and I'm worried about you being on the same slab of property as someone who obviously impacts you in a big way, and I can't tell if it's positive or negative."

For someone who told me she didn't have a lot of friends before coming to Meadowlark, Ada was a good one.

I let out a long sigh. "Look," I said. "You're right, Dusty impacts me, and it really isn't positive or negative . . . it just kind of *is*."

"Were you born being this cryptic? Or is it something you learned along the way?"

"Probably a little bit of both," I said. "I appreciate that you're worried about me, but I don't think you have to worry about Dusty and me."

"Why not?"

I shrugged. "Because he's a good person. It's not like he's living there to get closer to me. He's just doing his job."

"So you aren't even a little bit, like, apprehensive about this whole thing?"

"Of course I am," I said. "My high school boyfriend basically lives in my backyard. Wouldn't you be apprehensive? But really, I think any way I'm feeling right now has a lot more to do with me than with Dusty."

Ada pursed her lips. "Fine," she said. "I'll accept that answer. For now."

"And at the end of the day, this is about Riley. She deserves a house like that—a beautiful place to grow up."

"Okay then." Ada nodded. "Then that's what she'll get."

It took us about twenty minutes to get to Graham's. It was far out of town, like my parents', on a big piece of land with million-dollar views that we never would've used. The house was a new build—big and white and beautiful, but it had never felt like mine. Eventually, I think Graham would have floated the idea of us moving to Jackson Hole or Park City and keeping this as a second home. But that never would have happened. He didn't love Meadowlark, but I did.

Graham and I didn't have a bad relationship. It just . . . wasn't a relationship. Both of us were aware that it was convenient, easy, and both of us benefited from it. I liked Graham. He was nice, and there were times when I thought he was my friend, but I wasn't in love with him, and I knew I never would be. We both decided to settle for a half life, but if it meant our parents would leave us alone, then that would be nice enough. We would both get to exist in peace, which might not sound like a lot to some people, but it was a lot for me and even more for Graham.

Graham's parents were worse than mine, which is why I still couldn't figure out why he didn't show—what was worth more than the life we agreed to and wanted for each other.

I was so tangled up in my own thoughts that I didn't realize that Ada had already turned off the car and gotten out. I scrambled out behind her. She walked—stomped, actually, thanks to the platform Docs she loves so much—up to the front door. Her shoulders were back, and her head was held high; it reminded me to hold mine high, too.

Even though my life was shit, I took a moment to be proud of my friend and how much she'd grown into herself again since I'd met her.

Maybe I could do that, too.

Ada looked back at me. "You ready?"

No. "Yes," I said, a few steps behind her as she lifted her hand to knock on the front door.

Graham opened it less than a second later. He looked nice. He was handsome with his dark hair, classic haircut, and blue eyes. His face faltered a little bit when he saw me. That felt good.

"Hi, Camille," he said. It was always Camille. Never Cam.

"I'm . . ." Ada said slowly, "going to get the boxes out of the car." She walked back to the car, giving Graham and me some privacy—even though I knew she'd be doing her best to listen from where she was.

"Hello," I said with a small nod.

Graham slid his hands into his front pockets and pursed his lips. After a few seconds, he spoke. "I'm sorry," he whispered. I nodded. "I couldn't do it."

"Yeah," I said, straightening my spine a little. "So you said. In your note."

Graham flinched, and I let the uncomfortable silence continue for a few breaths. "Why?" I finally asked.

He brought a hand up and rubbed at the back of his neck. "I . . . met someone." I felt my eyes widen. "Nothing happened," he said quickly. "You're great, Cam, you're so great. I know our life would've been great, but . . ."

". . . it wouldn't be *that*." I finished for him.

His blue eyes looked sad. "Yeah," he said. "I know that this isn't what we planned, and I'm just so fucking sorry."

"I . . . get it," I said, and I did. I understood what he'd be giving up if he married me because I would have to give it up, too—love, passion, and all the uncertainty and heartbreak that came with it. The difference between Graham and me was that I wanted to give all that up. Life got so much easier when there were fewer possibilities—fewer choices to make, fewer chances that you'd make the wrong one.

"I should've told you earlier," he said.

"You should've," I agreed.

"If it makes you feel better, my parents are pissed," he said. "They're probably going to disown me."

If only. "Worth it, though?" I asked.

Graham's face went soft. "Yeah," he said.

I slid my engagement ring off my finger and handed it to him. He took it gently. It was a family heirloom—passed down through generations, so I couldn't keep it or pawn it or throw it into a lake. "This is yours," I said.

Graham nodded. "I'll let you get to it. Just leave your key under the mat when you're done. I'll be back in a few hours."

I nodded, and Graham walked past me and to his car. He gave me one last look before he got in and backed out of the driveway.

"So, I feel like that went as well as it could go?" Ada said, appearing next to me.

"You have got to stop eavesdropping," I said with an exaggerated eye roll. I swear, it was her favorite hobby since she'd moved to Meadowlark.

"I'll stop when I'm dead," she said as she pushed the front door of the house open. "Wes and Brooks will be here soon. Let's get your shit."

Chapter 14

Dusty

On Monday morning, I was tacking up Huey in the stables. I didn't have my own horse at Rebel Blue, which was normal for me, so I didn't mind. I liked riding all the different horses, depending on my mood or needs that day. Horses were like people. They each had their own distinct personalities—especially when they were working. Huey had become one of my favorite mounts, but he was also one of Emmy's, so we had this running thing going where whoever got to the stables first would take him so the other couldn't. Unfortunately for Emmy, I don't sleep well, and I get bored easily, so I always ended up at work way earlier than I needed to be.

I was taking a quick picture of Huey tacked up to send to Emmy when Gus and Amos walked in.

"Good morning," I said to both of them.

"Getting an early start?" Amos smiled at me. It was impossible not to be at ease when he was around. Gus, on the other hand, brought a little less ease to the table, but I don't think it was intentional.

"Yes, sir. I had to get to Huey before Emmy could," I said with a grin, and Amos let out a hearty laugh.

"Ah," he said, eyes gleaming. "I'm surprised she's still playing by the rules. Clementine usually finds a way to get what she wants."

"Did you just admit she's spoiled?" Gus asked.

Amos shook his head. "Not spoiled, loved."

"Right," Gus responded with an eye roll. His lip was twitching a little before he looked at me. "I'm surprised you have time to get here early. I heard you've got a lot going on." That felt like a direct nod to the fact that I was the caretaker for what was about to become Cam's house.

"It's nice of you to help Anne out," Amos said, shooting Gus a look. "That's what we wanted to talk to you about, actually." Cam? "A job," Amos finished.

"I thought I already had one of those here," I said.

"You do," Amos said. "And we appreciate you. You're great at managing the ranch hands and maintenance. You've filled a gap that we didn't know we had. Right, August?"

"Right," Gus said before he took a deep breath. "So we've been working on trying to get a horse sanctuary up and running here over the past couple of years." That didn't surprise me. Amos basically ran a non-official one anyway. He was constantly bringing horses home, and even when the horses he already had couldn't work anymore, he kept them. They all got to live out retirement in the hills of Rebel Blue, cared for by Amos himself and his daughter, who loved horses the same way he did. It was the same way I did, too.

I nodded. "This is a great place for a sanctuary. You have the room."

"And we can make more," Amos said, gesturing to the stables around us. The Ryders had three barns on the property: one for their horses, one for ranch hands to keep their horses if they had their own, and one that was currently empty. "You've worked at other sanctuaries before, right?"

"Yeah." I nodded. My favorite one was in Mexico. Most of the horses there had been found emaciated on the side of the road or had spent their lives tied to something. But, in this safe haven, they got to join a gaggle of animals running free around the place. My favorites were Mojo—a three-legged dog who was a food thief—and Choya, a goat that thought he was a dog. "A few. They were a great place to work."

"So would you be interested in helping us get Rebel Blue's version of one off the ground?"

"Not just off the ground," Gus said. "We don't have the capacity to do this on our own. This would be long term. And . . . I know you like to bounce around." The look Gus gave me was pointed, and my chest felt cold. I didn't have any plans to leave Meadowlark, but that didn't mean I didn't feel the urge to every now and then, especially when Gus was looking at me like that's exactly what he expected me to do.

But I was here, and I was staying. And if taking on some extra work was the way to prove that to everyone, then I'd take on some more work.

"Well," I said, "I'm here for the long haul."

Amos reached out and clapped me on the shoulder. "Good man," he said. "I'm not worried." When he said that, I swallowed. I didn't know that his approval or his faith in me meant so much, but when the steadiest man in the world tells you that he's confident in you, it does something to you.

"Ride out with me," Gus said. "And we'll talk about all the details."

"Sure thing," I said. "Thank you for the chance."

Amos brushed it off, and said, "There's no question that you're the man for the job," but when I looked over at Gus, he didn't look so sure.

I guess I'd just have to prove him wrong, then.

Chapter 15

Cam

Fifteen Years Ago

Dusty's arm was slung over my shoulder as we walked up to the front door of his house. It was my first time here. Even from the outside, the white farmhouse looked big and bright and warm.

"I have no idea what my mom is making for dinner," he said as he opened the door. "But if you don't like it, you don't have to eat it. She won't be offended, I promise."

Yeah, right—like I wasn't going to eat whatever she put in front of me no matter what. I wanted Dusty's mom to like me.

When we stepped into the house, I immediately felt like I'd been here before, even though I hadn't. It just felt that familiar. Unlike my house, which my parents paid people to keep so meticulously clean that it almost felt sterile, this one had signs of life everywhere. Shoes by the door, blankets and books on the floor.

"Is that you, bub?" I heard a woman call from farther inside the house.

"Yeah," Dusty called back. He dropped his arm from my shoulder and used a hand at the small of my back to guide me forward.

The kitchen was around the corner, and when we got there, Dusty's mom had her back to us as she worked at the stove. Her hair was long. It fell all the way to the middle of her back. Some of it was gray, and some of it was blond—now I knew where Dusty got his hair color from.

"Hey, Mom," he said as he walked toward her. He gave her a hug from the side, and she wrapped an arm around him the same way. Then she turned toward me and gave me a smile that could thaw a windshield on a winter day.

"And you must be Camille," she said as she put the wooden spoon on a spoon holder and walked toward me. I expected her to go for a handshake, but she didn't.

Instead, she pulled me into a hug. A tight, warm hug. I stayed still for a moment, surprised, but I recovered enough to hug her back quickly before she pulled away. Dusty was grinning at me.

"So nice to meet you, honey," she said. "We've heard so much about you. I'm Aggie."

Aggie and Dusty looked very much alike. They had the same angular features and slim build. I wondered if he got anything from his dad. "It's so nice to meet you, too," I said genuinely. "Thank you for having me."

"Of course. We're just waiting on Dusty's dad to get home and then we'll dig in. Dusty, honey, will you set the table?"

"Sure thing," he said. Aggie stayed by me.

"Do you prefer Camille or Cam?" she asked. "Dusty has used both."

No one had ever asked me that before. "Cam," I said.

"Cam it is, then." Aggie grinned at me. Was it normal for people to be this nice to people they just met?

Aggie and I chatted for a bit—about school and soccer. She asked if she could come to a game, and I told her I would love if she did.

When I heard the front door open again, I also heard two sets of feet come into the house. One of them ran toward the kitchen. When I saw the kid appear around the corner, I figured she was Greer—Dusty's little sister.

"Who are you?" she asked when she noticed an outsider in her kitchen. She and Dusty had the same eyes, but her hair was almost black and as long as her mom's.

"Greer," Aggie chastised.

"I'm Cam," I said. "It's nice to meet you."

Greer looked me up and down. "You're pretty," she said. Then a man came around the corner—Dusty's dad.

He put his hands on Greer's shoulders. "She comes off a little strong," he said to me. "But she means well."

Dusty's dad—Renny—was tall. His hair looked like it used to be dark, but now it was mostly gray. He was clean-shaven and wearing jeans and a T-shirt from the grocery store, along with his nametag. Both of his arms were full of faded tattoos.

"You must be Cam," he said to me. His eyes were bright. "We've heard a lot about you."

"All good things, I hope," I said, reaching out to shake Renny's hand.

"Good would be the understatement of the century," Renny said as he took my outstretched hand. When I looked over at Dusty, he looked like he might be blushing.

"Welcome. We're happy you're here," Renny said before moving past me to his wife. He gave Aggie a kiss on her temple and then her lips, and I realized I'd never seen my parents kiss.

When the oven timer went off, Greer and Dusty went to help their mom bring dishes over to the table—chicken, steamed broc-

coli, and one of those pasta side dishes from the box. I followed so I could help, too.

Dinner conversation flowed easily. Greer told everyone about the Bill Nye episode that she got to watch at school that day—the one about volcanoes; Aggie and Renny talked about their work, and Dusty told them about school. I chimed in when he was talking, and the way everyone at the table listened and leaned in to pay attention to me when I spoke felt . . . new. I wasn't used to it.

"How long have you two been married?" I asked Dusty's parents. They sat near each other at the table—Aggie at the head of the table and Renny to her right. They held hands on the table throughout the whole meal—except when one of them had to cut something.

"Twenty years." Renny smiled. "Of pure marital bliss. Isn't that right, scrumptious?"

Aggie rolled her eyes, but she was smiling. "That's right."

"Ew," Greer mumbled, and Dusty laughed.

"What about your parents, Cam? What do they do?" Aggie asked. I knew she was being nice, but I didn't want to talk about my parents. Not while I was here spending time with this family that actually felt like a family.

"My dad is the CEO of a bank," I said quickly. "And my mom does a lot of charity stuff."

"Do you have any siblings?"

"I have an older sister," I said. "Violet. She's in her second year at Yale."

"Damn," Renny said. "Your parents must be so proud of you both—Dusty tells us you're as smart as can be."

I looked over at Dusty, and he gave me a reassuring smile. "Um," I said, not really sure how to respond. "Yeah," is what I settled on.

"I'd love to meet them. Maybe at one of your games?" Aggie said. "I can ask them how they got so lucky with such a great girl."

"They, um . . ." I stumbled a little. "They're, um, really busy."

Aggie tilted her head when she looked at me, and I had a feeling she was figuring out way too much about me with that look.

"Well," she said after a few beats, "you're welcome here any-time."

"Yes, you are," Renny said. "Anyone who can get Dusty to be on his best behavior is a miracle worker in my book," and then he winked at his son. I loved watching this family—the ease with which they interacted with one another. I felt lucky to be here.

With Dusty.

"Who wants dessert?" Aggie asked after a second, and Greer's hand shot up.

Tonight was perfect.

Chapter 16

Dusty

The lights were on in the main house on the Wilson property. How did I know that? Because I'd been staring at them for the past hour. That meant she was here—she was moving in. She was going to be one hundred feet away from me for the foreseeable future.

I felt like I should go over there. I wanted to. It was better for us to acknowledge the fact that we would be living this close together sooner than later—right?

I was worried about just showing up, especially if Riley was there. But it's not like I'd stay. I just wanted to say, "Hey, this isn't weird"—even though it was weird—and then leave.

That was all.

I looked down at the stack of three wooden cutting boards that my mom had given me the other day. A housewarming gift, she said.

This didn't have to be a big deal. I'd bring over a gift from my mom. Cam liked my mom. She liked me, too, I think, but I think she hated that she liked me, which was complicated.

I dragged a hand down my face. *Get it together, Tucker.*

Whatever. I grabbed the cutting boards and went out my front door. It was warm in my little house, so the cold air was a shock to the system.

A good shock. A much-needed shock.

I was just going to go over there, give her the cutting boards, break the metaphorical ice, and then go back home.

When I got to her door, I didn't even pause. I didn't want to lose my nerve, so I quickly knocked.

I heard music coming through the walls and onto the porch, but I couldn't tell what it was. A few seconds later, I heard footsteps making their way toward me. When the door swung open, I had to pretend that I didn't feel like the wind had just been knocked out of me.

Cam looked perfect in a light blue sweatshirt, black leggings, and a familiar pair of dark gray wool socks that I clocked immediately. I didn't mind even a little bit that I'd never get them back.

"Oh," she said, blinking slowly. "Hi."

"Hey," I said. "I, um, thought we could get this part over with."

"What part?"

"You know, the 'we live on the same property but have spent the last year avoiding each other' part," I said. Even though I never avoided her, but it didn't feel like the right time to bring that up.

Cam nodded slowly. "And what are those?" she asked, nodding toward the stack of wooden cutting boards in my hands.

"Housewarming gifts," I said. "From my mom," I added quickly.

"Oh," she said. "That's, um, that's nice." Cam fiddled with her hands. I looked at them—no engagement ring. I could feel the hope monster climbing up my throat. I really had to get that under control. "Do you—do you want to come in?"

Did I? "Sure," I said. "Yeah."

Cam stepped to the side, and I walked into the house. There were boxes and plastic storage bins everywhere.

"Where's Riley?" I asked—there was no sign of Cam's mini-me anywhere.

"She's with her dad tonight," Cam said as she led me back to the kitchen. "I thought it might be an easier adjustment period if I had everything set up for her when she got here."

"And how's that going?" I asked.

Cam huffed a laugh. "Wes and Brooks had to take her bed apart to get it here, and I told them I could put it back together. Plot twist: I can't."

"Do you want me to give it a try?" I said. "I'm pretty good with beds." I didn't intend to make the joke, but I couldn't *not* take the opportunity.

"Shut up," Cam said, giving my shoulder a little shove. "You don't have any plans?"

"Just bringing you these cutting boards," I said, holding them up. Cam took them from me and set them on the kitchen table.

"These are beautiful," she said. "Like, they would be at least a hundred dollars at Williams-Sonoma. Will you tell Aggie thank you for me?"

I nodded. "Sure thing. She'll make you a thousand more if you want them."

"She's always been so good to me," Cam said thoughtfully. "She was with me when I found out I was pregnant, you know."

"She was?" I didn't know that. I was shocked that Cam had willingly given up that information to me—maybe I caught her at just the right time, or her soft spot for Aggie Tucker made her more forthcoming, or maybe it was the cutting boards; who knew? My mom had never told me. I wished I was there. I wished a lot of things when it came to Cam.

Cam nodded. "I ran into her when I was buying the pregnancy test at the pharmacy. She said she didn't want me to have to do it alone."

"She loves you," I said honestly. From the first time I brought Cam home, my mom thought she was magnificent. I did, too. "So," I said, "changing the subject—where's this bed that needs some attention?"

"Back bedroom," Cam said. "I have a tool kit in there. Do you want a drink or anything? I don't have much." She opened the fridge. "Two hard seltzers, three soft seltzers, and two Capri Suns. I need to get groceries before I grab Riley tomorrow."

"What flavor Capri Sun?" I asked.

"Pacific cooler," Cam said with a smile.

"Will Riley be mad if I have one?"

"It'll be our little secret," Cam responded as she tossed one of the juice pouches over to me. I caught it—thank god. It would have been embarrassing if I hadn't. Cam grabbed one of the seltzer waters and cracked it open before starting back toward Riley's bedroom. I followed and tried to keep my attention anywhere but on Cam's long legs.

The hallway off the living room had two bedrooms and a bathroom. There were boxes in both bedrooms. When we walked into Riley's room, it looked like a bomb had gone off.

All of the pieces of Riley's four-poster bed were laid flat on the hardwood floor. It was a light wood—probably walnut. It matched the tall dresser, nightstand, and desk. There was a mattress propped up against the wall, too. I could hear a refrain playing from a speaker in here—"You Have Stolen My Heart" by Dashboard Confessional—and for a second, I wasn't in this bedroom.

I was in the passenger seat of my Bronco. The windows were down, and Cam was driving us down a back road. She'd convinced me to let her drive, and I loved looking at her while she did. We were singing at the top of our lungs to a mix CD that she had made—the first of many.

". . . I literally cannot figure out where things go." Cam's voice pulled me back to the present. "I should've kept the instruction manual. This bag has all of the hardware and stuff in it," she said, handing me a bag.

"All right, I'll take care of this part," I said with a smile. When I made eye contact with Cam, her eyes dropped to my neck—the right side of my neck, specifically—just like they did when we were at Chili's—like she couldn't believe I still had it.

I wondered if she still had hers.

"How can I help?" she asked.

"Let me get the lay of the land, and we'll go from there," I said.

"So you're okay if I unpack some of her clothes and stuff?" Cam asked, and I nodded. She walked to the other side of the room, and we both got started on our respective tasks. As far as the bed went, it looked pretty easy to assemble. As far as Cam went, however, I didn't really know what to do.

I wasn't stupid enough to think that I still knew her the way I used to, but I wanted to. Know her, I mean—what her life was like now, if she was okay.

"So," I said, keeping my eyes on my task, "how's your week been?"

Cam laughed a little. She was sitting on the floor, pulling small clothes out of boxes and folding them. "Honestly, not the worst week of my life," she said. "Which pretty much tells you all you need to know about my life, I guess."

"I'd rather you tell me everything about your life," I said without thinking.

I thought she would clam up and stay quiet, but she didn't. Instead, she asked, "What do you want to know?"

I wanted to start with the basics—easy stuff that couldn't trip her up or cause her to stop talking to me. Just like I did back in high school. "Where are you working now?" I already knew, but I was trying to stay in the safe small talk territory.

"I'm a lawyer," she said. One of the Ashwoods' approved career paths—doctor, banker, accountant, lawyer. "A firm in Jackson Hole. I shadowed there over the summer before I took the bar again, and when I passed, they hired me as a junior associate."

"What kind of law do you practice or work with or whatever?"

"Real estate law, mostly," she said. "I work with estate holdings and stuff, too."

"Do you like it?"

I heard Cam sigh. "It's a good job with good people."

"That's not what I asked," I said. "Do you like your job? Do you like being a lawyer?"

"I like understanding the rule of law," she said. "I like how complex it can be and how many paths there are to different outcomes, but no, I don't always like my actual job very much."

"Why not?" I asked.

"Most of the time, it's pretty boring," she said. "I didn't have a lot of options when I graduated from law school and passed the bar because I couldn't move or take any sort of risk since I had Riley, so I just kind of got stuck doing what was available to me."

"That's . . . kind of a bummer," I said. "Why don't you look for something else?"

"It's fine, most of the time," she whispered. I almost didn't hear her. "I like the people, and I like what it gives me."

"What does it give you?" I asked.

"Security," she said. "In a lot of ways." Now that sounded like the remnants of Lillian and Rutherford's upbringing if I ever heard it. Always so focused on money and outcomes. Even though Cam was now living her own life, based on her new job and how she felt about it, it sounded like she was still following the lines they drew for her. Some things would never change for her.

"What's your favorite food?" I asked, changing the subject again. I glanced at Cam out of the corner of my eye and saw her shoulders drop slightly. She was skittish—you had to know when to push and when to pull.

"Still tomatoes," she said, and I laughed. She ate tomatoes like apples—it was the weirdest thing I'd ever seen. "And what's yours? Still anything blue raspberry flavored? Even though that's not even a real thing?"

"Yep," I said. "Blue dye does something to me—what can I say?" Cam shook her head, but she was smiling. "So do you like Bloody Marys now, too? I always thought you'd like those when I saw people order them."

"I do," she said. "There's nothing better than a giant Bloody Mary—with bacon or shrimp and a giant pickle."

I faked a shudder. "Pickles are gross."

"Pickles are delicious," Cam shot back. I smiled, fighting the urge to bring up Cam's pickle theory. She used to say that any successful relationship had a pickle lover and a pickle hater. She spent our time together stealing the pickles off of every sandwich I ever got at the diner. "So what about you?" she said.

"What about me?" I asked.

"Do you like what you do? Working at Rebel Blue?"

"I love it," I said honestly. "The Ryders are a good bunch to work for, and it's the most beautiful place on the planet." I thought about my conversation with Gus—about how he was offering me a chance and his trust to carve out a piece of Rebel Blue for myself. To make it something even more special. Excitement—and nerves—danced underneath my skin.

"High praise coming from someone who's been a cowboy all around the world."

I narrowed my eyes at her. "How do you know where I've been?" It was true that I'd been all over doing seasonal work as a cowboy and wrangler, but I didn't know she was keeping track.

"You hear things," she said. That was true—especially in Meadowlark. "And social media exists." I looked over at Cam. She had never followed me online, but sometimes I wondered if she ever scrolled through my page, since the texts I'd get from her always seemed to come after I'd posted something— not that I did that very often. Once I noticed the pattern, I posted just as often as it took to make sure she didn't completely disappear.

"Have you been keeping tabs on me?" I asked. I tried to sound playful, but I didn't know if I pulled it off. My heart kicked at my rib cage.

I watched Cam's cheeks flush. "Not in a creepy way," she said. "Just in a 'I wanted to make sure you were alive' sort of way." A smile crept up my face, and when Cam looked over at me, she rolled her eyes. "Oh, shut up," she said. "Like you've never done some good ol' fashioned social stalking."

She was right, of course, but I didn't think she wanted to hear about how when I saw she was pregnant, I felt like I got the wind knocked out of me. Or when I saw a picture of her, little Riley, and Gus without the context of their relationship, I nearly fell to my knees.

I was at a small ranch in Montana at the time. That made it worse, I think. Not only because of our history, but because, distance-wise, it was the closest I'd been to her in years, but I'd never felt farther away. By that point, I knew a baby existed, and I knew who her dad was, but that was the first time I'd seen the three of them together. In the picture, they were lying down, and Cam and Gus were each kissing one of Riley's chubby baby cheeks, and Riley was laughing. She was only a few months old, so she didn't have a ton of hair, but I could already tell she had Cam's curls.

All I'd wanted was a glimpse of Cam, and I ended up getting more than I bargained for. I felt like shit for a long time after that. But eventually, I decided I wanted her to be happy, and in the picture, at least, she looked happy. I just didn't want to hear about it or see it or know anything about her life. The next time she texted me—around the holidays—I didn't re-spond.

I didn't hear from her again until the next summer, on my birthday. By that time, my resolve had weakened. I decided that pieces of her were better than nothing at all, so I re-sponded with a quick "thank you" to her birthday wishes. I remember watching the three dots of her typing pulse for a few seconds before it went away.

"Your social media is on private these days," I said with a grin. Cam laughed, and I basked in it.

"See, you did it, too," she responded. "How's Greer, by the way?"

"She's good," I said. "Lives in Alaska. She works for the For-est Service—lives in a tiny cabin, worries about the planet, sends us pictures of giant grizzly bears that freak my mom out."

"So exactly where she should be, then?" Cam asked, and I nodded. "I'm sure it was hard for your mom when both of you were gone."

"Yeah," I said as I positioned a wooden dowel in part of the bed frame, which was almost ready for me to start putting the pieces together and securing them. "She jokes that she drove us away, but I hope she knows we just inherited her love for the big, wide world, you know?

"When I told her I was coming back," I continued, "she was ecstatic. The first words out of her mouth were something about her baby boy finally coming home or whatever, but the second ones were 'you're not living in my house.'"

Cam laughed again. "So you ended up living in a little house on Anne's property? Why not stay at Rebel Blue in the staff housing?"

I shrugged. "I've lived in staff or seasonal worker housing for upwards of ten years. I was more interested in living somewhere that finally felt like mine, where I could collect more belongings than what fit in a duffel bag or my car—a place I wanted to come home to at the end of the day."

Cam looked surprised before she glanced down at the clothes she was folding. I was surprised, too, when I found myself longing for home—for something more permanent. In some ways, I thought it meant that I'd finally healed enough to come back here. But when I looked at Cam, I still felt like the nineteen-year-old kid who got his heart obliterated, and I had to fight the urge to run—to run from her. "But how did you end up at Anne's, of all places?"

"I saw Anne at the grocery store when I was home once a few years ago. She was struggling to reach the loaf of bread she wanted, so I helped," I explained. "And then I walked around the rest of the grocery store with her to make sure she could get everything. We talked the whole time. She told me how her property was getting hard to manage on her own, with her kids and her grandkids all gone from Meadowlark, and by the time we made it to checkout, she offered me the cabin. I agreed to do anything she needed done around her house or the property for the foreseeable future." I was leaving a few details out of that story, but they didn't really matter right now.

"Sounds like a good deal," Cam said.

"It is."

"And have you accumulated more belongings?"

"A few—I bought my first mattress, some paperbacks, and a painting from Teddy a few months ago. I'm still working on it—being in one place. It took me six months to put my clothes in the dresser and closet."

"Well, I don't even have a mattress or a dresser, so you're ahead of me there," Cam said with a shrug.

"What?" I asked.

"I ordered one of those boxed mattresses online—the ones that come shrink-wrapped in a box—but it hasn't got here yet," Cam said. I guess that meant that she left all of her furniture behind—maybe it was her fiancé's? "But luckily I've got a few couches to choose from until it does."

Cam was tall—probably around five-ten—so sleeping on a couch all night wouldn't be comfortable.

"I'm sorry," I said, wracking my brain trying to remember if I knew anyone with an extra mattress or bedroom furniture. I could move my mattress here for her.

"It's okay," she said. "I ordered it when I first got to Gus and Teddy's, so it should get here soon."

"How was that?" I asked. "Staying with them."

"Easy," she said. "At least for a short period of time."

"How has it been? Adjusting to a new dynamic with them and Riley?" Gus and Teddy had gotten together earlier this year—shocked the hell out of everyone, except for me, maybe, but I hadn't observed the legendary days of their hatred for each other. I was more shocked by Brooks and Emmy, honestly.

"Also easy," Cam said. "Teddy loves Riley so much, and as a parent, it's really rewarding to watch your kid be showered with the type of love they deserve. Plus, Teddy is so different from Gus or me. She's creative and less . . . I don't know . . . restricted than both of us. I think it's good for Riley to have her around.

"Riley has a really good family," she continued. "The type of family I wish I could have had. When my mother heard about Gus's new relationship—or 'that man,' which is how she likes to refer to him—she made this stupid comment about how Teddy was going to be competition for me in my daughter's life—like Riley only had room for one maternal figure. I spiraled a little bit for a while. I wondered if my daughter would like . . . love Teddy more than me, I guess?"

It didn't surprise me that her thoughts went there. "But she doesn't," I said.

"Right," Cam said. "Maybe it's because Teddy has been around her entire life, but I don't think Riley ever had a 'Teddy is my shiny new toy' moment, and even if she did, it would've been normal. I don't know." Cam shook her head. "I feel like people expect it to be hard—adding someone else into the co-parent situation, and maybe it is sometimes, but it hasn't been for us, yet."

"And with Greg?" I asked, hating even bringing him up, but I wanted to know—even if it hurt.

"You mean Graham?" Cam asked. She was still smiling at me, so bringing him up didn't shut her down . . . yet.

"Whatever," I said.

"That was different. We weren't . . ." She stumbled and paused. "We weren't what Gus and Teddy are."

What did that mean? They were engaged. They were going to get married—legally bind themselves to each other. Cam must've seen the confusion on my face.

"How's the bed going?" There was the subject change. Cam didn't like being pushed, and I wouldn't push her. I wanted her to keep talking to me for as long as possible.

"Good," I said, looking down at it. "Come help me put it all together?"

"How much labor does that require?" she asked playfully.

"Lazy ass. All you have to do is hold the pieces together, and I'll secure them."

"Fine." She walked over to me and put her hands on her hips when she stopped next to me. I wished she'd step just a little bit closer, but it would have to do for now.

Five minutes later, we had a finished bed. We lifted the mattress onto it, and Cam grabbed some sheets and a quilt. She started to spread out the fitted sheet—sage green with small flowers all over it—and I took a corner. Same with the top sheet and the quilt, which was a light pink with small, embroidered flowers on it.

"Does Riley like flowers?" I asked.

"Yeah." Cam nodded. "She and Teddy did a wildflower hunt this summer, and she's been totally obsessed ever since. Personally, I love that her room always feels like summer now."

"Still your favorite season?" In my head, I was checking off the boxes of everything I knew about her that still remained true.

"Still my favorite season," Cam said. Summer, check; tomatoes, check; pickles, check.

When she looked at me, something flashed behind her brown eyes. Neither of us said anything. The only noise was the music from the speaker—"MakeDamnSure" by Taking Back Sunday. Another song from one of our mix CDs. Now that I thought about it, every song I heard was on one of our mix CDs.

Without thinking, I put my hand out, asking her to dance. I watched her face fall and her walls go up.

"I'm sorry," I said quickly, regret flooding me. "The song..." I trailed off.

"I know," she whispered.

"I'm sorry," I said again, swallowing hard. "That's not what I came over here for. I came over here to check on you, and then if that went well, I was going to ask if you thought we could be friends."

Cam's eyes flitted around the room—avoiding mine.

"C'mon, Ash," I said. "We were always friends before anything else."

I watched the wheels turn in her head. She bit her bottom lip and fiddled with her fingers again. In real time, I watched her weigh the pros and the cons, and I fought the urge to beg.

Say yes. Please.

"We have always been friends," she said, and I exhaled. "You're right."

"So?" I asked hopefully.

"Friends it is."

Chapter 17

Cam

Fifteen Years Ago

DUSTY: *Hike with me this weekend? Check yes or no (don't check no, please).*

CAM: *What are you, obsessed with hiking? You're insufferable. I don't even know if I like hiking.*

DUSTY: *Only one way to find out. I'll pick you up at eight.*

CAM: *In the morning?!*

DUSTY: *Yeah, sleepyhead. In the morning.*

CAM: *Okay, but park down the street.*

DUSTY: *That's getting kind of weird, Ash.*

CAM: *My parents aren't like yours. I'm protecting you, I promise.*

DUSTY: *Whatever you say. Wear good shoes.*

"Y*ou all right back there?" Dusty asked as we continued to trudge up the mountain. Well, I was trudging. Dusty was basically floating—the incline didn't seem to bother him at all.*

"All good," I huffed. "So do you do this a lot?"

"Hiking?" he asked.

I nodded, but then realized he couldn't see me, so I called up to him. "Yeah."

"A fair amount," he said. "There's not always a lot to do around here, you know? And even when there are things to do, it's normally stuff that you've already done at least once."

"But if you do this a lot, isn't this just another one of those things?"

"Yeah, but it's different every time you do it—I could hike up this trail every day and see or notice something new."

I took a second to look at the scene around me. I couldn't see that much on the trail—tall trees surrounded us—but we had to be pretty high up, considering we'd been walking for at least an hour.

It was beautiful, but I wasn't really sold on the whole hiking thing yet. I had homework to do.

"How much longer?" I asked.

Dusty laughed. "Like fifteen minutes. I thought you'd like this." I liked being with him. "Aren't you all about hard work and outcomes?"

"I like to see the outcomes," I said. "All I see are trees."

"Has anyone ever told you to enjoy the journey?"

"No," I answered honestly. "No one's ever said that to me."

Dusty stopped walking and turned around. I stopped when I was only a step or two away from him.

He looked down at me. "Well," Dusty said, as he brushed my cheek with the back of his knuckles, "enjoy the journey."

I rolled my eyes, and Dusty grinned when they came back around. "Let's keep walking so the journey doesn't take two more hours," I said.

"Fair," Dusty said as he turned and continued to lead the way. I also didn't know how long the person whose driveway we parked in would be okay with Dusty's Bronco in front of their house. I hoped they wouldn't mind if we parked there for a long time because the house mesmerized me and I wanted to explore every inch of the property when we went back to the car. When Dusty and I first pulled up, I immediately fell in love with the blue exterior, the way the house was surrounded by plants and trees. I can't explain it, but it felt like it had its own soul, like it was a living thing.

Dusty seemed to love driving me around, showing me new things. The first time I rode in his truck this past fall, I was kind of terrified. I wasn't used to cars that were that big or loud or bumpy.

Now, I'd count down the minutes until the next time I was in his passenger seat. I'd even made him a mix CD to listen to while he was driving because his radio was trash at picking up stations without static.

He had to drop me off down the street from my house when he would give me rides home, though. I didn't need my parents to find out about him or his loud Bronco. They wouldn't approve of Dusty or our friendship.

Because that's what Dusty and I were—friends. Good friends. He was probably my best friend, but I'd never had one of those before, so I couldn't tell for sure.

But it also felt like he was more.

I mean, we hadn't even kissed, but when he touched me, my stomach always flipped. I thought after a while, it would stop—that I would get used to it, the way he would cup my face or brush my hair behind my ear or hug me after we'd been apart for a while, but I didn't. My stomach somersaulted every time.

He came to almost every soccer game in the fall and we did

something nearly every Saturday that he didn't have to work—even in the dead of winter. In the colder months, Dusty bagged groceries and bussed tables at the diner. When it got warmer, he kept both of those jobs and bailed hay at Rebel Blue Ranch. Wes was one of Dusty's friends, so I knew about Rebel Blue, but I'd never been up there. Maybe he'd take me soon.

Unlike me, Dusty had a lot of friends, so being around him was good for me, I think, because it also meant that I was around other people. I didn't know if they were my friends, too, but I had Dusty, so I didn't feel like I needed more than that.

"I can hear you thinking back there," Dusty said. "What's rattling around in your head?"

"You," I said honestly.

"Anything good?" Dusty asked.

"Not a single thing," I lied. "All bad. Totally and completely bad."

"Liar," Dusty said. I could hear the smile in his voice. We walked a little bit longer, and the trees started to clear. There was a steep incline for a few minutes, and my lungs were working overtime, but we kept trekking.

As soon as we got to the top of the incline, we started to go back down—in between two large rock faces. The space between them was barely big enough for Dusty to fit through. "Careful," he said.

When he got through, he turned back around and stretched out his hand to help me the last few steps. I stepped out of the opening, and my jaw dropped.

"I told you that you'd like it," Dusty said, eyes on me.

"It's . . . wow." The view spread out before me was stunning. Unlike most of the other viewpoints I'd seen in Meadowlark, this one didn't face toward the town. We were on the back side of the mountain face, so there weren't any houses or buildings in the view, just

an expanse of evergreens and aspens and grasses and jagged and beautiful rocks—a river split the scene in half as it flowed below.

Dusty kept hold of my hand and pulled me toward the edge of the rock face we were on. I looked to where he was leading me and blinked a few times to make sure I was seeing things right. The way the rocks had eroded and broken had created something that kind of looked like a couch that sat looking over . . . everything.

"Watch your step," Dusty said. It was a good thing he had ahold on me because I was so distracted by what was in front of me that I think I could have very easily fallen off the cliff. When we sat down on the rocks, Dusty took off his backpack. He handed me a water bottle, which I took eagerly. He also had apples, peanut butter sandwiches, goldfish crackers, and blue raspberry sour straws.

I sat cross-legged and situated myself diagonally, so I could see both of the views—the mountains and Dusty. "I think I get it now," I said and then bit into an apple. I'd learned from Dusty's dad that he thought Pink Lady apples were the best, and now that I'd had them a few times, I agreed.

"What?" Dusty asked.

"Hiking," I said. "You didn't tell me we got views and snacks."

Dusty laughed. "So you like it?"

"I love it," I said.

"Good," he responded. "So really . . . what were you thinking about me back there?" He looked at me sideways as he ran his fingers through his mop of blond hair.

I took a deep breath. Dusty had gotten me out of the habit of censoring myself—at least around him. Maybe it was the notes or the fact that I felt closer to him than anyone else, but I didn't think there was anything he would judge me for.

"Why you haven't kissed me yet."

Dusty froze, but his gray eyes gleamed. "Do you want me to kiss you, Ash?" There it was—the nickname. I had recently folded one of my English papers in a way that cut off the latter half of my last name so it would fit inside my notebook. Dusty saw it on my desk and started calling me Ash. He'd finally found his nickname for me, the one that made him feel special.

I didn't tell him that he already was.

"Yeah," I said in a tone that I hoped communicated that was a stupid question. When he was quiet for a second, I quickly said, "But, like, only if you want to." Smooth.

"I want to," he said immediately. "I've always wanted to." There it was—the stomach flip.

"Then why haven't you?" My voice came out quieter than I expected.

I watched Dusty swallow. "Waiting for the right moment, I guess."

I gestured to the scene around us. "This feels like it could be the right moment," I said and moved a little closer to him. He moved closer to me, too. The air grew thin, and I knew it wasn't just the altitude.

"Yeah?" he asked. His voice was lower than I'd heard it.

I nodded. When he leaned forward, I paused. "I've never done this before," I blurted out. Oh god. That was embarrassing. "I don't know . . . do I move?"

Dusty smiled—the lopsided one that made my heart squeeze and my breath catch. "No, angel," he said quietly as he brought his hands up to each side of my face. "I'll come to you."

I tried to control my breath and my heartbeat, but there was no use—not with him. I watched his eyes scan my face before they landed on my mouth. He leaned in further, and I closed my eyes— half a second later, his lips were on mine.

It was pretty much the best first kiss ever. I didn't want to stop kissing him. I just did it over and over again—continuing long after we had left the rock couch, on our way back down the mountain, and in the front seat of Dusty's truck.

I barely noticed when he parked outside of my house because when the car was stopped, that meant I could start kissing him again.

So I did.

I pushed myself across the bench seat, so I was as close to him as I could get. His hands roamed—from my shoulders, to my back, to my waist. When he used his mouth to open mine a little, I felt a little bolt of electricity from the top of my head to the tips of my toes.

Why didn't we do this sooner? I wanted to spend every spare second I had with my mouth attached to his to make up for lost time.

A bang on Dusty's passenger-side window startled both of us, and when I looked back at it—oh, shit—I saw my mother.

Shit. Shit. Shit.

"Camille Ashwood, get out of this car. Right now." She was yelling. My mother didn't yell—it was normally just cold disappointment.

Dusty's arm was still wrapped around me, and when my mother spoke, it got tighter. "Is that your mom?" His voice sounded shocked, maybe even kind of scared.

I nodded and looked back at him. "Let's get out of here," I said.

"What?" he asked.

"Take me somewhere. Today has been so . . . amazing, and I can't deal with her right now," I said. "Please." My mom hit Dusty's window again. She tried to open the passenger-side door, but it was locked.

"Ash, I . . . I can't. She's your mother. I think it'll just make things worse. I'll come get you tonight, okay? Maybe after everything has . . . died down?"

I felt my eyes well with tears, but I nodded.

Dusty kissed me again—he didn't care that my mom was watching. "I'll get you out of here someday, I promise."

Chapter 18

Cam

Riley and I were perusing the aisles at the craft supply store in town this morning. I could count the number of times I'd come in here on one hand. This week was Riley's last week of school before the holiday break, and one of her friends taught her how to make friendship bracelets out of embroidery thread, and she was determined to make as many as she could for Christmas gifts.

"Daddy will want a green one," she said as she pulled a couple of different green embroidery flosses off their hooks.

"Good choices," I said. So far, we had a slew of pinks, purples, and reds. The greens would be perfect for Gus, and I grabbed a couple of yellows, too. "Are they all going to be monochromatic?" I asked and Riley looked up at me, confused. "One color or different versions of the same color." I nodded toward her hands. "Like how those are all green but different greens."

"Mon-o-chruh-mat-ik," Riley repeated quietly to herself—memorizing the word and storing it away. Smart girl. "No.

Auntie and Teddy and Ada are going to get rainbow ones," she said.

"They'll love that," I said. "What about Papa?"

"Yellow, I think," she said with a nod. "Because he said he misses the sun and summer."

"That's thoughtful, Riles," I said.

"What color do you think Dusty will want?" she asked as we went back to perusing. I froze.

"U-uh," I stuttered. "I didn't know you were making one for Dusty."

"I have to make him one," Riley said. "He lives in our back-yard, Mom." Good point. "Do you know his favorite color?"

"Blue," I said without thinking. Images of blue sour straws on a hike, blue Jolly Ranchers in a truck's center console, and a blue margarita at Chili's flashed through my head. "His favorite color is blue."

After we bought out half the embroidery floss in the store, Riley and I walked down the street to the coffee shop. It hadn't snowed in a few days, so the sidewalks and roads were mostly clear, but it was cold as shit—even though the sun was out. I held Riley's gloved hand in mine as we walked. Well, I walked. Riley had some pep in her step today—and every day—and her walk was more of a half skip.

It was little things like that, or the way she squealed when she ran, that made my heart swell up in my chest. To me, it meant that she felt safe and happy—loved. I never would've done any of that as a kid. When she talked constantly or danced in the kitchen without any sort of inhibition, I hoped that she never lost her joy.

A bell rang as we opened the door to the coffee shop. We were immediately hit with warmth and the smell of coffee and warm sugar. Even though The Bean had always been a Meadowlark institution, it had come under new ownership a few years ago, and they had really stepped up their game.

Once we were inside, I let go of Riley's hand, and she made a beeline for the pastry case—checking out all of her options before we ordered.

I felt eyes on me as I waited in line. It hadn't been that long since the not-wedding, and people clearly still hadn't moved on. I didn't want to know what they were saying—I didn't care. Well, I did care, actually. Deeply. But it was easier to pretend that I didn't.

After a minute, Riley scampered back to me. There was only one person ahead of me now. "So," she said, "what if you get something and I get something, and then we split it?"

"Excellent idea, Sunshine," I said. "What do you have your eye on?"

"The chocolate cake," Riley said, smiling wide. The chocolate cake in question had chocolate ganache with a layer of strawberry compote between the two layers. "It's decadent," Riley said with a nod.

"That's a good word," I said.

"Teddy taught it to me."

It was our turn now, and the cashier waved me up to the register. "Hi," she said. "What can I get for you guys today?"

"You go first, Sunshine," I said to Riley. She liked to order for herself.

"Um . . ." Riley said. "Can I have a small vanilla steamer and a piece of the chocolate cake, please?"

"Sure thing," the cashier said with a smile. "And for you?"

"I'll have a small latte with skim milk, please, and . . ." I looked over at the pastry case. "A slice of coffee cake, please."

"Absolutely. It'll be right out."

Once we sat down, Riley was able to remove a few of her layers to reveal her white knit sweater with a red heart in the middle.

"Are you excited to have a break from school?"

Riley nodded. "Yeah, but I like school, too. This week was fun. We watched the Grinch and frosted cookies and made ornaments."

"I love the ornament," I said. Riley's teacher had each student make a small stocking from felt and decorate it. Then, she cut a little circle out of the front and put Riley's school picture in it.

Riley told the teacher she needed to make two because her parents didn't live in the same house, and the teacher let her, so Gus and I each got a very glittery stocking ornament.

"And we colored, too," Riley said. "A lot of coloring."

"Is that your favorite thing to do at school, do you think?" I asked. "The art stuff?" Riley's adjustment to first grade had been a little bit rocky. The first day of the second week of school, I walked into her room to wake her up, and she told me she was too sick to go. She didn't have a fever or a runny nose and she said her stomach didn't hurt, but she looked at me, and her big green eyes were full of tears, so I let her stay home.

I had to work, but I set her up on the couch with a few movies and some saltines while I got some things done in my office. When I got to a place where I could stop for the day, I went out and lay on the couch with her. After a few minutes, she burst into tears and confessed that she wasn't really sick. I held her tight and let her cry before I asked her why she didn't want to go to school.

She wiped her nose and said, "I didn't know that being in first grade meant that I had to go to school all day." The year before, Riley had only been in morning kindergarten. She was absolutely torn up about the fact that she had to be in school for seven hours.

I watched Riley's face morph into her thinking one—cutest face in the world, by the way. "I like library time, too," she said. "And my teacher says that I'm good at math."

She didn't get that from me. I hated math.

"Do you like math?"

Riley shrugged. "I like that I can do other stuff when I finish it early." Ah, she had a strategy. Now that was like me. I loved that she was using the analytical part of her brain; except, in her case, she was doing it to do things she loved, as opposed to when I was growing up, when all I used it for was to get other people to love me.

I always thought maybe if I changed this or did that—got the highest grades, ran the fastest, and did the most—I would be the best. Then my parents would have to be proud of me if I was the best, right?

You would think. Generally, I only really got a rise out of my parents when I was doing something wrong, so in adulthood, I think I just tried to keep them happy. That way, they'd leave me alone.

I never wanted my daughter to feel that way. I wanted her to enjoy spending Saturday mornings with me at the craft store. I never wanted her to feel like we couldn't share a brownie and a coffee cake or sit at a table and enjoy each other's company. Personally, I can't say I ever enjoyed my parents' company, and I would guess they probably felt the same.

Like any parent, I had expectations for my daughter. I expected her to be kind and curious and hardworking. I had hopes for her, too. I hoped she would never feel unloved or disposable. I hoped she had dreams and that she was brave enough to go after them.

But I never wanted the hopes and expectations I had for her to overshadow the hopes and expectations she had for herself. Because if I did my job right, she would have them, and they would be wonderful.

I never really saw myself as a parent, but when I was younger, I wondered if I was capable of being a good one—like Dusty's parents. They were the first example I had of parents who were ... there. My parents had always been more of a presence in my life versus being actually present. They inform every decision I make because they're on my mind almost constantly—even though I don't see or hear from them very often. I feel like I live my life like they're watching—in an ominous way.

I'm sure they've been proud of me at some points or found joy in something I achieved, but I don't think they knew how to communicate those things. I think they only knew how to communicate disappointment, which I understood now as kind of a double-edged sword for them and for me.

On one hand, I hated it when they were disappointed or upset with me, but when they were displeased, I got the attention that I used to crave so badly.

Sometimes I found myself wondering if I used to use Dusty

as a weapon against my parents, especially after my mother found us kissing in his Bronco. Once he was no longer a secret, our relationship became the only way I had ever successfully worked against their wishes, to stand up for myself. But I think he saw himself as more of a shield—something that could protect me.

I hoped my daughter never needed either of those things.

"I love you, Sunshine," I said. "You know that, right?"

Riley's forehead wrinkled. "Duh," she said right as an employee dropped our drinks and pastries off at our table in mismatched mugs and on mismatched plates.

"I like plates like this," Riley said.

"Plates like what?"

"Plates that don't match. Can we get some for our new house?"

"Have you seen our plates, Sunshine?" I laughed. I was definitely not a mismatched plates type of woman.

"Yeah. They're all white and boring," Riley said. Her eyes were alight.

"Ouch, kid," I said. "You think my plates are boring?"

Riley nodded enthusiastically. "Really boring," she said. "We should get rainbow plates!"

"What if we compromise and get some pastel plates or something? Or something with a pattern?"

"Pastel is light colors, right?" Riley asked, and I nodded. "Okay. Pastels are good." When she took a sip of her steamer, which was just steamed milk and vanilla syrup, my seven-year-old looked like she was seventeen.

I swiped a bite of Riley's chocolate cake. "Oh that's good," I said.

"Hey!" she exclaimed. "I haven't even had any yet." I

shrugged, and Riley took the first bite of my coffee cake with a grin. As she chewed, she nodded and smiled.

"Good?" I asked.

"Good," she said. Then, each of us got a bite of our own cake on our forks.

"Cheers," I said, and we clinked our forks together.

Chapter 19

Cam

Fifteen Years Ago

When I was in private school, I loved spring break. I didn't really have anything from school to miss back then, but now, I did. I had friends—well, I had Chloe. We stayed pretty close after soccer season was over, and, of course, I had Dusty.

I was counting down the days until school started, so I could see him.

"You seem distracted, Camille," my mom said from the other side of the dining table. It was the last Saturday morning of the break. I'd go back to school on Monday—thank god. The two of us were eating breakfast together. It was the one day out of the entire year that we ever did so. My dad was working. Yup, on Saturday. He always seemed to find a reason to work on the weekends, yet he was always miraculously done when it was time for him and my mom to go to a fancy party with their fancy friends while I stayed home.

"Just tired," I responded while I speared a strawberry off my plate. We had the same breakfast every Saturday and Sunday. My mom had a lot of stupid rules about food, so fruit, two eggs, and wheat toast it was. During the week, it was yogurt.

"Why could you possibly be tired?" she asked, but I knew she didn't need an answer to chastise me for something—going to bed too late, drinking too much caffeine, snoozing my alarm because she read somewhere that actually made you more tired—so I stayed quiet and kept picking at my breakfast.

"Your father got the phone bill a few days ago," Lillian said after a few beats. "He wanted me to ask you why you seem to be sending so many more texts."

Of course, my dad couldn't ask me that himself. It seemed like the novelty of having a daughter wore off for him a little more each year, and so his investment in our relationship wore off as well.

"Don't we have unlimited texts?"

"That's not the point. The point is that I've noticed your grades slipped a little this semester. At a public school," she said with disgust. I got an A minus in AP Calculus. "And now apparently you've sent more than ten thousand texts per month since October. I'm seeing a pattern."

I shrugged. "I send a lot of texts for soccer."

My mother pursed her lips, like she didn't believe me. "I certainly hope you're not getting distracted, Camille. By anything . . . or anyone." She raised her eyebrows, and the image of my mother banging on Dusty's window flashed through my mind.

I'd never seen her like that before. After I got out of the car, she yanked me into the house by the top of my arm, and when the front door shut behind us, I expected her to yell.

She didn't. She did something worse. She went deathly calm and said, "You are so disappointing."

Later, I had to have a talk with both her and my father, where both of them were sure to tell me exactly how disappointing I was and how they didn't know how I could be so reckless. They informed me I was to keep my distance (as if I could ever do that with Dusty), or else there'd be consequences, their threat vague enough to be darkly ominous. I almost wished for my mom to get angry again—to show she cared or something—but she didn't. And my dad? Well, he looked bored and disgusted.

I'd never felt so small.

My mother's voice broke through the memory. "You're a senior. You need to have an unwavering eye on your future."

"I do," I said. I had an "unwavering eye" toward school being back in session.

"I hope so," she said. "Because in order for us to continue supporting your decisions to live out this silly Meadowlark . . . fantasy, not to mention financing your life, we have standards that we expect you to meet."

The closer I got to graduating, the more my parents liked to remind me of my trust fund. They dangled it in front of me like a carrot—like it was the only reason I would do anything. They didn't know I would do anything just to feel like they were proud of me. I wanted my dad to read the paper I wrote for AP English that I left on his desk. I wanted my mom to take me dress shopping to go to a school dance. I wanted to eat breakfast with both of them on a Saturday and have a pleasant conversation about our favorite parts of the week and make fun plans for the weekend.

"I understand," I said after a second.

"And I'm serious about that boy," Lillian said. "You're better than him, Camille—even if you don't know how to act like it yet."

My food turned to ash in my mouth.

After breakfast, I spent most of the day in my room watching movies. I texted Dusty, but he was at work. I hoped someday I wouldn't have to spend so much time alone.

Chapter 20

Dusty

This year, my mom and I were celebrating Christmas at the Ryders'. She'd been doing this since my dad died six years ago, but I'd always been gone over the holidays. This was the first year that I was home for them.

I headed over there around three. Amos always gave ranch hands the day off, so he, Gus, and Wes worked in the morning, doing everything they could with a skeleton crew.

When I pulled in front of the Big House, I noticed Gus's, Wes's and Luke's trucks. I also saw my mom's old Toyota Highlander. But there was no sign of Cam's sleek SUV.

I ignored the disappointment gnawing at my insides.

I grabbed the small bag of gifts from my backseat, and made my way down the shoveled path to the front door. I didn't bother knocking—just pushed open the door, and let the warmth of the Big House envelop me.

It didn't matter who you were, when you walked into the Big House, it felt like home—whether you'd never been here before or had crossed the threshold countless times. It always smelled like leather conditioner and pie crust. Today, it also smelled like a lot of good food.

Voices and laughter carried down the hallway. I slipped off my coat and hung it on one of the hooks near the door before making my way into the heart of the home.

"Take your coat off, Luke," Emmy said. She and Brooks were sitting at the kitchen table. It looked like they were playing cards. "You're going to get hot."

"No," Brooks said.

"Please," Emmy countered, and batted her eyelashes.

"Fine," Brooks grumbled. He unzipped the Carhartt coat he was wearing to reveal a cream-colored fisherman's sweater, which looked exactly like the one Teddy had given to me to wear.

"You've got to be shitting me," Gus said from the couch. He was wearing the same goddamn sweater.

Teddy—who was sitting on the floor in the living room doing a puzzle with Riley—and Emmy both burst into laughter. Ada joined in from where she was helping in the kitchen because Wes was wearing the same sweater, too.

"You all look so cute in your matching sweaters," Teddy said on a laugh. She wiped a tear from her eye. "Including you, Dusty." She waved at me. I should've known to be more suspicious of a gift from Teddy a few days before Christmas.

"Oh god, not you, too," Gus said when he looked at me. I couldn't help but laugh.

"I'm changing," Brooks said, standing from the table.

"No, you're not," Emmy said, pulling him back down. She laughed and gave him a kiss on the cheek. "I like it." Brooks immediately relented.

"It's a nice sweater," Wes said with a shrug and slung an

arm around Ada's shoulders. "Good choice, sweetheart. Dusty," he said, looking over at me, "good to see you."

After that, there were a bunch of hellos and hugs exchanged. Amos was manning the stove, a kitchen towel draped over his shoulder. My mom and Hank were on the love seat opposite Gus. I walked into the living room and leaned down to give my mom a kiss on the cheek and give Hank a handshake.

"Hi, honey," she said.

"Hey, Mom." I sat on the floor next to Teddy and Riley. "What's going on here?" I asked.

"It's a puzzle," Riley said.

"Yeah, dummy," Teddy said. "Can't you tell?"

"Thanks for clearing that up," I said. "What's the puzzle a picture of?"

"Rebel Blue," Riley said. "My mom got it for Papa."

"Amos, what soap is in the guest bathroom? It smells so good." Cam's voice came from behind me, and my spine went straight. "Oh my god. Is that the same exact sweater?" Everyone laughed again.

She was here.

I turned around. She was wearing a light gray sweater and black jeans. I let my eyes track down her body, even though I shouldn't have. Her snowman socks took me by surprise, and I smiled.

"Oh," she said. "Hi."

"Hey." I waved. Cam swallowed and gave me a sheepish wave. When she turned to go into the kitchen, Riley called after her.

"Mom, you were doing the puzzle with us!" I watched Cam take a deep breath, and when I turned back to Teddy, she was fighting a smile.

I must've taken Cam's spot without knowing. After a few seconds of hesitation, she came and sat on the ground next to me. I hadn't realized that almost everyone had stopped talking until Cam sat down and the chatter started again.

"How many pieces is this?" I asked her.

"Twenty-five hundred, I think," she said.

"We're sorting out the edges right now," Riley told me. "Well, me and Teddy are sorting out the edges. You and my mom can find middle chunks and put them together."

"Sir, yes sir," I said with a salute and looked over at Cam, who was looking at her daughter with a hell of a lot of love.

I hoped I wasn't looking at Cam the same way.

We sat down at the dinner table a few hours later. Amos and Hank were at each end of the table, then Riley, Gus, Teddy, Emmy, and Brooks on one side. Then, my mom next to Hank, Ada, Wes, Cam, and me. Ours were the last two seats left, and based on the wink Teddy gave me, it was on purpose. *Jesus Christ.*

I don't know what I expected—it was basically impossible for anyone at this table to mind their own damn business. Not that I was complaining, but I worried Cam would feel smothered or uncomfortable—especially because everyone else at this table, except for Amos and Riley, was coupled up.

The spread of food was amazing. Amos didn't know how to half-ass meals. There was prime rib, turkey, a few different types of potatoes, stuffing, multiple roasted vegetables, and homemade rolls with shiny golden tops.

There was chatter going on all around the table—except between Cam and me. Great.

"So," I said, trying to crack the tension a little bit, "how are you liking the house?"

She didn't look at me when she answered. "It's great. Riley really likes it. I'm excited for when it gets warmer."

I nodded. "You'll have to take her up the trails when the snow melts," I said. To anyone else, it would've been a throwaway thing to say—like talking about the weather. But to us, it mattered.

I had shown Cam every trail behind the Wilson house. When I watched a blush creep up her cheeks, I knew she was thinking about something we shared at the top of my favorite one.

"Yeah," she said. "I've told her about a couple of them. She, um, wants to see the rock couch."

I grinned. "That's a good one."

Cam gave me a small smile in return, and my brain short-circuited enough that I dropped a dollop of mashed potatoes and gravy on my denim-clad thigh.

"Goddammit," I muttered, but Cam laughed, and suddenly I didn't care about the potatoes.

Every time Cam and I saw each other now, there was always a moment of awkwardness, which would make me wonder if we'd changed too much, if too much time had passed. But then we'd get through it (or in this case, I'd make a fool of myself), and we'd find that familiar sense of comfort and ease.

This was nice, this new fragile friendship we'd been building. It's not like we could avoid each other anymore (well, she couldn't try to avoid me like she had been); we were sharing the same square plot of land. With every wave when I left my house in the morning, or quick passing chat in the yard, it felt like we were finally getting used to each other again. Our presence in each other's lives was small, much smaller than it ever used to be. But it was constant, and that felt good, after so much distance for so many years.

In a lot of ways, I felt like we were as close as we could be to being friends again. But I didn't know if we'd gotten there by ourselves or if we were just giving in to the fact that our lives had begun to overlap too much for us to ignore it. But it didn't matter to me how we'd gotten there if the outcome was the same.

"Good thing you didn't get any on your sweater," Cam said. "Then you'd have to change."

"And that would be a damn shame." I shook my head. "Were you in on this?"

"Me?" Cam put her hand over her heart in faux shock. "Never." That meant she knew I was coming, and she came anyway. That made me happy. I didn't fight the smile that crept onto my face, and I didn't try to look anywhere but at her. It felt like another step in the right direction, another hunk of ice thawing. "It looks good on you, though—the color."

"I don't know," I said, trying to regulate my heartbeat. "I feel like the cream color kind of washes me out."

Cam shook her head and shrugged. "No. It looks good."

"Thanks," I responded, and I hoped she couldn't see my heart swell through this stupid sweater. "You, uh, you look nice, too."

I watched the blush creep up Cam's cheeks. I swear, that was one of my favorite colors. She opened her mouth to respond but was interrupted by Amos scooting his chair back from the table and standing up.

"I just wanted to take a minute," he said, "to thank all of you for spending your holiday here. When Stella and I got married, Aggie made us this table that you're all sitting at." I looked over at my mom, whose hands were clasped under her chin as she smiled at her old friend. "It hasn't moved from this spot for nearly forty years. When we first saw it, both Stella and I thought that we'd never be able to fill it with people—it was so big, and at that time, it was just the two of us."

"So, today, when I look around and see this full table"—Amos scrunched his nose a little bit—"it makes this old man's heart feel damn close to bursting. Stella taught me that the family you choose is just as important—sometimes more—than the one you're born with. Everyone here is part of that family that Stella and I dreamed about." Amos lifted his pint glass, and the rest of us followed suit. "Cheers," he said.

"Cheers," everyone at the table said in unison and began clinking their glasses together. When I clinked my glass with Cam's, her eyes didn't leave mine until after she took a sip of her wine.

After dinner, everyone dispersed throughout the house—to take a nap or read or watch football. I gave Emmy, Teddy, and Ada their presents—small leather jewelry cases—then went to find Cam.

I found her at the back of the house—in a little alcove with big windows and a beautiful view of the winter wonderland outside. She was sitting on the couch and looking out the window. God, she was stunning. My footsteps faltered when I saw her. She looked up.

She smiled at me—the same small smile she gave me at the dinner table.

"Hey," she said.

"Hey. I, um, have something for you," I said, holding up the large canvas bag I was carrying. "Can I?" I asked, motioning at the open spot on the love seat next to her.

"Oh, yeah, of course," she said. "You didn't have to get me anything. I'm not really a presents girl, you know."

"I know," I said as I sat down next to her. But I knew Cam actually loved presents. "And I didn't get you anything . . . technically."

Cam tilted her head and studied me, confused. "Close your eyes," I said. Instead of doing what I said, she just narrowed them.

"Why?" she asked.

"Just do it." I laughed. "And put your hands out."

"You don't have a snake or anything in there, do you?" she asked, eyeing the bag that I'd set between us.

I rolled my eyes. "Yeah, I've been keeping a live animal in this canvas bag all day, just for a chance to scare you with it."

"You never know," she said.

"Close your eyes, Ash," I said. Cam made a big show of being annoyed, letting out a huff, before she finally did what I asked. "Hands," I said.

Cam put her hands out. I took a deep breath before setting her pile of gifts into them. "Open," I said, and when Cam looked down, her mouth dropped open slightly.

"Oh my god," she said as she set everything on her lap. There was a medium-size shoulder bag, a laptop sleeve, and a padfolio—all genuine soft leather. All made, start to finish, by me—cut, stained a deep, rich brown, and branded with a small monogram.

I watched her drag her fingers over the surface of every-thing, but she stayed silent. I started to feel embarrassed. Was this silly? Did I spend hours making things that she wouldn't even like or use? Was it weird that I'd made her something personal instead of just buying her something generic and easy?

"These are . . . beautiful, Dusty," she said as she examined the padfolio more closely. "But you said you didn't buy me anything."

"I didn't," I affirmed.

Cam looked at me. "Did you . . . did you make these?" I nod-ded, still feeling shy. Cam looked back down at her gifts. "Holy shit. These look like they cost a fortune." She looked back up at me. "And believe me, I would know."

"You like them?" I asked.

She was earnest when she said, "I love them, Dusty." Her hands were still rubbing the leather and tracking the stitches. When she made it to the snap on the padfolio, she unclasped it and opened the cover. Her smile widened. "College-ruled paper?"

"You and I both know wide-ruled paper sucks ass."

Cam laughed. "And this pen." She pulled it out of its loop.

"My mom made that," I said. It was a skinny wooden pen with a mountain scene carved into it. "I put a point five pen tip in there. I didn't know if that was still your preference, so I have some other ones, and we can change it," I said quickly.

"Point five is perfect," she said. "Seriously, thank you. This is the most thoughtful gift." She leaned forward—to hug me, I think, but then paused—like she wasn't quite sure.

I leaned forward, too. "You started it," I said. "Now it would just be weird if we didn't." Friends hugged, right? And friends got each other presents—after all, I made something for Emmy, Teddy, and Ada, too.

Cam rolled her eyes again, but it looked like she was trying not to smile. "Right," she said, so I took the opportunity to fold her into my arms. She smelled so good—earthy and expensive. When I felt her relax against me, I felt like I was holding the world. God, she turned me into a cliché motherfucker.

"This is all amazing, Dusty. Thank you."

"You're welcome," I murmured. I tried not to make it obvious that I was smelling her hair like a creep.

"I'm sorry I didn't get you anything," she said. I didn't have the balls to tell her that this was enough. Cam wasn't moving away, so I rubbed my hands up and down her back. She held me tighter. "I didn't know you did this."

"Leatherwork?" I asked.

"Yeah."

"I picked it up in Buenos Aires."

I let my eyes flutter closed, memorizing this moment—thinking about how I had so many memories of her in my arms, but they were all from then. This was now.

And it was everything.

"You feel different," she whispered.

"So do you," I said. "Good different or bad different?"

"Good different, I think," she said. "More substantial."

"Are you saying I was scrawny, angel?" I felt her laugh against my chest—the vibrations made my entire body relax. I thought she hugged me tighter for a second, too.

Right then, we heard little footsteps scurrying down the hall. "Momma!" Riley's voice carried to us, and Cam immediately pushed away from me.

I thought her sudden absence would make me feel empty, but I just felt normal. Maybe empty was my normal. It wasn't the first time I'd wondered this.

I think that's why I came home. When you're constantly on the move, it's hard to stay full. There's not enough time to let everything settle. I liked that when I was younger—gathering people, places, and experiences—enjoying them while I was there and then moving on. I didn't really offer anything a sense of permanence.

Over the past few years, though, it started to get to me. Everything—even the most wonderful things—felt kind of . . . hollow. But until last year, I just kept moving. It was like inertia or whatever. I had been in motion, so I was going to stay in motion. But when Gus called, I finally saw an opportunity to stay still, to come home.

I expected to start to feel restless at some point—to feel the desire to start moving again. And even though I felt it a few times, it was fleeting. Especially right now, when Cam was within reach—physically, at least.

"I can't find Dusty," Riley said as she appeared in the entry to the alcove. When she saw me, she grinned. "Oh. Never mind."

"What's up, Sunshine?" Cam asked, and Riley bounded toward us. When she jumped onto the couch, she situated herself right between Cam and me. Cam lovingly ran a hand over Riley's hair.

"I want to give Dusty his present," she whispered to Cam—not very quietly, though.

Cam smiled. "Good idea," she whispered back.

Riley turned to me and held out a small, balled fist. I held my hand out, and she dropped a small loop of fabric into it.

"It's a friendship bracelet," Riley said. "I made it." I looked down at the bracelet. It was different shades of blue all wrapped around each other. "My mom said blue is your favorite color."

"Your mom is right," I said, glancing at Cam, who looked embarrassed. "This is badass," I said. Riley blushed. "Thank you so much for making it for me. Will you put it on?"

Riley nodded excitedly, like that was the best thing I could've possibly said. I gave the bracelet back to her and held out one of my hands.

"You have pretty drawings," she said as she looked down my arm and hand.

"Thank you," I said. "I like them, too." Riley looped the bracelet around my wrist, but when it was time to tie the knot, she started having a little trouble.

She turned to Cam, who was watching the two of us intently. "Can you help me, Mom?" Cam nodded and took the two ends of the bracelet from Riley. Goosebumps rose on my skin when her fingers grazed it. I hoped she couldn't see.

Cam tied the two ends of the bracelet into a tight, neat knot. This bracelet wasn't going anywhere.

"You know," I said to Riley, "you and I think alike." I reached into my pocket.

"Why?" she asked, tilting her head—just like Cam had done earlier.

"Because I made you a bracelet, too." I pulled the small leather bracelet out. It was the same base color as Cam's gifts, but had lighter flowers carved into it to create a two-toned effect.

Riley's eyes lit up, and her joy was contagious. She went to grab the bracelet out of my hand, but Cam stopped her with a "Riley," and a quintessential mom look. "What do you say?"

Riley looked up at me. "Thank you," she said excitedly. I could've sworn she was almost vibrating. It was cute as hell.

"You're welcome," I said. "Can I?" I gestured to her arm, and Riley held it out. The bracelet closure was a small ruby, Riley's—and my—birthstone, that went through a loop.

"It's beautiful, Dusty," Cam said. When I looked up at her, she was looking at me the way I had been dreaming she would since I came home.

So are you, I thought.

Chapter 21

Cam

I grabbed another blanket and snuggled deeper into the couch in my living room. The house was quiet. Riley was at Gus's for New Year's Eve. They invited me, of course, but honestly, a nice, quiet evening at home felt like the perfect way to ring in the new year—especially after the year I'd had.

I'd gotten a lot done today—cleaned the house, organized the library, and even finished a few case briefings that I sent to the junior partner at my firm. Now, I was waiting for my dinner—a one-pan chicken and veggies recipe that I made at least once a week—to finish up in the oven.

The only downside was that the house was fucking cold (and that I still didn't have a bed frame, but I preferred to ignore that). I'd checked the thermostat, and it said sixty-eight degrees, but it felt a hell of a lot colder than that. I was layered up—leggings, sweatpants, long-sleeved shirt, fleece pullover, and my new favorite big warm wool socks. I was under three blankets, and I was still freezing. My nose felt cold to the touch.

I stared at the big black hole that was the wood-burning

fireplace. I'd been making aggressive eye contact with it since the house's temperature started to drop this afternoon. It would definitely help. At the very least, it would warm the living room up.

But the fireplace came with strings attached—well, one string attached. A very handsome and kind and flirty string.

Being with Dusty on Christmas was . . . nice. He was so kind, and I liked getting to know the man who still had parts of the boy I used to love—maybe the most important parts.

He still made me laugh and knew how to make me feel so comfortable—whether it was after my not-wedding, building Riley's bed, or around a holiday dinner table. He made me feel at ease, and he didn't even have to try.

But I was also reminded that there were years between us—years where he didn't stay put for longer than a season, where he went off to Buenos Aires and learned new skills and god knows what else, and he was happy doing that. I didn't know how someone who seemingly loved to hop around as much as Dusty did could be happy in one place for very long. And that made me feel unsteady.

But then there was the gift he made for me. Incredible. That handmade, genuine, quality leather set would've cost thousands in a store. But he made it just for me. I'd been using the pieces every day since. I'd probably use them for the rest of my life. And the day after Christmas, I found a bottle of leather conditioner and a cloth on my front porch with a note.

I forgot to give this to you yesterday. Use this once a month or whenever your leather is starting to look a little worse for wear. I hope they last forever.
Dusty

But there was a big difference between acknowledging a thoughtful gift and showing up on his doorstep on New Year's Eve and asking him to light my fire—my actual fire, not a metaphorical one. I flopped down on the couch and covered my head with my blankets.

Maybe I could just ask him to teach me, and then I could do it myself? Anne didn't have to know that, right?

Who was I kidding? I loved rules. Even the thought of not following the ones that Anne had laid out for me gave me hives. What an annoying fucking quality to have.

I closed my eyes under the blanket. Dusty probably wasn't even home. It was New Year's Eve, after all. He was probably out doing . . . actually, I didn't want to know what he was doing. What if he was with a woman? Would I care? No.

Yes.

But I didn't have a right to care. An image of Dusty at the Devil's Boot with some faceless woman, grabbing her and kissing her at midnight, made my stomach turn. God, this was ridiculous. I was ridiculous. It wasn't like he and I were anything more than . . . friends. Right? I think it's safe to say we had regained some semblance of friendship. But sometimes, it still felt like there was something . . . else . . . bubbling beneath the surface.

I couldn't believe I could still feel so drawn to him. Dusty wasn't the only man I'd ever loved, but I had to admit that he was the one that I compared every other love to.

And none of them ever measured up.

I used to say it was just because he was my first—that there was no way it could've been as good as I remembered. It was all nostalgia and youth. And that was probably at least partly true. But even now, Dusty still felt like . . . more. More than I was able to understand logically. And more wasn't really an option for me at the moment—at least, I didn't want it to be. I was happy to have him back in my life, but I just wanted to be able to maintain something stable and easy between the two of us.

Okay, I would look out the kitchen window, and if his light was on, I would ask him to start the fireplace. If it was off, I would leave a note for Gus to find with my last will and testament because I would freeze to death before morning.

Perfect.

I took a deep breath before whipping the blankets off myself and heading to the kitchen before I could second-guess it.

As I peered out the window, I saw a soft orange glow coming from Dusty's little house.

Well, fuck.

Here I go, I guess.

I slipped on a pair of snow boots that I kept by the back door, turned off the oven so I didn't burn the house down, since, you know, that's exactly what I was trying to avoid by enlisting Dusty's help.

It wasn't until I was halfway across the snowy yard that I remembered that I was wearing nothing, well, cute. Too late now.

I'd obviously seen the small house before, but I'd never been this close to it. It was small, brown, and brick, and couldn't be bigger than a few hundred square feet. There was a pathway through a thicket of trees from my house to his. Dusty had shoveled it.

When I got to his door, I hesitated—even though it was freezing, or below freezing, rather. It was just a fire. This would be fine.

I took a deep breath before raising my arm and tapping on his door three times. The sound made me think about when Dusty knocked on the bathroom door of the Devil's Boot on my wedding day. Was that really just a month ago? I wondered what that day would've looked like if Dusty hadn't rescued me. Because that's exactly what he did: rescue me. Now, when I thought of that day, I didn't think about Graham or the fact that he didn't show up. I thought about Dusty and the fact that he did.

He always showed up.

The door opened a few seconds later, and I could feel the warmth coming out of his house. I guess he didn't have any heating problems.

"Ash, hey," he said. "Everything okay?"

"Yeah." I nodded. "I'm sorry to bother you, but . . ."

"Your heater is on the fritz." He shook his head and stepped aside. "Come in. Get warm for a minute." I hesitated for half a second, but my chattering teeth and numb nose made it impossible for me to say no or back out.

I let the warmth of his house envelop me as Dusty shut his front door. My eyes wandered as I took everything in. Right inside the door, there was a small kitchen to the right with a half sink and the smallest oven and stovetop that I'd ever seen. His bed was pressed against the back wall. There was a patchwork quilt covering it. At the foot of his bed was a two-seat leather couch and a coffee table. There was a bookshelf in the other corner, as well as a small desk with a reading lamp.

The place was pretty bare. Still it felt homey. Maybe it was because of the size—or the temperature. I noticed that he had a wood-burning fireplace, too. It was a third the size of mine, on the wall to the right of his bed, and it was doing its job quite effectively.

"How long has the heater been out?" he asked.

"Oh, um, I don't really know," I said. "It was pretty cold when I woke up this morning, but started to get unbearable like an hour ago."

"You've been in the cold all day?" I shrugged, and Dusty shook his head. "Why didn't you come get me earlier?"

"It's New Year's Eve. I didn't want to bother you."

Dusty sighed. "Sit by the fire for a bit."

"Can I take my boots off? I don't want to track snow all over your house."

"Yeah, of course. I'll make you some tea."

I slipped off my boots, and when I looked down at my feet, I hoped he wouldn't notice I was wearing his socks. Again. They were just so warm.

Dusty stepped into his kitchen as I walked toward the couch. When I sat down, I watched him pull out an electric kettle and fill it with water. I noticed that his hair was damp— like he'd just gotten out of the shower.

"Earl Grey okay?" he called over his shoulder.

"Yeah," I said. "Thank you."

Dusty pulled a mug out of one of his cabinets. "I'm sorry about the heater," he said. "Sometimes, when it gets too cold, it starts to overwork itself and blows its own fuse."

"When did you add HVAC to your extensive résumé?" I asked.

"Somewhere between Montana and Australia," Dusty said. "You learn to fix a lot of random things when you're not quite sure what your living situation is going to look like."

I scanned the house again. This time, my eyes landed on the coffee table in front of me. There was a small wooden box on top of it, maybe the size of a shoe box. It was covered in stickers. I spotted a couple of bands, cities, and a "love your mother" sticker featuring planet Earth.

"Are these stickers from all the places you've been?" I asked as I reached forward and picked up the box. A few things rattled around inside softly.

"Yeah," Dusty said without looking at me. "I didn't take a lot from place to place, but I always had that box, so it kind of became my scrapbook."

"Did your mom make it?" I asked.

"I made that one, actually. The workmanship is shoddy, but it did its job." Dusty was walking toward me now, with one steaming mug in his hand. He set it on the coffee table in front of me.

"What's in here?" I asked.

Dusty sat on the other side of the couch. "Nothing," he said.

I gave the box a light shake. "Doesn't sound like nothing."

Dusty swallowed. He looked . . . nervous? Only for a second, though; I watched him brush it off before saying, "Stop snooping, weirdo," and he reached to take the box from me.

I pulled the box away, but one of Dusty's hands grazed the top, and it slid back a few inches. It was full enough that a few folded papers fell out. They fell right between Dusty and me. It felt like slow motion. One of them landed on the couch, and I saw "Ash" written on the outside fold.

My heart stopped. I lowered the box slowly back into my lap and pushed the sliding lid off all the way. It was full of folded notes. Everything was folded in a triangle—the same way Dusty used to fold notes when he passed them to me in class. Some looked older than others—more worn, but every one that I could see had something in common—my name scrawled across the front.

"What are these?" I asked.

It was so quiet in his house, I felt like I could hear his heartbeat. "Notes," he said after a few seconds.

"Why is my name on them?"

"Why do you think?" Dusty asked.

Coming over here had been a mistake—thinking I could be here without feeling anything was a mistake.

"I should go," I said, putting the box on the coffee table and standing up.

"Wait," Dusty said and grabbed my hand softly. "Don't go. Please." I don't know what made me sit back down—maybe the pain in his voice or maybe because I was still freezing.

But Dusty's pain wasn't something I ever wanted to see or hear or contribute to again.

My hand was still in his, and one of my knees was pressed against his on the couch. "What are they?" I whispered.

Dusty let out a long, deep breath. "Ash, even after everything went sideways, I didn't stop wanting to be with you. I didn't stop missing you. Adjusting to a world without you in it sucked," he said quietly. The fireplace crackled and snapped.

"Even months and years later, when something happened to me or I had something that I wanted to talk about, you were the person I wanted to tell. So I did. I wrote notes like I used to. I told you about my jobs and my life and, sometimes, I told you how much I missed you and how fucking annoying it was that you hadn't faded from my mind or my heart—even a little bit. I knew I'd never send them, but I don't know, something about it was just . . . comforting, I guess."

"Why do you keep them?"

Dusty leaned forward until our foreheads were touching. I didn't pull away. "Because they're all I had left of you." I felt his breath against my face. "Do you want me to be all the way honest, or do you want me to stop there?"

I swallowed. I knew this could quickly turn into too much too fast, but I couldn't help but want more from him. I wanted to hear everything about what he'd felt over the past fifteen years. I wanted to know if he thought of me as much as I thought of him. I guess I just wanted to know that I wasn't alone in the aftermath of us.

"All the way honest," I whispered.

Dusty closed his eyes tight. "They reminded me that it was all real—no matter how much time people spent telling me that we were too young or that it would never work out." I hated that those people were right. "The notes made you feel real. I needed it all to be real for the pain to be worth it."

"Was it?" I asked. My eyes fluttered closed, and I brought my hands up to each side of his face. He held my wrists. "Worth it."

Dusty laughed a little, but it sounded pained. "I'll let you know if it ever stops."

I could hear my heartbeat in my ears—almost like it was trying to tell me what to do and drown out the noise from my head at the same time. My head wanted to run—to hightail it across my yard, slam my door, and hide from Dusty Tucker while I still had a chance. My heart? It wanted this moment to last as long as possible. It was overwhelming—how right it felt to be this close to him. "Does this make it better or worse?" I asked, rubbing my thumbs back and forth on his cheeks.

"Worse," he said. His voice was strangled and rough.

"And if . . . I kissed you right now?" I whispered, knowing that if I said it louder, I'd lose this moment of courage.

"Worse," Dusty said again on a shaky breath, but then said, "but do it anyway."

I inhaled deeply—breathing him in. He smelled clean and dewy. He used to smell like Axe, which I loved then, but I liked this version better.

I was so close to pressing my mouth against his for the first time in fifteen years. Would it feel familiar or new?

But when Dusty leaned toward me and his eyelids fluttered closed, the heartbeat in my ears turned into alarm bells. A flashing caution sign. *Danger zone. Don't cross. You won't come back from it this time.* I pulled away. I dropped my hands to my lap. "I'm sorry," I said. "I don't . . . I want to, but I . . ." I didn't really know what to say.

It was like me pulling back allowed the oxygen to reach me again. I blinked slowly—trying to process what had just happened, how close I'd come to upsetting the precarious balance that Dusty and I had found for something as fleeting as a kiss.

"I can't . . ." I started, but I couldn't finish, so I stood up quickly. "I'm sorry," I said. "You're right. I don't know what that was."

Dusty rubbed a hand at the back of his neck. "Old habits die hard?" he said. He was trying to smile, but it didn't reach his eyes. I recognized it—the pain. Would I ever stop hurting him? "Let's go look at your heater."

Chapter 22

Dusty

DUSTY: I need your help with something.

TEDDY: Yes, you should get a haircut.

TEDDY: You're looking a little raggedy.

DUSTY: Thanks for the advice, but that's not what I need help with.

TEDDY: That's what you think.

TEDDY: What's up?

Instead of giving Teddy more chances to roast me via text, I decided to call her. "Teddy Andersen speaking," she said as a greeting.

I rolled my eyes, and I hoped she could hear it somehow. "Can you find out if Cam still doesn't have a bed frame?" I asked. After the almost-kiss on New Year's Eve, I was trying to let her control the distance or proximity we had to each other. So far, we landed right in the middle of the two. She didn't avoid me completely—she and Riley brought me leftovers from a dinner they made a couple of days ago—but I didn't see her as much as I had around the holidays.

I didn't know what exactly made her pull back the other night. Had she just gotten swept up in the moment? Had I freaked her out with all my stupid notes? Or was there something that worried her, so much so that she was ready to run back into the cold night? I mean, she had just broken off an engagement, for fuck's sake. She didn't need me falling all over her. Whatever it was, I wanted to put her at ease and show her it was okay. Even if I had nearly leapt at the chance to put my lips on hers again, I could still be her friend, without letting everything I felt for her get in the way.

"Probably. Why?"

"I was at my mom's this morning, and she had a client commission a bed frame in December, but she hasn't been able to get hold of them since then. We're past the thirty-day holding period that she enforces for pickup, so now it's fair game for anyone who wants it."

"That's convenient," Teddy said. "That Cam needed a bed frame and your mom happened to build one that you could give her the day before her birthday."

"Yeah, I guess it is," I said. I really hadn't thought that much about it. I told my mom about Cam's bed situation after I helped put together Riley's room. Well, actually, I told Greer, and she told my mom.

"And really lucky that the client just didn't respond, even though a custom bed is a big purchase."

"Do you have a point, Teddy?"

"I just think Aggie has a vested interest in this entire situation, that's all."

"What 'entire situation'?"

"The Cam and Dusty situation, obviously."

"There is no Cam and Dusty situation," I said. "My mom

would do this for anyone, you know that. She loves to give stuff away. I'm pretty sure you have a nightstand that got left behind by someone."

"Yeah, but I think she'd prefer to do it for Cam."

"Can you find out for me or not?" If someone knew their friend needed a bed frame, and they just happened to have access to one, they'd give it to their friend, right? That's all this had to be.

"Give me ten minutes," Teddy said and then hung up.

An hour later, my mom and I pulled up in front of Cam's house with a deconstructed walnut bed frame in the back of my dad's old truck. That was one of the drawbacks of the Bronco—no truck bed. Luckily, Renny Tucker's old pickup was still kicking.

Cam must've heard us pull in because she came out the front door. When she saw my mom, she beamed. Was I jealous of my mom? That was pathetic.

Aggie hopped out of the truck and made her way to Cam. The two hugged tightly. "Happy almost birthday, honey," she said to Cam.

"Thank you," Cam responded. "And thank you for saving me! I am so sick of sleeping on a mattress on the floor, but I can't find anything I like."

My mom gestured toward the truck. "Well, let's go see if this is your taste." She linked her arm through Cam's and started leading her my way.

"Hey," I said as the two of them approached. "Happy birth-day eve." My heart started kicking up dust in my chest. It had started doing that again ever since New Year's. Standing this

close to her, I felt the sting of rejection. But I kept telling myself she was right to pull away; she had always been the
smarter one. Otherwise, we could have upset whatever careful balance we had struck, and the last thing I wanted was for
her to disappear from my life. Again.

It just sucked that I couldn't stop thinking about how close
I had come to finding out if she still tasted the same.

"Thanks," Cam said with a genuine smile in my direction.
Take that, Mom. I walked to the back of the truck and pulled
the tailgate down so Cam could see the bed frame. It was
stained a deep cognac and built in a mid-century style. "Oh
my god," she said. "This is beautiful, Aggie. I can't believe that
someone wouldn't want it."

My mom had a gleam in her eye that I couldn't quite place.
"It's all yours, honey," she said to Cam. "Dusty, you can get this
inside, can't you?"

"Yes, ma'am." The bed was heavy, but I got it in the truck by
myself with some finagling and willpower, so I was sure I
could get it out—especially if Cam was watching.

"Are you sure?" Cam said. "I can help."

"No, no," my mom said with a shake of her head. "He's got
it. Why don't you give me the tour of your new house?"

Cam gave me a look for assurance, and I nodded.

I watched as the two of them walked into the house, heads
close together like they were conspiring. It made my heart
swell up in my chest. The love my mom had for Cam had
always been so evident. It made me happy that they had
continued a relationship of their own, even when I wasn't
around.

I broke a sweat getting the four pieces of the bed up the porch steps and into Cam's room. I tried not to think about the fact that I was in her bedroom while I was putting everything together. Luckily, it was quick work this time, unlike Riley's bed. My mom had built this with these sort of Lincoln Log contraptions that slid into each other and locked into place easily—no hardware required.

When I was done, my mom and Cam were sitting at her kitchen table. It looked like they'd pulled out a set of dominoes.

"Everything good, Dusty?" my mom asked when she saw me.

"All good," I said.

"See?" she said. "I told you he could manage."

"You raised a hell of a man," Cam said with a grin. "That is the second bed he's put together in my house with no help."

"You helped a little with the last one," I said, smiling.

"Not really," she said. "But I appreciate you saying so."

"Grab a chair, Dusty," my mom said. "Come play with us."

My mom's purse was on the chair next to her, so I had no choice but to sit by Cam—not that I minded.

"Oh, this is so nice," my mom mused. "To see you two together again. Makes my old heart happy."

I opened my mouth to say something, but nothing came out. I was scared my mom's comment would spook Cam, send her spiraling far away again, into the recesses of her brain. I didn't know how to respond, but that didn't matter because Cam did it for me.

"Yeah," she said with a quick look in my direction. "It is nice."

Chapter 23

Cam

March in Meadowlark was normally cold and dreary. This year, it was warmer than normal—less snow, but also more rain. Everything was still brown—there wasn't enough sun to bring the earth back to life quite yet, but I was enjoying every time it would peek through the clouds.

I was on my way to pick up Riley at Rebel Blue. It was Saturday, so she had riding lessons with Emmy. It wasn't warm enough for outdoor lessons yet, so Riley was in the indoor arena, but the side panels had already been removed, so you could see in from outside. I parked my car at the Big House and walked over to watch. My face was cold, but I didn't mind. The air was fresher up here—I felt freer.

Both Emmy and Riley were in the center of the arena while Riley's horse, Sweetwater, was walking around them in a circle. When I got close, Emmy noticed me and waved, but she didn't say anything. She let Riley keep her focus, so I stayed quiet, too.

Riley's thick eyebrows were knitted together—watching

Sweetwater's every move—and it made me smile. We had the same thinking face. It was easy for me to see Gus in her—honestly, it was easier to see any of the Ryders in her than it was for me to see myself in my daughter sometimes. But that face was all me.

Emmy walked up to the horse and grabbed her halter. "Good job, Sunshine," she said. "Let's practice leading, okay?" Riley nodded and walked over to Sweetwater. "And your mom is watching." Riley's head snapped over to me, and she gave me a big ol' smile. My daughter's smile could warm me up no matter what the temperature.

I leaned up against the fence, and Emmy walked over to me. "Hey," she said.

"Hey," I said. "How's she doing?"

"She's a natural." Emmy smiled.

"Of course she is," I said. I watched as Riley led Sweetwater around the arena in a circle. They were an adorable pair. "It doesn't hurt that she's got a good teacher, too."

The sound of a truck caught my attention. I looked up and out in the pasture and saw Dusty. He was standing on the back of a flatbed truck that was stacked high with hay. It looked like he was pushing chunks of it off the back of the truck based on the way the horses were following him.

It'd been about two months since New Year's Eve. I'd decided that both of us had just gotten carried away that night—especially me. The cold had made me a little crazy.

I just didn't want things to change between us. I was trying to be happy with what we were without letting myself long for more.

But when it came to Dusty, I'd been secretly wishing for more for years—wishing I could see him, wishing he would come home, wishing that, one day, he would respond to more than one of my texts, and we could talk. Now, I had all of those things, but they came with the fear that I would lose him again.

The fear was almost debilitating, but so was the desire to be close to him—so much so that when it was just me alone with my thoughts, I wished I hadn't pulled away.

Since then, though, things had been okay. It was like both of us decided to be content with pieces of each other, so I just had to stop my mind from imagining what the fuller picture could look like if we ever tried to put those pieces together again.

I was grateful when Aggie and he brought me the bed frame, and we had fun playing dominoes for an hour afterward. It felt like a perfect birthday. We texted. He came over sometimes—to check the heater, patch a leak under the sink; things like that. Things with Dusty felt aggressively normal. We were friends . . . but that didn't mean I minded when he flirted with me a bit. That was just Dusty. He couldn't help it. It felt good, a little confidence boost, but even more so, it felt safe. Flirting was harmless. And I just pretended I didn't notice the way his eyes lingered on me or the disappointment in his face when it was time to leave.

It was a foolproof system, if I do say so myself.

The truck was going slowly, but when I tried to see who was driving, no one was there. "What's going on over there?" I nodded toward Dusty.

"Luke and Dusty's prized possession," Emmy said on a laugh. "They jimmy-rigged the engine, so when whoever is on the back pulls on a string, it gives the truck gas, so they can do feeding with one person instead of two."

I watched Dusty kick hay off the back of the truck, and then I saw it when the truck slowed, his arm moved, pulling on the string, and the truck went forward again.

"Clever," I said with a nod, not taking my eyes off Dusty. God, he was pretty. He was wearing a dark green trucker hat, brown work jacket, and worn denim jeans.

"He looks good up there, no?" Emmy said, and my eyes whipped to hers. She had a knowing smirk on her face.

"Clementine Ryder," I said, shocked. "I don't know what you're talking about."

"You're blushing," she said with a laugh. "It's good, though. I like the open staring more than the stolen glances you two have been giving each other." My mouth fell open. "What?" Emmy said. "I saw you two on Christmas."

"I don't know what you're talking about. Dusty and I are *friends*," I emphasized. Emmy let out a disbelieving snort. "Whatever, I'm telling Brooks."

Emmy shrugged and bit down on her lip. "I like what happens when he gets jealous."

"Gross," I said with an eye roll. "Go be in love somewhere else."

"I've got ten more minutes of a riding lesson to teach, so will do," Emmy said, walking away toward where Riley was leading Sweetwater. "Plus, it looks like you're going to have company."

"What?" I asked and followed Emmy's gaze over my shoulder. Dusty was a few paces away. Oh.

"Hey, Dusty," Emmy said with a wave over her shoulder.

"Hey, Em," he said. "Cam." He nodded at me.

"Hey," I said. Why did my voice sound higher? And was

I . . . sweating? God, that was embarrassing. "Happy Saturday." Shit. That was even worse.

Dusty's eyebrows went up in amusement. "Happy Saturday. What brings you up here?"

I nodded toward Riley. "My weekend," I said.

"Ah," he responded. "She's good. I saw her mount earlier on Maple. She's got a good seat."

I laughed. "I wish I knew what that meant, but I'll take your word for it. I don't even know what she's doing right now." I didn't know a thing about horses, but I loved to watch them. They were majestic as hell.

Dusty looked over at Riley and Emmy. "Groundwork," he said. "Helps build trust between a horse and its rider." Dusty shook his head. "Emmy looks just like her mom out there."

I tilted my head. "Did you know Stella?" I asked.

"Yeah." Dusty nodded. "I took riding lessons from her as a kid, so I was in the exact same spot Riley was."

"I didn't know that," I said. The image of a smaller Dusty flashed into my mind, leading a horse around the arena like Riley had done. "Emmy told me about your, um, ingenuity," I said, gesturing toward the utility truck.

Dusty smiled, and when he lifted up his old trucker hat to smooth his hair back before adjusting it on his head, I could only hope I wasn't visibly drooling. Especially when his jacket moved up on his arm a little bit, showing that the blue friendship bracelet that Riley had made him for Christmas was still there. "It's actually super fucking helpful," he said.

"How do you get off of it?" I asked. "Like if it just keeps moving?"

"If you don't pull on the string for a while, she gets really slow, so you just hop off the back, run toward the driver's side, and throw her in park."

"I wish I would've seen that part," I said with a laugh.

"So you were watching me?" Dusty said with a smirk.

I rolled my eyes. "You know," I said. "Someone standing on the back of a moving truck with no one in the driver's seat is a bit of a spectacle."

"All I care about is that it made you look," Dusty said, and I felt it in my spine.

"Shameless flirt," I said with a push on his shoulder. He caught my hand and held it there for a second before letting go.

For a second, I wished he hadn't let go, and then immediately got frustrated with myself. *Friend, Cam,* I reminded myself. *This is your friend. You're just having fun with your friend.*

"You like it when I flirt with you," Dusty said with a smile.

"Shut up," was the only response I could come up with. Because he was right. He'd always seen me so clearly.

Dusty laughed a little. "I'm going easy on you," he said.

"Believe me, I'm aware," I responded. Dusty had fifteen more years of flirting experience under his belt, and I was a little scared of what he might have learned. I also didn't want to think about who he'd learned it from—or with.

"Let me know when you're ready for me to dial it up," he said with a wink. My only defense mechanism was another eye roll, and Dusty's response was to laugh again. My cheeks were hot, and I could only hope they weren't as red as they felt. If they were, I'd blame it on the cold.

"So I was wondering—" Dusty started to say but was interrupted by Riley climbing onto the other side of the fence and putting her arms around my neck for a hug.

"Did you see me leading Sweetwater, Mom?" she asked excitedly.

"I did." I squeezed her back with one arm. "I'm so proud of you."

"Did you see?" Riley looked over at Dusty with a giant grin on her face. One side of Dusty's mouth tilted up as he nodded.

"You're a natural," he said.

"That's what auntie says," Riley told him matter-of-factly. "She also said I had to wait a minute before I came over here so you guys could talk. I waited like five whole minutes."

In Riley time, that meant she waited approximately thirty seconds. We were working on the whole patience thing.

I looked over at Emmy, who was close enough to hear. She had a small smile on her face. Meddling little shit.

"Look what I'm wearing." Riley held out her wrist to Dusty and pushed up the sleeve of her coat a little. The leather bracelet Dusty had made for her was on her wrist. She refused to take it off, which I secretly loved most of the time. It would get a little heated at bathtime when I asked her to take it off, but when I told her that water might ruin it, she'd allow me to take it off her for five minutes.

Dusty held out his wrist the same way, so she could see his blue bracelet. "I'm wearing mine, too," he said with a grin. "I love it."

My sassy and spunky daughter went bashful, and it made me smile. The Dusty Tucker effect seemed to take hold of her, too. Just like her mom. She detached from me and scooted her little feet along the fence, getting closer to Dusty. When she swung her leg over, Dusty put a hand on her back, so she wouldn't fall as she brought over the other one. Instead of climbing down like she always did, she reached one arm back to Dusty, who grabbed her with care and set her softly on the ground.

"Thank you," she said as she looked up at him. Where did these manners come from? Riley stepped toward me and looped her hand in mine. "Are you done working?" she asked.

Dusty shook his head. "Not quite. I've gotta help your auntie get the horses back to the stables."

"Oh." Riley looked disappointed. "Mom takes me to the coffee shop after lessons. You could probably come if you want. She likes you."

I looked down at Riley, mouth agape. I heard Emmy stifle a laugh behind us, and when I turned to look at her, she shrugged with a grin.

When I turned back, Dusty's eyes were on me. They were alight. "Next time," he said, not breaking eye contact with me for a few seconds—long enough that I was grateful there were only two people around to see it. When he finally broke it, he looked down at Riley. "You did good today, kid," he said and ruffled her hair. She giggled. He was good with her. It didn't shock me, necessarily, but it did make me realize how much things had changed. Dusty felt so . . . steady now. When we were together, I always knew I could depend on him, but he was also just . . . Dusty. He was fun and flirty and spontaneous back then—all things I wasn't. And he was those things still, but he was also different. I couldn't put my finger on it, but there was something about him now. He seemed even sturdier, unyielding, as if he was a ship incapable of sinking. I couldn't explain it, but I also didn't know: Could a ship like that stay anchored in the harbor, or would it eventually yearn to drift off toward the open waters and new horizons?

"I'll see you guys later." Then he hopped over the fence

with as much grace as an actual ballerina and walked toward Emmy, who had four horses on hitching posts at the end of the arena.

"Bye," I said, and Riley gave him a wave as we started to walk away. I looked back just in time to see Dusty ride out of the arena toward the stables. The horse he was on had another horse tied to it. He looked at ease as he rode. Beautiful, even.

I sighed. Beautiful and my personal Achilles' heel, just like he'd always been.

Chapter 24

Cam

Fifteen Years Ago

We had a test in English today—*six short-answer questions and four long-essay questions about* Animal Farm. *I had trouble focusing because I could feel Dusty at the desk right behind me. I wondered what he was thinking about—probably the test, which was also what I should have been thinking about, but I was mostly just thinking about him.*

I'd never really experienced something like this before—something exciting and butterfly-inducing and totally consuming.

I loved it.

I might have loved him, too, but I didn't know for sure. Did that exist at seventeen? Did it exist at all? I didn't know if I'd ever seen it—at least not between two people. My parents loved things, money, but I didn't think they loved each other.

Or me.

I heard a chair scoot back—Dusty's chair, I was pretty sure. It was confirmed when I saw a familiar pair of worn-out Levis and mop of blond hair making their way toward Mr. Watson's desk.

Dusty dropped his test in the box on the desk before turning around and coming back toward me—toward his desk, I mean. I tried not to look at him.

When he walked past, he dropped a piece of paper that was folded into a triangle onto my desk, and my heart jumped a little bit. I eyed it for a second. Should I open it now? Wait until I finished my test?

It couldn't hurt to just take a peek . . . right?

I reached for the note, but before I could grab it, someone else did. When I looked up, I was met with a very annoyed Mr. Watson. Shit.

"Passing notes, Miss Ashwood?"

"N-no." Well, kind of. "It's nothing, sir."

"You know the rules." I did. If you passed notes, they got read in front of the class. Oh god. I wanted to wither and die right in the middle of the classroom. If he read that note out loud, I would. I didn't even know what it said, but at this point, I didn't want to know.

Yes, I did.

"It's not—I mean," I stammered. "I didn't—"

"It's from me, sir," Dusty said. I felt him stand behind me.

I swore Mr. Watson rolled his eyes. "All right, then, Mr. Tucker. Would you like to share with the class or shall I?"

Dusty was quiet for a second. Mr. Watson started to unfold the paper. "I haven't stopped thinking about kissing you," Dusty blurted out, and Mr. Watson's face blanched. It even took me a minute to catch up.

"I hope you're talking about the contents of the note, Mr. Tucker."

"Yes, sir," Dusty said. He took a step forward—I saw his shoe in my periphery, and then he kneeled right next to my desk.

"I haven't stopped thinking about kissing you," Dusty said again. This time, his gray eyes were on mine. "I think about it all the time, actually. I think there's something wrong with me.

"I think about you when I wake up and when I go to sleep. During the day, you just stand at the front of my brain, and I can't shake it. When I'm with you, I don't want it to end, and when I'm not, I just want to see you again.

"Is it stupid for me to write this in a note that I'm going to give you in English class? Probably. But I like writing to you. I like that these are just ours . . . well, not anymore obviously," Dusty added, smiling a little.

"I can't say for sure, but I think I'm in love with you." My breath caught in my throat. The smile on my face was big and reckless, and my cheeks burned with embarrassment and excitement.

"I'm going to kiss you now," Dusty said, and I nodded eagerly. He rose and took my face in his hands before his mouth landed on mine. I forgot we were in class. I forgot people were watching us. I forgot where I was completely.

Dusty just made me brave, I guess.

Cheers erupted around us. Our classmates clapped and whooped. I heard Chloe's familiar yell.

We only kissed for a second before Mr. Watson cleared his throat. "All right, you two, that's enough," he said. Dusty pulled back. He was grinning. "Mr. Tucker, please return to your seat, and Miss Ashwood"—he looked at me—"I'd recommend finishing your exam."

Before Mr. Watson walked away, he handed the note back to Dusty.

Chapter 25

Dusty

After I saw Cam and Riley at Rebel Blue, Emmy and I cleaned stalls and groomed the horses. It was too early for them to start losing their winter coats, so I didn't end the day with a mouth full of horse hair, which was nice.

"So," Emmy said as we were walking back toward the Big House—toward our trucks, "anything new and noteworthy to report on you and Cam?" Emmy and I had gotten closer since I came home. We worked together a lot. I was usually with her or Gus, so basically the same person in a different font. Stubborn, hardworking, hotheaded, kind—all qualities that I liked about both of them.

"You're hanging out with Teddy too much," I said as I shook my head. "Where's your subtlety? Your finesse?"

"You two dance around each other enough, so I figure straightforward is the way to go here."

Huh. I couldn't really argue with her there, except for one small correction. "I don't dance around her nearly as much as she dances around me, you know." Actually, there was minimal dancing these days, but I was still worried that one wrong move would spook her.

"Are you okay with that?" Emmy asked.

I shrugged. I hadn't really talked about this with anyone, but I liked that Emmy asked. "I don't blame her. She's had a weird couple of months, but she gives me just enough that I can't help but let a little hope slip through all the cracks, you know?"

Emmy nodded. "Hope is good, though, right?"

"Depends," I said with a shrug.

"On what?"

"On whether or not you're hoping for something that's never going to happen." Sometimes, I wondered if I'd spent fifteen years building Cam up in my head and that when I came home, I'd realize that.

Now that I was here, I didn't feel that way at all. I almost felt like the feelings I had for her back then were just a solid foundation for the new ones to build upon.

I just didn't know if she was standing on that foundation with me. I thought she might be. I saw the way she looked at me. She *had* leaned in to kiss me (as I reminded myself every night when I'd replay that moment before bed, trying to forget the moment when she had pulled away). When we talked, it felt like she was holding herself back—like she was afraid to let herself fall again. I understood it. I empathized with it. I was trying to be patient, but I didn't know what to think anymore.

Honestly, it frustrated me. I was the one who had been trying to convince her that we could be friends. But now, I was worried I'd given her a way out, a path to escape her feelings for me, and she seemed hell-bent on taking it. And I felt like I didn't really have any choice but to let her.

I had pushed, and she'd pulled away.

I already knew how this story ended.

Emmy shrugged. "I think it'll work itself out," she said.

"That's . . . optimistic," I responded.

"I'm all about love conquering all these days." Emmy laughed. "I don't know. I just think you and Cam are tied together in so many ways—in even more ways than Luke and I were. You guys actually liked each other. I don't think those ties exist for nothing, you know?"

"Are you going soft on me, Ryder?" I asked sarcastically. I'd always known Emmy to be stubborn and fierce, but I liked seeing how much she'd grown into herself since I'd been gone. "You basically made yourself a human shield between Cam and me when I crashed your girls' night last year." I remembered the way Emmy placed herself protectively between the two of us. As much as it threw me in the moment, I liked seeing that Cam had found a place and people that would protect her. Especially if I couldn't fill that role anymore.

"Well, she was engaged. I thought she was happy, and I didn't need you stepping in and fucking it all up."

"Was she not happy?" I asked. I didn't know anything about Cam's engagement. I didn't know how she and Graham met, how long they were together—nothing. But in the past couple months, Cam didn't seem to give any indication that she was a heartbroken woman. She seemed . . . fine. Not sad, just run-down.

Emmy was quiet for a second before she answered. "I've been thinking a lot about it since the wedding day. I just . . . I think there was more to her engagement than any of us knew, and I don't know if she would've chosen it if she didn't have a reason."

My thoughts immediately went to Cam's parents. To be blunt, the Ashwoods fucking sucked ass. They were somehow completely absent and totally controlling all at once. They dangled money like a carrot but never approval or love or affection. As a teenager, I don't think I really understood how bad being in that house was for her. I knew she didn't like her parents, but I don't think I understood how detrimental it was to feel like love had to be earned.

I think my parents saw it, though. I think that's why they always let Cam stay for dinner and put her report cards on the fridge. I think that's why my dad taught her to change a flat tire and why my mom went to her soccer games.

There were parts of Cam that I had to grow up to understand. I think I was finally starting to do just that.

"That bums me out," I said to Emmy with a sigh.

"Me too," Emmy agreed. "So don't give up yet, okay?" And with that, we went our separate ways for the day.

When I got home, I noticed a small human playing on the rocks outside of my front door. What was Riley doing there?

I got out of my truck and started walking toward her. She waved at me excitedly as I got closer. "What's up, kid?" I asked. "Everything all right?"

"I'm bored," she said with a huff. "And I can't reach the Fruit Roll-Ups in the pantry."

"A tragedy," I responded. "Where's your mom?"

"She's asleep in her office." Riley sighed.

My spine straightened. "Is she okay?"

Riley nodded. "She was working. I think she got tired."

"You didn't wake her up?"

"She doesn't wake me up when I'm tired." Riley lifted her small shoulders in a shrug. "Can you come get me a Fruit Roll-Up?"

"Yeah, kid," I said with a nod. "Let me change my clothes, and I'll meet you back there."

"I'll wait," Riley said and sat down on one of the rocks. I hurried into my house and took off my coat and whipped my long-sleeved thermal over my head before grabbing a pair of sweatpants and a hoodie. I smelled like horses, but I didn't want to shower. I wanted to get Riley her Fruit Roll-Up and make sure Cam was okay.

I swung the door back open less than two minutes later. Riley popped up from her seat on the rock, and before I knew it, she had slipped her small hand into mine and was walking me back toward her house.

"How was the coffee shop?" I asked as she walked.

"It was okay," Riley said. "I tried a hazelnut steamer today."

"You didn't like it?" I asked, based on her tone. She shook her head. "I don't like hazelnut, either. What flavor do you normally get?"

"Vanilla," she said.

"You can't go wrong with a classic."

"I think so, too," Riley said. "But my mom says I have to try something new once a week."

"That's a good rule," I said. "Because you wouldn't know if you didn't like it if you never tried it."

"Sometimes I like the new stuff, though, like olives. Do you like olives?"

I wrinkled my nose. "No, not at all."

"Teddy doesn't, either, but my mom and dad do," Riley said. We were close to her house now. "So I'm like them."

"They're good people to be like," I said as I pushed the back door of Cam's house open. Music was playing from a speaker, and it was nice and warm. Good. The heater hadn't gone out again. "All right, kid. Show me where these Fruit Roll-Ups are."

Riley let go of my hand and scampered toward the pantry. I followed her as she pointed to a white box of Fruit Roll-Ups on the top shelf. I reached for it and brought it down to her level.

When Riley put her hand inside the box, she closed her eyes as she shuffled around, and a smile tugged at the corner of my mouth. An image of a seventeen-year-old Cam came to my mind, her eyes closed as she dug through a giant bag of saltwater taffy after one of our hikes. She didn't know what flavor she wanted, so I told her to let fate decide.

I said the same thing to Riley now, and she looked up at me with big green eyes.

"That's what my mom always says!" I felt like someone had just kicked the back of my knees. Even when we weren't near each other, Cam appeared in so many parts of my life. I always got ice cream in a cup with a cone on top because Cam had taught me that you got all the benefits of a cone without all the mess. I always hit my dashboard when I went through a yellow light because we used to pretend it would supercharge us to make it through the intersection before it changed to red. It never occurred to me that I would show up in her life in the same way.

Until now.

"You can have one, too," Riley said, and I smiled.

"Thanks, kid." I grabbed a blue Fruit Roll-Up out of the box before I put it back on the shelf. I watched Riley launch—literally, there was no other word for it—onto one of the couches in front of the TV. I wanted that kind of energy.

"I'm going to check on your mom quick, okay?" Riley peeled open her Fruit Roll-Up and nodded. I walked down the hallway at the end of the living room. The door to Cam's office was open, and a soft glow was coming from it—more than just the light in the room.

When I peeked inside, I saw it was a happy light on her desk, which was piled high with papers and file folders. I scanned the room and saw her asleep in a chair by the window. Her hair was pulled up, and she had her glasses on. An open file folder with papers spilling out was lying on her chest, and her mouth was slightly open. She wasn't snoring—yet.

I walked through the door as quietly as I could, so I could take the files off her. I tried to keep everything in order as best I could as I set it on the floor next to her. I pulled a blanket out of the basket by her chair—I picked the soft one—and laid it over her.

I thought for a second that maybe I should wake her, but I decided against it. She was obviously tired. I could hang out with Riley—it's not like I was doing anything tonight.

I looked at her one last time before I walked back out to the living room. It was the most peaceful and calm I'd seen her since I came home.

As I walked out, I turned off the lights and closed the door—not all the way, but enough that maybe any noise wouldn't wake her up.

Riley had the TV remote in her hand when I walked back out into the living room. "Can you help me with this?" she said. "I don't know how it works."

I walked over and flopped onto the couch next to her. I held my hand out for the remote, and Riley slapped it onto my palm. "What should we watch?" I asked.

Riley shrugged. "What do you like to watch?"

"I don't know," I said honestly. "I haven't had a TV in like ten years, kid."

Riley giggled. "You're old. Are you as old as my dad?"

"Not that old," I said. "Maybe you're just young." I turned on the TV and started going through the guide.

"I'm going to be eight soon," she said. "I'm already seven and a half."

"You're going to be eight in July," I said. "That's like months from now. My birthday is then, too."

"How old are you going to be?"

"Thirty-two," I said.

"Old." Riley nodded.

"Your mom is older than me, you know," I said—only by six months, but still.

"My mom isn't old," Riley said.

"Well, she's older than me, so I guess that means I'm not old, either." Riley folded her arms and rolled her eyes, and I tried not to laugh.

"How do you feel about *Mythbusters*?" I asked as I scrolled.

"I don't know what that is."

"*Pawn Stars*?"

"I like stars." Riley shrugged.

"*Pawn Stars* it is," I said and pushed down on the enter button on the remote. After a few minutes, Riley asked, "What's a pawn shop?"

"It's a place where people go to sell their stuff, but normally, they don't get as much money as they want or need."

"Why?"

"Because the shops have to make a profit, and they're usually kind of shady."

"What's a profit?"

"Um," I said. "It's how people make money on stuff—like your shirt probably costs a few dollars for someone to make and then they sell it for ten."

"Like the clothes Teddy makes?" Riley asked.

"Yeah, so Teddy sells people clothes for more money than it cost her to make them." There was a whole nuanced discussion in here about cost versus labor, but maybe we'd save that for when she was eight. "So she can get paid for making them. Make sense?"

Riley nodded. "Why are people selling their stuff?"

I shrugged. "Maybe they need some extra cash or maybe they just don't need that thing anymore."

"Like a garage sale?" I nodded. "Ada likes those. People in town have them sometimes."

"They do." I nodded.

"Do we have a pawn shop?" Riley looked up at me. Her eyebrows had knitted together, and she had bitten down on her bottom lip. When I blinked, it was like my vision was flashing between seeing her and Cam.

"We do," I said after I found my footing again. "But you can only get to it from the alley behind the diner. It doesn't have a front entrance."

"I want to go there," she said.

"I'll take you," I responded. Dahlia, the shop owner, would probably love a visit from Riley—especially if Wayne had been in with all of his scrap metal that day asking for a cool grand. "They've got a good vinyl collection."

"My dad has vinyls. We could get him one."

"We could. What do you think he would like?" I put my arm over the back of the couch.

"Conway Twitty or Billy Idol," she said, and I grinned. This kid was getting raised right, that was for damn sure.

Riley scooted closer to me until she could lay her head on my chest. When she did, I froze. I wasn't around a lot of kids. I didn't really know what to do, so I just let her stay there. We watched a few episodes in a row of *Pawn Stars*. Riley asked a lot of questions. I had a good time trying to figure out how to answer them.

"Why doesn't he pay them what they ask for?"

"Because he's gotta negotiate," I said. "What the person asks for is just a starting point."

"Can I negotiate?"

"What do you want to negotiate?" I asked, amused.

"Bedtime," she said.

"I bet you could," I said. "You just gotta know what to ask for—like if you want to stay up thirty minutes later, ask for an hour."

"Why?"

"Because then you can knock your parents down like this guy does to his customers." I could almost hear the wheels in Riley's head turning.

We ate a couple more Fruit Roll-Ups, and I made her a

sandwich when she said she was hungry. Not long after that, she fell asleep curled into my side. Just when I was about to join her in snoozeville, I heard panicked steps coming down the hallway.

Cam appeared a second later, looking stressed and frazzled, and like she was about to yell. When she saw me, I brought my finger up to my lips in a "shh" motion, and then pointed to Riley asleep next to me.

I watched Cam's shoulders drop as she exhaled. "Should I take her to her bed?" I whispered, and Cam nodded. I maneuvered Riley into my arms and tried not to jostle her too much. When I stood up from the couch, Cam's eyes were moving from Riley's face to mine—like she didn't quite know where to look, but the expression in her eyes didn't change. It looked a lot like love.

I tried not to think about it as I moved past her. She followed me down the hallway to Riley's room and pushed the door open for me. When I set Riley in her bed, she moved a little, grabbed a stuffed horse that was next to her and pulled it close, but she didn't wake up. I pulled her blanket up over her and met Cam in the hallway as I shut the door softly behind me.

"Wait," I said. "Does she sleep with her door shut? I saw this thing a few years ago about a house that had a fire and the door being shut to the kid's room kept him safe, so now I always shut doors, but I can open it if you want me to."

I was rambling. Why was I rambling?

"It's okay. She sleeps with her door shut," Cam whispered.

We walked back down the hallway to the living room together. "She, um, she was waiting outside of my house when I got back," I explained. "She wanted a Fruit Roll-Up and couldn't reach the box."

Cam dragged a hand down her face. She looked exhausted. "I can't believe I fell asleep." She sat on the armrest of one of her couches. "I was doing briefs at my desk, and I thought moving to my chair wouldn't hurt, and when I checked on Riley, she was going buck-wild in a couple of her coloring books."

"It's okay," I said to her. "You were tired."

"I don't get to be tired," she said. "I don't get to fall asleep in my office—not with my daughter here." Cam let out a heavy sigh, and I watched the tension return to her shoulders. "A million things could've gone wrong. She could've tried to climb up to reach the Fruit Roll-Ups and fallen and broken her arm. She could've decided she wanted to roam farther than your house."

"Hey," I said and put my hands on each of her shoulders. "None of those things happened. You have a smart and thoughtful kid, Cam. She didn't want to wake you up. She came and got me. We watched *Pawn Stars,* and she fell asleep on the couch. It's okay."

"You don't get it, Dusty," she fired back. "You're not a parent."

"No, I'm not," I said, "but I'm also not an idiot, so I know this isn't worth getting worked up for." I brought my hands to her face without thinking about it. "And next time you're tired and you need a nap, you come get me, okay? And I'll come sit on your couch with Riley. I've watched Riley's village work for Gus, so let me be the part of it that works for you, all right?"

Cam's nostrils flared, but then her eyes went soft. "Thank you—for taking care of her. She likes you, you know."

"I'm glad," I said. "I hope you're still thanking me when she's trying to negotiate a new bedtime."

Cam gave me a puzzled look. "What do you mean?"

"Don't worry about it," I said. "Is there anything else I can help you with? With work, or whatever?"

"No," Cam said and rubbed a hand over her face. "I don't want you to bore yourself to death."

"If it's so boring, why don't you do something else?" I asked. "Maybe something where you don't have to work so much? Or that makes you happier and less sleepy?" I tried to keep it light.

I watched her shoulders deflate—so much for light. "Honestly, I don't really know where to start," she said. "I don't really know if there's anything else I want to do. It just feels easier to just do this and know that I've got a secure job, even if I don't love it."

"That feels like a really half-assed way to live, Ash, and I've never really known you to half-ass anything."

Cam sighed and shrugged, as if she was depleted. "I didn't mean to dump all of that on you," she said. "I just keep waiting for things to slow down a bit, but they haven't. And I have to see my parents next week, so I'm more keyed up than usual."

"Why?" I asked. "Not why are you keyed up—I get it—why do you have to see them?" From the outside, it didn't seem like Cam's relationship with her parents had changed that much, so I wondered why she was still trying.

"They have this annual fundraising gala thing in Jackson Hole," she said with a wave of her hand. "They raise a lot of money for childhood cancer research, so I don't mind going. I just wish I could go . . . without talking to them."

"Are they still . . ."

I didn't finish my sentence before Cam said, "Yeah. They're mostly the same."

"Anything I can do to help?" I asked.

Cam started to shake her head but then bit at the inside of her cheek. "Maybe . . ." She trailed off for a second. "Do you . . . maybe . . . want to come with me?"

I blinked a few times, shocked that she would ask. "Oh. Uh. Y-yeah," I said quickly. "Yeah, I'll go."

"Really?" She sounded as shocked as I felt.

"Really."

"You'd have to wear a tux," she said.

"Sounds like a nightmare," I responded in a chipper voice. "But maybe we can make it less of one."

Chapter 26

Cam

Fifteen Years Ago

Ash,

I know we've already graduated, but I decided I'm going to keep sending you notes. I'm not exactly sure when I'm going to give you this one. Maybe when you come visit me at work today. The day is going to go by so slow waiting for you. I could just text you, and I probably will, but I dunno . . . I like the notes. I like that they feel special and that they feel like ours, you know?

Anyway, this note has a point.

My parents are going out of town for their anniversary this weekend, and Greer is staying with a friend. And for the first time, probably ever, I don't have to work on Saturday or Sunday. Think you can get away long enough to spend some time with me?

Check yes or no, and bring this back to me before Friday—with snack requests. I'm also going to (try) to make

you dinner. No promises it'll be any good, though. I hope
you'll love me anyway.
   I love you,
   Dusty

W*hen I pulled into Dusty's driveway, it was just after six.
My parents got me a car for graduation—a sporty BMW
three series that had more buttons than I knew what to do with. I
liked the car. I was grateful for it. They said I'd need it when I went
to Vanderbilt this fall, which was probably true, but it came with
one giant stipulation: I wasn't allowed to see Dusty.*

*To say my parents didn't approve of our relationship was the
understatement of the century, but I didn't care. As far as they
knew, Dusty and I broke up when we graduated. What they didn't
know wouldn't hurt them. It wasn't my fault that my dad was out
of town and my mom would get home from the country club late
enough that she'd assume I was already in bed. Being with Dusty
was worth everything, so risking my car to see him felt like the
easiest thing in the world.*

What did a car matter compared to somebody I loved?

*Especially because we didn't have much longer together—at
least in Meadowlark. I wanted to spend every second with him. He
was leaving for guide school in Montana right after his birthday.*

*God, I loved him so much. When I thought about both of us
leaving, my heart sunk so low that I felt an echo in my chest when
I breathed.*

I shook those thoughts out of my head and got out of my car.

*Dusty must've heard the car door shut because next thing I
knew, he was walking out the front door, kissing me on the cheek,
and taking my duffel bag from me. I was going to stay for the whole
weekend.*

"Hey, angel," he said as he pulled me close. "I missed you."

"I missed you, too," I said. Now that school was out, I didn't see Dusty every day. He worked a lot—trying to save up money. I visited him when he worked at the diner. He would get me a chocolate shake or a blue raspberry rainbow, and I would read while he worked. But I didn't get to see him on the days that he worked at the grocery store or Rebel Blue.

I took my time taking him in. He was wearing a pair of faded blue jeans and a worn white T-shirt. It had holes in it, a few peppered along the neckline. It looked perfect on him. When I was with Dusty, my head went quiet in the best way possible—like there was nothing I was dealing with that couldn't wait until tomorrow. I also felt the most like myself around him. I didn't have to be so . . . clenched, I guess.

It was freeing and wonderful, and I wanted to feel this way forever.

When we got inside, Dusty dropped my bag to the floor and brought his lips down on mine. I wondered if I would like kissing as much as I did if I wasn't kissing Dusty. I didn't have any other experience to compare it to, but I didn't think I would. His tongue swept inside my mouth, and I gripped his shirt.

Soon, my back was pressed against the wall right next to the front door. One of Dusty's hands was on my waist and the other was on the back of my neck—both holding me to him. My hands ran up and down his chest, getting lower every time I brought them back down.

When I reached the top of his jeans, I slid each of my pointer fingers inside of the waistband of his briefs.

"Whoa there, angel," he said against my mouth. "Slow down."

"We've been going slow," I said. "So, so, so slow." Not to be dramatic, but I felt like I'd been trying to get into Dusty's pants for a *while. He made me feel safe and respected and loved. I wanted this with him.*

We'd done other stuff, and so far, it had all been amazing. But every time we got close to sliding home, Dusty stopped us—like he was doing now. When he stepped back, his eyes looked wild, and I'd sufficiently mussed his hair. His expression was kind of . . . pained?

I felt the insecurity creep up my body, and I folded my arms over my chest. I looked down at the floor. "Do you . . ." I started. "D-do you not, um, want to . . . with me?" I finally managed to get out. As soon as I said it, I felt like crawling into the deepest hole I could find and burying myself alive. I couldn't look at him, so I slid my back down the wall until I was seated on the floor. I put my head on my knees and wrapped my arms around my shins.

"Ash," Dusty said softly. "No." His voice was soft, but close, which meant he had met me on the floor. "Look at me, angel."

I shook my head, embarrassed. "Ash," he said more firmly. "Look at me. Please." I let out a sigh. I couldn't refuse him, so I lifted my gaze to his.

"I want you." His gray eyes were glued to mine. "I want you so bad—in all of the ways. I love you, and I want to be close to you like that. I'm ready to be close to you like that."

"So why won't you?"

"I know we don't like to talk about it, but I'm going to Montana next month, and you're going to college in the fall," he said. "I don't want to have sex with you and then leave a few weeks later."

"But you're not leaving me," I said. "You're just leaving. We're going to stay together. We'll talk all the time, and we'll visit each other."

Dusty swallowed. "I know," he said. "And I'm so glad about that. I just . . . I love you so much, and I want our first time to be special.

I don't want you to feel like I'm just going to like . . . hit it and quit it."

A laugh bubbled out of me. It was loud and free. "Hit it and quit it?" I said between inhales.

Dusty's mouth tilted. "You know what I mean," he said. "I respect you and shit, and I need you to know that and feel that, okay?"

I pushed up on my knees, so Dusty and I were face-to-face. God, he was so good. I studied him for a second: his eyebrows that were a few shades darker than his hair, the silver ring through his right nostril, the tiny scar underneath his left eye that he got from running into the corner of a table when he was little. "I love you, too," I said. "I know what I am to you, Dusty. The fact that we're going to be apart for a little doesn't change that—not for me."

"Not for me, either," he said softly.

I put my hands on either side of his face. "Okay, then," I said and then kissed him again. Less urgently this time. I let my mouth linger on his as the heat started to build between us again. His hands roamed over my body and mine explored his.

"Wait," he said and then pulled away again. "Before we go too far, I need to show you something."

I huffed impatiently. "You're a real mood-killer, Tucker, you know that?"

He laughed a little before he stood and brought me with him. "I think you're going to like this," he said. He looped his fingers through mine and started pulling me toward the back of the house. When we reached the back door, he said, "Close your eyes," and I gave him a look. "I've got you."

I rolled my eyes dramatically before squeezing them shut. Dusty grabbed my other hand, so he was holding on to both of them now.

I heard the back door open, and he carefully guided me outside. I took a few steps until I felt the ground beneath my feet change from cement to grass.

"Okay," Dusty said. "Open."

When I opened my eyes, I couldn't believe it. It looked so dreamy back here. Dusty had used a couple of sheets and rope to create an open tent-like structure using the branches of the big oak tree by Aggie's workshop. From what I could see, it looked like every pillow and blanket in the Tucker household was inside of it. There was a picnic blanket with snacks on it, too.

"Oh my god, Dusty," I said on a gasp. "This is beautiful." When I looked over at him, he was grinning wide.

"Look that way," he said, nodding toward the back of the house. When I did, I noticed another white sheet hanging on the back of the house with a small projector a few feet behind it. I couldn't believe he did all of this. It was perfect.

I started pulling him toward the blankets inside the tent, and the two of us flopped down onto them as soon as they were within reach. Then we were kissing again. I had my hands on his face and my leg hitched up around his hips, using everything I had to pull him closer to me.

One of his hands slid into the back pocket of my jeans and brought the middle of our bodies together. I gasped.

I started kissing his neck. I had left Dusty with a visible hickey more than once, but I didn't care. "Are you sure?" he asked. His voice was breathy and strained.

"Yes," I said with a small bite where I'd been kissing him. He groaned, and I felt powerful. "Are you?"

"Yes. Yes. Yes," he said quickly. "I've never done this before."

"I know," I said. "Neither have I." I liked that I was going to be his first and he was going to be mine. My last, too. I knew it.

Then he rolled himself on top of me. When his gray eyes landed on mine, I felt like we were the only two people in the world. The affection in his gaze made it hard to swallow.

"If you change your mind, you have to tell me. We have to talk to each other, okay? I don't want to hurt you."

"Okay," I said. My voice was choked up with emotion. I didn't know where it came from. He kissed me again, slower this time. I put my hands under his shirt and slid it up his back. He broke away from our kiss to pull it all the way off. God, he was beautiful.

And he was all mine.

We went slowly. And when our bodies were joined, Dusty put a hand on my cheek and looked straight into my soul. "I'll love you until we're dust, Camille Ashwood."

Chapter 27

Cam

With the number of butterflies in my stomach, you would've thought I was about to jump out of a plane or off a cliff—not that I was about to attend a fancy-ass gala with my high school boyfriend and current . . . friend.

"That dress is amazing on you," Ada said through my phone screen. We were on FaceTime—Riley was on her lap. Ada and Wes were taking Riley for the night. It was technically my weekend, and I'd asked Gus for a lot since the not-wedding and the move.

I hated the mom-guilt that I felt for spending half of the time that I got with my daughter away from her. Knowing my parents, they probably planned this timing of the gala on purpose.

"What do you think, Sunshine?" I pulled this dress out of the back of my closet. I'd never worn it before. I bought it when I thought I'd be married and attending this gala with my husband. It was a stunner—satin, cobalt blue, one shoulder, and clung to my body until mid-thigh.

"You're a knockout," Riley said, and I laughed.

"Where did you hear that?" I asked. She absorbed every little thing.

"Dad says it to Teddy." She shrugged.

"And it works here, too," Ada said. "How are you feeling?"

"Good," I responded and held two different earring options—one in each hand—up to the screen: one with a teardrop diamond and the other with two small diamonds and a sapphire in the middle. Both Ada and Riley pointed to the sapphires, so I put them in.

Ada arched a dark brow at me. She wasn't a fan of my one-word answers.

"Are you and Dusty going on a date, Mom?" Riley asked out of the blue.

My eyes widened. "U-um," I stammered. "No, Sunshine, we're not going on a date. Dusty and I have been friends for a long time," I said. Ada rolled her eyes and looked like she was fighting a smile.

"Oh," Riley said. I couldn't tell for sure, but it looked like she . . . deflated a little bit? "I like Dusty."

"Me too," Ada said, and I gave her a look.

My doorbell rang—saved by the bell. "I've got to go, Sunshine. Have fun tonight, okay?"

"I will. Uncle Wes said we're making s'mores and that Loretta could sit by us." Loretta was Wes's bottle calf from last year. Riley was obsessed with her.

"I love you, Sunshine. I'll see you in the morning."

I hung up the phone. I shot off a quick text to Dusty, telling him to come in and that I'd be out there in a second.

I slipped on a pair of nude slingbacks and checked my hair and makeup for the thousandth time. I loved getting ready—

doing my own makeup and hair, spending time on myself. For my hair, I'd gone with a full blowout and then did my best attempt at some soft old Hollywood waves. I pulled my hair back on one side—the same side that my shoulder was exposed on—and I loved the way it looked.

I took one last look in the mirror, but before I walked out of my bedroom, I realized that I hadn't put my necklace on. I quickly grabbed it off my dresser—I'd put it on in the car—and grabbed my clutch.

Dusty had his back to me when I walked toward the entryway. He was looking out the window—there was still a decent amount of snow, but the sun was breaking through more and more every day.

Half of his blond hair was pulled back into a bun at the back of his head. His broad shoulders filled out his suit perfectly and when he turned, I lost my breath.

A lock of hair that was too short to be pulled back fell down the side of his angular face. Without his hair down, his eyes were even more striking than usual. I watched them drink me in.

He brought a hand to his chest—the one with the rose tattooed on it—and his mouth dropped open a little bit. "You look . . ." He swallowed, and I tracked the movement of his Adam's apple. "God, you look stunning, Ash."

Dusty's voice was almost awestruck, and it made me want to run and hide but also bask in it.

"Thank you," I said, running my eyes up and down his form. On further inspection, he wasn't wearing just a suit—it was a tux. I didn't think he'd actually wear one. He wasn't a tux sort of guy. "You, too—where'd you get a tux?"

Dusty flashed me a grin. "I'm full of surprises." He saw the necklace in my hand and nodded toward it. "Do you want me to put that on?"

"I don't think it goes with your outfit," I said.

Dusty reached out, and I tried to dodge him, but he softly flicked my nose. "Smartass," he said. "Give it here," he said with a palm out. I dropped the necklace into his palm, and he used the other hand to motion for me to turn around. I did.

After a moment, I felt Dusty's fingers on my shoulder, moving my hair to one side. I remembered him unzipping my wedding dress a few months ago.

He always seemed to show up right when I needed him.

Goosebumps rose on my skin as his fingers dragged across it, and I had to fight the shiver vibrating through my spine. I closed my eyes and basked in his featherlight touch.

I felt the necklace at my throat, pulled taut as Dusty fiddled with the clasp. My breath caught, and I tried not to let the room go sideways. Once he'd gotten the clasp fastened, he dropped the necklace, and it found the proper place on my neck. I didn't move for a moment, and neither did he.

When I turned around to face him, he said, "You're beautiful, Ash," and I rolled my eyes, trying to regain the playful mood. Suddenly, Dusty gripped my chin firmly.

"Don't do that," he said. "Don't hide from me. I want to see you."

I should've tried to pull away, but I didn't. Instead, I let my eyes grab hold of his, just like his hand held my chin and refused to let go.

His eyes moved over my face like he was memorizing me and this moment, then they'd come back to mine every few seconds. I was helpless when his hands were on me, so we stood in my entryway, and I let him see me.

"You're beautiful," Dusty said again. "So fucking beautiful." He leaned forward, and I waited for my brain to go into fight or flight, like it had the last time we were this close. But it didn't. It welcomed him into my space—it wanted him there.

"W-we should get going," I stammered out. One of the corners of Dusty's mouth lifted.

"We should," Dusty said. "Where are your keys?" We were taking my car—better gas mileage, and probably more reliable, but don't tell Dusty I said that about his Bronco.

I fumbled with my clutch and somehow was able to get my keys out, and Dusty gently took them from me.

"Oh," I said. "I can drive."

Dusty looked at me like that was ridiculous. "I don't think so," he said. "Let's get you a coat and then we'll go."

I grabbed a long wool coat from the hall closet, and Dusty helped me slip it on. Apparently, I couldn't do anything by myself when he was around.

I didn't mind.

I kept the entryway light on, and we went out the front door, which Dusty locked, and then he led me to my car with a hand on the small of my back. He opened the door for me and made sure I was inside before shutting it.

When he crossed the front of the car to get to the driver's side, I watched him through the windshield and came to the same conclusion that I'd come to over and over again: He was beautiful, too.

"Ready?" he said when he got in the car.

"Ready," I responded. And with him, I might actually be.

⭐

It took us a little over two hours to get to the venue in Jackson. Dusty and I talked the whole way—about Riley, Rebel Blue, getting the yard ready for spring, a porch swing, Fall Out Boy's evolution into emo dads—that sort of stuff.

We were in a heated debate about the merits of Nicolas Cage's filmography and whether or not *National Treasure Three* would ever happen. Dusty took the turn into the lodge where the event was being held. It was a log cabin–style building—rustic, timeless, and grand.

When my car rolled to a stop, silence fell over our conversation. I felt the weight of who we'd find inside creep back onto my shoulders.

"So," he said after a minute, "is it true that this place won an architectural award for their bathrooms?"

I couldn't help but laugh. "What are you talking about?"

"Bathrooms," he said with a smile. "I heard they have back-lit white onyx and gold-plated sinks."

"They do," I supplied. "The bathrooms are actually annoyingly gorgeous."

"Annoying," he repeated, and I gave him a small smile. I knew what he was doing—lifting the weight again. "Are you sure you want to do this?"

"No," I said honestly, but I was hoping this might help change my parents' opinion of me. Maybe they'd see that I was fine. I didn't make it down the aisle, and everyone survived. I still had a good job, and I lived in a house I loved. I was happy. Maybe they'd see that was more important than their expectations of me.

Even though I wasn't quite happy—not yet. But I thought that I could be.

"You don't have to do this," Dusty said. "We can go hit up a middle-class chain restaurant instead."

I shook my head. "I have to," I said, and when I looked over at Dusty, I thought I saw him physically bite his tongue. I knew how he felt about my parents. I didn't need to hear it right now. They would probably think I brought him to piss them off on purpose, but I didn't. I brought him because even though I could do this alone—I could do everything alone— I liked that I didn't have to.

"Okay, then," Dusty said. "Let's go check out these bath-rooms."

Chapter 28

Cam

The inside of the lodge was beautiful. It was gorgeous on a normal day, but tonight, it was sparkling. White and red rose flower arrangements, frosted glasses, and bubbly champagne. The Ashwoods spared no expense—they never did.

Dusty checked my coat for me and then returned to my side. "Do you want a drink?" he asked, and I nodded. He grabbed two flutes of champagne off a tray as a waiter passed by. I watched the waiter give Dusty a double take. The tattoos on his neck and hands were the only ones visible at the moment, but that was enough for him to stand out—plus the long hair and the nose ring.

Dusty didn't seem to notice, though. His eyes were just on me. "What do you think your parents will think when they see me here?" He took a sip of champagne and placed his hand on the middle of my back.

"They'll live," I said, taking a shaggy breath, as if trying to convince myself. Dusty was what got me here, so for that, they should at least be kind of grateful.

"I love to see that spine, Ash . . . and feel it," Dusty said. His hand dipped a little lower just as I took a sip of champagne, which was not great timing, because it caught in my throat, and I started to cough.

"Easy there, killer." Dusty laughed. He took the champagne flute out of my hand and set both of our glasses on a table. "Dance with me."

This time, when he stretched out his hand, I took it and let him lead me to the dance floor.

The song was a simple waltz, but I didn't expect Dusty to know that, so I just put my arms over his shoulders so we could step and sway to the music. But Dusty took one of my hands in his and placed the other on my waist before he started leading us.

"You know how to waltz?" I asked.

"Full of surprises." He grinned, and I let out a shocked laugh. He was a little fumbly, but mostly, he was good—more than passable. "I used to watch YouTube videos when we were in high school," he said. "I remembered you saying that you had to dance whenever your parents had or went to an event, and I wanted to be prepared . . . just in case I ever got to go with you."

"You mean in case I ever forced you to come with me?"

Dusty shook his head. "No. You're a privilege, Cam. Being in your presence is a goddamn honor." I looked over his shoulder instead of at him. What the hell was I supposed to say to that?

"I can't believe you did that when you were so young . . . for someone who wasn't even a sure thing," I said.

I felt his shoulder shrug under my hand. "You've always been a sure thing to me," he said softly.

"Dusty . . ." I trailed off. "You can't talk like that."

"Like what?" he asked.

"Like we're more than what we are," I said.

"I think you're going to have to enlighten me then," he responded. "What are we?"

"Friends." I sighed. "We're friends. Aren't we?"

"Ash, I tried friends. I really did. But friends don't feel the way I do about you," he said as he pulled me even closer to him. Our bodies were touching now. "Or the way you feel about me." I could feel his breath on my face. "I've waited half a lifetime for you, Cam."

Dusty breathed me in. "And I would wait a whole one if I thought I had to, but here we are. Together. No distance, no timing, no ring . . . nothing is keeping us apart." Our dancing had slowed and the song had changed, but we were still out on the dance floor. Dusty used his finger to lift my chin, gently this time. "Except you," he whispered.

I refused to meet his eyes. *Except me.*

"So I need you to look at me, Ash." It was like my eyes couldn't help but give in to him. "And I need you to tell me why."

Because I'm not the girl you fell in love with. Because I don't even know who I am. Because loving you is the bravest thing I've ever done, and I'm not brave anymore.

Because I can't take the pain of losing you again.

"Well, isn't this a surprise." My mother's voice cleared our bubble, and I instinctively pulled away from Dusty—putting more distance between us than just physical. I tried to pretend I didn't see his face fall, but he quickly steeled his expression. I tried to do the same.

"Hi, Mom," I said as I leaned in to give my mother a kiss on each cheek. "You look beautiful." And she did. Lillian Ashwood was dripping in understated beauty. She was wearing a floor-length silver gown that was impeccably tailored to her slender frame, and a diamond choker that my father gave her for one of their earlier anniversaries, and matching earrings.

"You look . . ." She surveyed my appearance. I was used to this perusal and instinctively tried to brace myself for whatever was coming. "Comfortable" was what she settled on.

"Camille," my father said next to her.

"Dad," I said as I looked over at him. I looked most like him with my dark hair and features and my height. He ignored me. His eyes were shooting daggers at the man I was with.

"Mr. and Mrs. Ashwood." Dusty nodded. No pleasantries or good-to-see-yous, not between these three.

"Interesting to see you here, Mr. Tucker. I don't think you were on the invite list," my father said. "You don't quite fit in."

"And thank God for that," Dusty said. "I'm Cam's plus one."

With that, my parents started to strategically shepherd us to the outer space of the room—off the dance floor and into the shadows—where they'd always preferred to keep me. As we walked, Dusty's hand found its way to the small of my back again. I focused on that feeling—channeled everything I had into his touch on my spine.

"You didn't tell us you were bringing anyone, dear," my mother said. Her voice and face were tight. "There are a few lovely bachelors here tonight that I think you should meet."

I felt my shoulders sag.

My dad didn't say anything. He was still sizing up Dusty.

"Please . . . not right now," I said as firmly as I could, but it was meek at best.

"Not ever, actually," Dusty said. His jaw was set.

"This is none of your concern," my father responded.

"Cam is my concern," Dusty said. "She always has been." Right then, a waiter, who either didn't notice the tense posture of our quad or didn't care, held a tray up for us. I reached out to take something off it. I didn't even know what it was—I just needed something to do with my hands.

"That's fried, Camille," my mother chimed in. "Best to wait for something else to come around." My hand stopped mid-air, and I brought it back to my side.

"You are a piece of work, Lillian," Dusty said, and I went all the way still. "You always have been."

"I beg your pardon?" my mother said as she brought her hand up to her chest. Aghast was the word I'd use.

"I can't believe I ever thought that it would just be better, easier for Cam to try to ignore your bullshit. I guess I was young, stupid. But I'm not anymore. I've changed, but you haven't, and I'm tired of seeing the way you tear this woman down and saying nothing about it."

"You have no right to talk to us this way," my father said. I could practically see the steam coming out of his ears.

"No, Rutherford, that's where you're wrong. It's you that doesn't have a right to talk to me or Cam or any other person that way," Dusty said. The arm around my waist pulled me closer to him.

"Now you listen." My father put his pudgy finger in Dusty's face, but Dusty cut him off.

"No, I think I'm done listening. I know Cam is. You have an incredible daughter, and both of us have better things to do than *listen* to the two of you any longer."

Dusty grabbed my hand and started walking away. "Camille," my mother said—I could tell she wanted to yell, but she didn't want to attract attention. "Camille Montgomery Ashwood, you do not walk away from us."

Dusty looked at me. His eyes danced. *Say something,* they pleaded. With him, maybe I could be brave again.

"Tonight, I do," I said back. I heard my mom stomp her foot, but I didn't care. All I cared about was Dusty's laugh as it drifted back to my ears.

I didn't know where we were going, but I let him lead me. We rounded a few corners, went down a flight of stairs, and down a hallway.

"Where are we going?" I asked. With the amount of adrenaline coursing through my veins, you would think that I had just jumped out of an airplane—not said something mildly defiant to my parents.

"To check out some award-winning architecture," he responded. Then he pushed open a door and pulled me in behind him.

When the door shut, Dusty pressed me against it. It was darker in here—not pitch-black, but dark enough that my eyes needed a second to adjust. I blinked a few times. There was some light in here, coming from a counter.

Backlit white onyx.

"I'm sorry about that," he said. He was closer to me than he'd been in a long time.

"No you're not," I breathed.

Dusty grinned. "No, I'm not," he said, and then he kissed me, like really kissed me. His hands were in my hair, pulling my head back to give him all the leverage he needed to dominate my mouth. I held on to his wrists and tried to keep up. "I told you I'd get you out of there—like I always do." he said.

Soon, there was an arm wrapped around my waist, hoisting

me up, and my legs wrapped around Dusty. I pulled my mouth away from his and started kissing his jaw and then his neck. When I reached the base of his throat, Dusty whimpered.

"Angel," he breathed, and it hit me right in the chest. I missed that. I missed him. I missed us. "Maybe we're getting carried away."

"Maybe," I said against his skin, but I didn't care. I licked my way back up his neck and found his mouth again. He bit my lip, and I groaned. Dusty's hips rolled into me, and I groaned again. "God," I breathed.

I lost track of time. We could've been in there for five minutes or five hours when I made the move to push off Dusty's tux jacket, and I felt the air shift. It started to buzz and tremble around us.

Dusty pulled me away from the door. I wrapped my legs tighter around him, and my dress hiked higher up my hips as he carried me to the glowing counter. Before he set me down, he pushed it all the way up, so it was bunched at my waist, exposing my thin black panties. When my bare skin hit the counter, I gasped into his mouth.

His hands gripped my thighs so tightly it almost hurt.

"Angel," he moaned. "We can't do this. Not here."

"Yes we can," I said, looking up at him. He brought a hand up to my face, brushing my lower lip with his thumb. He was looking at me like I was the only thing keeping him tethered to the planet—but also terrified I might suddenly disappear.

I held his hand to my face for a moment before I sucked his thumb into my mouth.

"Fuck," he gritted out and then kissed me again. Hard. "Are you sure?" he asked.

"I'm sure," I said. "I'm always sure with you."

"I promise I didn't bring you in here for this," he said against my mouth. I laughed a little.

"Sure," I said sarcastically, even though I believed him. "Now stop talking." I moved my hand to cup him through his pants to emphasize my point.

"Point taken," he groaned and kissed me again. One of his fingers skated up the inside of my thigh, and I knew I was wet for him. When he reached my underwear, I gasped. "Should I take these off or just move them out of the way?" Dusty asked. His voice was low. "Decisions, decisions."

"Better make one fast," I breathed.

Dusty stopped what he was doing and put a hand on my neck; his thumb pressed into the bottom of my chin. "I've been waiting for this for over a decade, angel," he said. His other hand pushed my underwear to the side. "I don't want to do anything fast with you." He dragged a knuckle up my center, and I inhaled sharply. His grip on my neck tightened at the same time he pushed a finger inside of me.

"Oh," I gasped.

"Beautiful," Dusty murmured as he looked down at me. "Fucking beautiful," and then his mouth was on mine again. His tongue worked inside my mouth while his finger worked inside of me. My breath got faster, and my body started to move of its own accord.

When he slid a second finger inside of me, my head fell back on a moan. "That's right, angel," he said as he licked and sucked at my neck. "Let me hear you. Don't be shy. You never were before with me." His thumb pressed on my clit, and I didn't recognize the sound that came out of my body.

"Dusty," I panted, and he bit down on my neck.

"Again," he growled against my skin. "Say it again."

I clutched at his back, trying to grab on to his shirt to steady myself. "Dusty," I said again.

More. I wanted more. I spread my legs wider.

I felt it when Dusty's mouth left my skin, but I didn't have time to wonder where it went because when I brought my head back up, I saw him drop to his knees, pull me to the edge of the counter, and then his mouth was back on me. I was lost to the sensation of it all—of the ways he felt familiar and new all at once. It was like my body remembered him and reacted accordingly.

He used one of his hands to keep my underwear out of the way as he licked up my slit. I watched with rapt attention as he devoured me with his mouth and fucked me with his fingers.

The sight of him, with my legs over his shoulders and his eyes closed in pleasure, made my hips buck. "Oh my god," I panted as his fingers went in and out of me—their rapid but steady pace felt so different from the languidness of his tongue, and I couldn't get enough. I didn't even register the sounds I was making or the way my body was writhing. I was just focused on him. I stared at Dusty between my legs until pressure started to travel down my spine.

"Dusty . . ." I moaned again, and my eyes rolled back. I couldn't tell if I was shaking or if it was the world around me, but something was definitely falling apart. Dusty put pressure on my clit using the pad of his tongue before he sucked my clit into his mouth, and I broke apart.

I wasn't used to this. The way my body fell apart under Dusty's touch felt foreign and wonderful. Not that it hadn't been incredible before, but there was something to be said for being older and wiser and more experienced.

And he kept going. He didn't let up—forcing me to ride the

wave of my orgasm. He made it last—wringing every ounce out of me. When I finally came down, Dusty's mouth was still on me, and it felt like too much. I needed something different—something more. I wanted him inside of me.

"Dusty," I panted. "I can't—" I stumbled. "—No more, please," I gasped.

Dusty lifted his head from between my legs slowly and grinned up at me. "Sorry," he said, even though he didn't sound sorry at all. "I've missed . . . doing that."

"Noted," I breathed.

As he rose from his knees, he wiped his mouth with the back of his hand, and if I wasn't already seated, I probably would have collapsed.

"You're, um . . ." God, why couldn't I make my voice sound normal? "You're still . . . very good at it." That felt like a stupid thing to say. "I—I mean—"

Dusty kissed me then, stopping my idiot blabbering. It was soft and tender and made me feel like I was a puddle on the floor of this very beautiful bathroom. "I've been waiting a long time to get my mouth on you again," he whispered darkly. "And I'm nowhere close to done."

I wrapped one arm around his neck and pulled him closer and used my other hand to try to unbutton his pants.

A knock at the door startled both of us out of the kiss. "Anyone in here?" a man's voice called. I slapped my hands over my mouth and started to giggle.

"Occupied," Dusty called back. When his eyes met mine, he shook his head and started to laugh, too.

He pressed his forehead to mine, and I felt him breathe me in. "Let's get out of here."

Chapter 29

Cam

Fifteen Years Ago

Before I met Dusty, I never would have entered any sort of tattoo shop. But now, here I was, sitting next to him while he added more ink to his arm. This one was a creepy-looking moth with skulls on it near his shoulder. I already loved it. I loved everything about him.

The hand attached to the arm that wasn't getting tattooed was resting on my thigh. I thought he would tense up or something, but he didn't. He was relaxed. Sometimes his eyes were closed, and sometimes they were on me.

Both of us were trying not to think about the fact that he was leaving in a week.

The artist working on him was an older guy named Shannon who was covered in tattoos. He even had the words "OLD SCHOOL" tattooed around the back of his head.

"What if I got one for you?" Dusty said out of nowhere.

I looked at him questioningly. "A tattoo?"

"Yeah." He nodded.

"That's . . . um . . ."

"Permanent." Shannon finished for me.

"Yeah," I said, nodding at the tattoo artist. "Permanent."

Dusty shrugged with one of his shoulders. "So are we."

Even though he was leaving, I couldn't argue with that. We felt permanent. I thought that would scare me, but it didn't. It made me feel like I could take on anything as long as I had Dusty.

"I'll get one, too," I said, almost without thinking. I thought once the words were out of my mouth, I'd want to take them back. But I didn't.

"Seriously?" Dusty said after a few seconds.

"Seriously," I said. "We're permanent."

"Oh lord," Shannon said under his breath.

"What do you think?" Dusty said.

"I think it's stupid," Shannon said as he worked. I felt my shoulders fall a little. Maybe it was. "But sometimes the stupid things push us forward, so if you want 'em, I'll do 'em."

My heart started to pick up speed. Was I really going to do this? When I looked at Dusty he was grinning, and that's when I knew the answer. Yeah. Yeah, I was.

I grinned back at him.

"Any ideas, Shan?" Dusty asked, but his eyes were still on me.

"No full names," he said. "I still haven't figured out how to cover up or change Betty's name on my arm."

"Betty from the diner?" I asked, shocked. Shannon nodded, and Dusty and I both burst into laughter.

"Hold still, kid," he said to Dusty. "I'm almost done."

"Sorry," Dusty said, still laughing, and then he turned to me. "What if I got an A for Ash?"

"Feels a little Scarlet Letter, don't you think?" I said.

"But it works because we started passing notes in English, and we read The Scarlet Letter.*" He smiled earnestly, his eyes sparkling. How lucky was I to find a man like him, a love like this, so early? And how was I supposed to be thousands of miles apart from him? How was I supposed to say goodbye?*

"Where will you get it?" I asked.

Dusty brought his right hand up to the side of his neck and tapped at it with his pointer finger. "Right where you like to kiss me."

Less than an hour later, Dusty had two new tattoos, and I had my first one: the letter T on my hip. For Tuck or Tucker or Dusty's full name. It didn't hurt as bad as I was expecting. Plus, the pain didn't matter. Now I had a symbol of the mark Dusty left on me. Forever. I was changed now . . . and I knew I never wanted to go back.

When I looked at it in the mirror after we were done and before Shannon covered it to heal, I'd never felt more beautiful or more powerful or more me.

"Dusty," I said as we walked toward his car, hand in hand.

"What's up, angel?" he asked, and I pulled him to me, careful to avoid the cling wrap and gauze on his neck. When I looked up at him, I felt resolute.

"I want to go with you," I said.

"Where? Are you hungry? Do you want to go get something to eat?"

"No, Dusty. I want to go with you to Montana. Next week. Take me with you."

Chapter 30

Cam

When Dusty and I grabbed our coats and ran out the gala doors, we were met with a wall of falling snow. The flakes were huge, and I could barely see in front of me. There were at least six inches piled up in the parking lot. Dusty pulled me closer to him and used the arm around my waist to lift me into a fireman's carry.

"Those shoes you're wearing won't make it through the snow," he said. I let my head fall back with a laugh, and my feet kicked involuntarily.

I tried to look forward, but the snow got in my face, so I looked up at Dusty instead. I looked at his sharp jawline, and his Adam's apple moved as he swallowed. I wanted to memorize how he looked right now—this close to me. I used one of my hands to push down the white collar of his tux so I could see the entirety of his "A" tattoo. I pulled myself closer to him so I could kiss it again.

"Ash," Dusty breathed when I did.

"I forgot how much I loved this," I said as I kissed it again. Dusty groaned, and I watched his jaw flex.

"I didn't," he said. He managed to keep hold of me as he reached into his pocket and grabbed the keys to my car. I heard it unlock. I reached out to open the door, and when I did, Dusty set me carefully inside.

"You have four-wheel drive, right?" Dusty asked. One of his hands was on my hip, and the other was on the side of my neck.

"Obviously," I responded. "We live in Wyoming."

"Smartass," he said and then kissed me quickly—like he would do it a million more times. It felt so natural, but the effect it had on me was anything but.

I brought my hands up to his suit jacket and held him to me for a second. He let me. He didn't ask me why—just stood in the snow while I sat in the car and let me breathe him in—let me imprint this moment in my brain. When I let him go, he flashed me a smile. "Put your seatbelt on, angel."

Whatever bubble we were in right now, I didn't want it to pop.

Then he pulled back and shut my door softly. I did what he said. When he got in the car and started it, he reached over and turned my seat warmer on for me before grabbing the snow brush out of the backseat and getting back out to clear the car off.

I watched him through the windows as he cleared them. I didn't know if anyone else had ever cleared my car off for me. I had gotten used to doing it myself—just like everything else. For a second, it scared me, how easy it would be to get used to this—to have someone turn my seat warmer on and clear off my car, who could drive when I didn't want to.

Did I want that? I always thought that if I could take care of myself and my daughter, if I never had to depend on anyone, then I'd never run the risk of disappointing anyone, either. I was sick of feeling like such a disappointment, at least in the eyes of my parents. But I had to admit: It made me feel extremely lonely sometimes. What if there was a different way? A way that allowed me to share the load, to give up full control every once in a while?

When Dusty got back in the car, he shook the snow out of his hair and rubbed his hands together before grabbing one of mine. The two silver rings on his hand were ice cold, and I loved the way they felt against my skin.

"Ready?" he asked, and I nodded—grateful again that he was here. I hated driving in the snow. I should probably be used to it after all this time, but it still scared the shit out of me. But when I looked at Dusty, he was calm and in control of the car.

"Can you check the weather alerts for the highway?" he asked. "Honestly, I would be shocked if the canyon isn't closed."

"I think we should just get a hotel," I said. "Even if the canyon is open, I don't think it's safe to go all the way home tonight." I pulled out my phone and searched for hotels nearby. "Is that okay with you?"

"Uh, yeah," he said. "If that's okay with you." I kept scrolling as Dusty started driving closer to town. There wasn't anything around the ski resort, and it would probably take us at least thirty minutes to get farther down the mountain toward some sort of civilization.

"What have we got?"

"No dice so far." I let out a sigh. "There don't seem to be any good options."

"Have you tried, you know, just looking out the window for a neon vacancy sign through the snow?"

I actually laughed out loud at that. "Yeah, no," I said. "That's not for me." Neon signs did not usually match up with my preference for crisp white bedsheets and fluffy robes.

Dusty chuckled and shook his head. "You know . . . there's a motel like ten minutes up the road. I bet we might have some luck there."

I groaned but when I looked up from my phone and saw what the road ahead of us looked like—a total whiteout—I relented: "Okay."

"I promise it's not bad," Dusty said. "Probably one of the nicer places I've stayed in my life."

"Yeah, but you're not fussy like me," I said.

"I don't think you're fussy," Dusty responded. "You know what you like and you have preferences."

"So you don't think I'm a snob?" I asked.

Dusty shot me a quick grin before his eyes were back on the road. "I didn't say that," he said. "But I just happen to like your version of snobbery, I guess."

He seemed to be chewing on something in thought before he spoke again.

"Speaking of snobs . . . what was the deal with your parents tonight?" Dusty asked. "They were trying to set you up? I mean, clearly they were not happy to see me, but to try to show you off like you're some sort of piece of meat in the marriage mart seems a little old school . . . even for them."

"I don't want to talk about it," I said. My go-to answer for anything and everything having to do with my parents.

"No," Dusty responded immediately. He sounded more frustrated than he did a second ago. "We're not doing that anymore. I need you to talk about it. I need you to talk to *me*." His voice cracked, and I felt like I was two feet tall.

I took a deep breath. At least he was driving, so I didn't have to look at his face. Maybe it was time for me to talk about this—and talking to Dusty seemed to be easier than talking to anyone else. "A couple of years ago, I was thinking about what I wanted for Riley and her future, and I met Graham pretty soon after that. We had a lot in common when it came to our parents—they weren't very present in our lives, but they tried to be very present in our decisions. We didn't, um, click . . . romantically, but when we went to this event together that both of our parents were at, they were thrilled. As soon as my dad saw me with Graham, I think wheels started turning about how this could benefit him. Graham said the same thing about his dad.

"And both of us had the stipulation of parental approval for partners in our . . . um, trust funds. So we just kind of fell into this weird relationship where we both knew we were using each other, but we were okay with it, because it was the first time either of us had gotten any peace from our parents." After our confrontation at the gala, though, I was realizing that I created a lot of the noise that I felt around my parents. Everything I did was informed by my efforts to avoid their disappointment or criticism. If I could stay close enough to the lines of what they deemed appropriate, they'd leave me alone. I could keep them at a safe distance. And if I did something they actually *wanted,* like align myself with a suitable man who could benefit their financial future, I thought I'd get even more than that—I thought I might be able to finally make them happy. Maybe I could replace all of their disappointment with something better. But, of course, I should have known: I'd never actually be able to make them happy. So when Graham brought up getting married, it seemed like a good idea. And I decided to seize the opportunity to ensure some sort of inheritance from them for Riley—more than enough money for college and a nice nest egg."

I glanced at Dusty's hands on the steering wheel out of the corner of my eye—they clenched the wheel harder.

"So we got engaged. Things were fine. Both of us felt . . . okay. Maybe not happy, but content, at least."

"But he called off the wedding."

"He met someone," I whispered. Someone who made him realize that the chance at a full life was worth more than a guarantee of a half one.

"So you were going to get married to someone you didn't love so your daughter could have some money?" Dusty asked. His tone was sharp, and it cut me.

He made it sound so simple, but it wasn't. "You wouldn't get it," I said defensively.

"Explain it to me then," he said. "Because, you're right, I really don't get it. It's not like you're Riley's only parent. It's not like Gus doesn't have money. I get that the Ryders don't have Ashwood money, but they're stable. Riley was always going to be taken care of because of that." Dusty turned off the highway.

"I wanted to take care of her, too," I said. "And I didn't have anything then. I decided to put law school on hold for a while when I got pregnant, and then for the first few years after Riley was born, I needed to focus on learning how to be a mom. So I just . . . I didn't want to be a burden to the Ryders. I felt insecure about the fact that I had just gotten plopped into this family that cared for me right away; I was . . . just preparing for when the other boot would drop."

"But now you do just fine. You became a lawyer—you make good money. Even if you fucking hate it. Even if Gus wasn't in the picture, Riley would be okay." His deep voice rumbled in frustration.

"I don't hate it!"

Dusty scoffed.

"I'm sorry, but why are you mad?" I asked.

"Why am I mad?" he parroted back. "I'm not mad. I'm pissed. I'm pissed that after all these years, you still don't seem to see yourself clearly. I'm pissed that your parents imprinted this ridiculous idea on you that love has to be earned and not just freely given. I'm mad that you were going to settle for a life you didn't love because it was more convenient for you. And I'm pissed that you, of all people, would think your daughter needs all the things that you had. I was there, Cam. You had everything that money could buy and you still weren't happy. Riley has support. She has security, *and* she has an army of people who would do anything for her."

"I was just being practical," I said defensively.

"Fuck practicality," Dusty said softly. Too softly. It was eerily calm after his outburst, and I felt the familiar ache of the past fifteen years push its way back into my bones as Dusty maneuvered my car into a snow-covered parking lot. He cut the engine before the car was all the way in park.

Then he got out of the car. I expected him to stalk away, but he didn't. He walked around the front of my car, opened my door for me, and picked me up out of the car—still not letting me trudge through the snow even though I could feel his anger in his tense shoulders.

We walked inside a dimly lit lobby that smelled just left of normal. As soon as we were in, Dusty set me down and walked ahead. There was a woman at the front desk with jet black hair and a septum piercing. The only noise I could hear was the faint music leaking out of the headphones she had on and her chewing her gum.

The woman looked up when we got to the front desk. Her nametag said "Mal." She did a double take at the sight of Dusty.

"Hi," he said. "Do you have two rooms for the night?" I don't know why this request slapped me so hard across the face, but it did.

"Um." Mal scrambled for her computer. "We only have one room available for tonight. The snow pushed a lot of people off the road," she said. I saw Dusty's shoulders roll back and down in frustration. Mal looked past him and saw me. She looked between the two of us—probably sensing the tension. "But it's got two beds," she said.

"That's fine," Dusty gritted out.

"Great," Mal said. "I just need some information from you." I listened as Dusty listed off his first and last name and gave Mal his driver's license. "Cash or card?" she said.

"Cash," Dusty responded and pulled his wallet out of the inside pocket of his tux. I watched him pull out a hundred and put it on the counter. Mal slid a key across it at the same time.

"You're going to be in room forty-eight," she said. "You can go out the back door behind me. The walkway is covered, so you don't have to worry about the snow. Your room is going to be toward the right, nearly at the end of the walkway."

"Thank you," Dusty said as he swiped the key off the desk. He looked back at me and gave me a nod before walking toward the back door. I followed. When we got outside, I went to walk on the outside of him, but he put a hand on my waist and gently pushed me to his other side, farther from the elements—as if making sure I was safe. We walked in silence.

When we got closer to the end of the walkway, I started looking at the room numbers, until I saw ours. The four was metal, but it looked like the eight had fallen off.

Dusty put the key in the doorknob and pushed it open. He let me go in first. He was right—it wasn't bad at all. It was rustic, with flannel quilts on the beds and wood-paneled walls, but it was also clean and cozy.

"I'm going to raid the vending machine," Dusty said, his voice still hard. I hated it, and I hated that it was directed at me. "Get us some waters and some snacks. Any requests?"

My stomach growled at the mention of snacks. "If they have those little powdered donuts, I want those," I said. Dusty didn't respond. He just nodded and left me alone in the motel room.

I sighed as I flopped down on one of the beds and slipped my shoes off. Dusty's words rang in my head over and over again, banging on the sides of my skull like a drum. I couldn't deal with that right now.

I got up, walked to the back of the room, and turned on the light in the bathroom, which was also surprisingly clean and nice-looking. Thank god. I needed a shower. I turned on the water before walking back out to the bed. I slipped off my coat and dug through my purse.

You'll never catch me leaving my house without these five things: a makeup wipe, contact lens solution, a claw clip, some sort of moisturizer, and at least eight Chapsticks and lip balms. Right now, I was immensely grateful for that.

Back in the bathroom, I slipped my dress off—thank god it was a side zip. I put my hair up and stepped into the shower, letting the warm water cascade down my body. I rubbed at my shoulders and held my face under the stream of water.

I tried to empty my mind. Well, I tried to push everything I was feeling into a little compartment that I could shut and lock. That's where I kept everything about Dusty—shut tight and locked away. Out of sight, out of mind. *Just like his little wooden box*. Goddammit.

But Dusty was no longer out of sight. He was here. With me. And he took up every spare part of my mind.

I didn't know how long I stayed in the shower, but once my skin was an angry shade of red from the hot water and it was hard to breathe from all the steam, I turned the water off, got out, and wrapped myself in a towel.

When I opened the bathroom door, steam billowed out. Dusty had returned from his vending machine run. There was an array of snacks set on top of the mini fridge—including mini powdered donuts.

The man himself was lying on the bed. He had taken his suit jacket and shirt off, and he was bare-chested with his hands behind his head on the pillow. It was the first time I'd seen him with his shirt off as an adult. His chest and stomach were just like the rest of him—toned and smattered in tattoos. The dagger that stretched from a few inches above his belly button to his sternum caught my eye. His eyes were closed. When he heard me, he sighed before blinking them open.

"I want to talk to you," he said without looking at me. His eyes were on the ceiling.

"Okay," I said softly.

"And I need you to talk back." He looked at me this time, and I watched his eyes give me a once-over. I padded over to the other bed and sat on the edge of it, facing him.

"Okay."

"I'm sorry for raising my voice at you," he said.

"You didn't," I said.

"But I got mad," he responded. "I just . . . For the past year I've been trying to keep my distance from you because you were engaged, and I didn't know I could actually be friends with you without wanting something you couldn't give. It just hurt, I guess, knowing that you were picking somebody you didn't even love over . . . well, over me—over even being my friend.

"And I'm so fucking mad at you for thinking that was all you deserved." I looked down at my bare feet. I didn't know what to say to that.

"What am I to you, Ash?" he asked. "And if you say that we're just friends, I swear to God, I'm going to make Mal find me another room—I don't care if I have to sleep in the same bed as a random trucker."

"I don't know," I said honestly.

"What do you want me to be?"

"I don't know," I said again. This time, I wasn't honest, and he must've heard it.

"I don't believe you," he said. "Try again." His eyes were on me, and they showed no sign of letting up. This was the first time he'd pushed me—really pushed me—since we started being in each other's lives again. He was the only one who knew how and when to do it.

I sighed. I couldn't run from him, and I didn't really want to. Not again. I met his gaze, and for the first time in years, I unlocked the little box in my head, and I was totally and completely honest with myself. "Everything," I whispered. "I want you to be everything."

His eyes stayed on mine as he got off the bed and kneeled in front of me. His hands were on either side of my thighs. "I'm ready for that," he said. "Are you?"

"No," I said honestly. "But I think—I think I'm getting there." I saw something flash in his eyes: hope. Dusty laid his head on my lap, and I brought my hand up to stroke his hair and the side of his face without thinking about it.

"I missed you," he whispered. "I loved traveling around the world, Ash. I really did." His hands on my thighs squeezed them a little tighter. "I loved meeting new people and seeing parts of the world that teenage me could only dream about in this small town. I loved sleeping under the stars and listening to cowboy poetry and getting stupid tattoos.

"But most of all, I love that at the end of it, I got to come back here. To you." *But would he stay?* He nuzzled his nose into my bare thigh.

"Dusty . . ." I breathed. He lifted his head and looked at me. I held his face in my hands. "Your tattoos aren't stupid," I said, and the grin that stretched across his face could've powered me for weeks straight.

"Do you . . ." He swallowed nervously. "Still have yours?"

"Yeah," I whispered. "I do."

"Can I see it?" he asked. I nodded, and both of us stood

from the bed. It felt like someone had cranked the heat up in the room. Before I lost my nerve, I dropped my towel, and Dusty's eyes wasted no time in darting to my left hip. Right next to the bone, a small, black "T" in the same font as the "A" on his neck.

I couldn't tell if he dropped to his knees again on purpose or if it was the sight of it that did him in, but now he was eye level with my tattoo. I felt his thumb brush over it as he stared at it in disbelief. The sound that left his throat was somewhere between a groan and a whimper as he brought his lips to it. He kissed and licked and sucked at it as I knotted my fingers in his hair.

"Get back on the bed," he said against my skin.

"Which one?" I asked on a breathy laugh.

"Mine," he said on a growl. "I want you in mine." He stood and gripped my waist, turning me so my back was toward his bed before lifting me up and tossing me onto it. A shocked laugh came out of me as my back hit the mattress, but it got cut off by Dusty getting on top of me and sealing his mouth to mine.

It was intentional, slow, and hungry. He kissed me like he was starving but wanted to savor every last bit of his meal.

"I missed you," he said against my mouth. "I missed you every day."

I gripped his shoulders. "I'm here now," I said. "We're here now." He kept kissing me slowly. He moved from my mouth to my cheeks to my neck and chest—tasting me. I felt the tip of his tongue and the edge of his teeth. He hadn't even put his hands on me, and I was already gasping underneath him.

He pushed up on his hands so he was hovering above me.

His eyes dragged down my body, and it felt just like his tongue. "You're so beautiful," he said.

When we were in the bathroom at the gala, things were going so fast. We were so frenzied and hot that I forgot that my body was something I was usually self-conscious about—when I was naked, at least. I waited for the doubt to creep in—after all, my body had changed completely since he'd last seen it, because I'd carried a whole-ass baby in it—but it didn't show up.

When Dusty told me I was beautiful, I believed him.

"So are you," I said. I looked up at him, at his inked arms and chest. I traced the dagger on his sternum with my fingers, and he closed his eyes. His nostrils flared. "I want to know all about these."

"We have time," he said and then he was kissing me again. Dusty was the one who taught me how much I liked kissing, and damn, did I still. Mostly him, especially him.

One of his hands started to wander—across my collarbone, down the side of my abdomen, to my thigh—while the other kept him hovering above me. He touched me reverently, like he couldn't believe I was here with him.

I couldn't believe it, either. But I wanted more, so I dragged my fingernails down his spine and grabbed his hips. I tried to tug on them so they were flush with mine, but he stayed steady.

"Don't rush me," he said against my ear. "I want to spend all night worshipping your body—learning all of the things I don't know about it and remembering all of the things that I do."

"Can you at least do that with your pants off?" I breathed.

Dusty lifted his head from where he was kissing my neck

and looked down at me. He brought his hand to the side of my face and brushed his thumb over my bottom lip. "Open," he said, so I did—always the rule follower. He pushed his thumb into my mouth, and I immediately bit down and sucked on it. A growl came from Dusty's throat. "I'm not a fumbling teenager anymore, angel, and when I tell you I want to take my time, I'm going to take my time, and you're going to love it. And then, when you're ready, I want you to take what you want. I want you to take everything from me that you've missed in the last fifteen years, yeah?"

He pulled his thumb out of my mouth, so I could answer. "Yeah," I breathed.

"That's my girl," he said, and then he kissed me again. Harder this time, and when his hand found the wetness between my legs, my back arched, and I moaned under him.

"I have a condom in my wallet," he said.

"Were you hoping to get lucky tonight?" I asked playfully. Dusty's tongue went inside my mouth at the same time one of his fingers went inside of me, and I went boneless on a moan.

"I always feel lucky with you," he said. "But no, it's been in there for a while. I'm all clear, though."

"I have an IUD," I said. "But . . ." I trailed off, suddenly nervous and shy. Dusty caught on immediately. He rolled on his side and pulled me with him so we were facing each other. I instinctively hitched my leg up around his thigh.

"But what?"

I felt a blush creeping up my cheeks. I'd never said this to anyone before—I wasn't usually vocal at any point in the bedroom. At least not since Dusty. "I don't want you to come inside of me," I whispered. "I, um, I don't want any more babies."

Dusty paused for a second and looked at me thoughtfully.

"You got it, angel," he said and kissed me again. "Thank you for telling me that. I want you to tell me stuff like that always, okay? Can you do that for me?" I nodded, but Dusty said, "Words, angel."

"Yes," I said. "I'll tell you."

"Thank you," he said with his mouth on mine. He kissed me for a while—exploring my mouth with his tongue and my body with his fingers. I was so turned on, and my hips started moving of their own accord whenever his fingers got close to my center.

I brought my hands to his waist and started unbuttoning his pants. He let me. I looked down when I pushed them down his hips and saw his cock straining against his black briefs. "Still a briefs man?" I asked.

"Some things never change." I heard the smile in his voice. He helped me get his pants down and off him. Then I took them from him and threw them across the room. His laugh rumbled through me. "That was aggressive. I like it."

"I want you" is how I responded. With my fingers knotted in his hair, I pulled him to me again. Our bodies were flush, and it wasn't enough. I wanted to be closer to him. I wanted it all.

Dusty's finger slipped inside of me again, and both of us moaned. I moved my hips against his hand. "That's it," he said. "That's my girl." Another finger, another moan. More kisses, more teeth.

My hips moved faster, and Dusty kept pace with his fingers. "God," I groaned. "More, Dusty. Please." He pulled his fingers out of me, but before I had time to miss them, he gripped my ass and rolled me on top of him. I gasped at the contact I made with his hard cock.

I sat up and let my head fall back and grinded against him.

"Oh, fuck, angel," he said through gritted teeth. "That's right. I'm yours. You've spent too much time giving yourself to others. Now take what you want. Take it from me. Grind on my cock." I moaned at his words. I didn't know I liked that. "God, you're beautiful, Cam. I love the way you look right now." I looked down at him. His arms were flexed as he gripped my hips, and his jaw was tight—like he was focusing hard on something.

"I can feel how wet you are through my briefs," he said as he tilted his head back. "God damn."

Between the rhythm I'd found, the stimulation on my clit, and Dusty's words, I was close to coming for the second time tonight, and I wanted it. I wanted it so bad. "Can I come like this?" I asked.

"You can come however you want, angel. Keep going. Keep riding me." My breath picked up, and I started to feel a familiar squeeze at the base of my spine. "That's it, baby. You're so close, aren't you? I can feel it. Fuck."

"Yeah," I whimpered. Dusty's grip tightened on my hips as their movement became more sporadic and jerky. The squeeze in my spine got more intense as it moved lower. "Oh my god," I moaned. "Oh my god, oh my god."

"That's it, baby. That's it." I fell forward so my hands were on either side of Dusty's head. I could barely hold myself up as I came. My body shook, and I closed my eyes.

When I opened them, Dusty was looking up at me like I was the most beautiful thing he'd ever seen. I didn't have a chance to take it in before he flipped me on my back again. He stood and pushed his briefs down his legs, and his dick sprung free, and then he was on me again.

"I want to be inside you," he said. I reached down and

grasped his dick. When my hand made contact, Dusty swore through gritted teeth. I guided him toward my entrance.

"I'm ready," I said. "I want you. Please."

"You had to throw in the please," he said with a breathy laugh. "Such a good fucking girl." When the tip of his cock slipped inside of me, both of us gasped. He went tortuously slow. I tried to lift my hips, but he held them down—taking his sweet time.

"You feel so fucking good," he said, and my back arched on a moan. "That's it, angel. I can't wait for you to take every inch of me."

"I want to," I said. "Please, Dusty. Faster."

Instead of doing what I wanted, Dusty pulled all the way out of me, and I let out a frustrated huff. "What did I say about rushing me?"

"To not," I huffed.

"That's right," he said as he started pushing inside of me again. God, it was too much. "Look at me, Cam. I want to see you."

I met his eyes, and the affection in them would've melted me into a puddle on the bed if I wasn't already liquid. I felt so many things at once—turned on, frustrated, adored—I almost couldn't handle it.

He pushed farther inside of me, and when he was fully seated, we both felt it. He collapsed on top of me for a second with a groan. "I just need a second," he said. "Give me just a second."

I trailed my fingertips up and down his spine. I felt goosebumps rise in their wake. I would give him as long as he needed. I loved this. I think I still loved him, but I couldn't fully think about that yet. Not now.

When he started to move inside of me, he pushed up on his arms again. He thrusted in and out of me slowly, with one hand on the side of my neck. The cool metal of his rings pressed against my neck made me shiver, and we both moaned as he moved. Fuck, we were loud. I didn't know what time it was, but I felt bad for the people in the room next to us.

I kept my eyes on him the best I could, but every once in a while, they would roll back. When they did, he would lean down and kiss me, reminding me that he wanted my eyes on him.

"That's right," he said. "Don't hide from me." His hips picked up the pace, and I tried to match him thrust for thrust. The noises that came out of him were obscene. I wanted to memorize them—to listen to them over and over again. "You're doing so good, angel. You're doing so good for me."

His words cascaded over me like hot water. I pushed my hips up into him, trying to meet in the middle.

Dusty whimpered. "Fuck, baby," he said. "You've gotta warn me if you're going to do that. Oh my god." Seeing how he reacted made me feel powerful, so I kept going—kept meeting him thrust for thrust. "Just a few more and then I'll pull out— just a few more, okay?"

"Yes," I moaned.

"Where do you want me, angel? Tell me where to go."

"On my stomach, please. I want to feel you."

"Fuck, there you go again." His thrusts became more sporadic as he lost control. He sank his teeth into his bottom lip and gasped. His moans and gasps got higher and more frequent—like he was barely in control. "Good god, woman," he groaned as he pulled out. He took his hand off my throat and grasped his length. He gave it one hard jerk before I felt warmth all over my stomach.

I watched his face as he came, the way he heaved and gasped. God, he was beautiful. His arms shook as he held himself above me. When his eyes met mine after a minute, they were hooded and dazed.

I moved my hand down to my stomach and dragged a finger through the mess there before bringing it back up to my mouth and tasting him.

"Fuck," he gritted out and then brought his mouth down on mine. "You are so fucking hot." He kissed me for a while, until both of our breathing slowed. "Wait here," he said and then got off the bed. I heard water running in the bathroom.

I stared at the motel ceiling, trying to process what had just happened, but my brain was fried. I was just . . . content. Happy, even. When Dusty returned, he cleaned me up with care before getting in bed next to me and pulling me to him.

He held me close and moved his hands gently up and down my spine as I laid my head on his chest. "You did so good, angel," he said with a kiss to my forehead. "You're perfect. You're so fucking perfect." I wrapped my arms around him tight. *Perfect.* I knew nothing or nobody actually could be perfect, especially not me. But with Dusty, I felt pretty close to it.

"I missed you," I whispered, finally getting brave enough to say it in the dead of night. His heartbeat was against my ear, and I heard it skip.

"I've been waiting to hear that for fifteen years," he said softly.

"Thank you for coming back," I whispered.

Chapter 31

Cam

Fourteen Years Ago

Ash,
It's a long one today. I probably won't be home
until you're asleep.
I miss you. I love you.
Dusty

I stared at the note from Dusty that he'd left on the kitchen counter of our small one-bedroom apartment. We'd been here since we came to Montana in July, and it was nearly November. Dusty ended up getting a job as a wilderness guide for the rest of the summer and into fall. We were planning to stay here for the winter and then try to go to Colorado or northern California for summer.

Seasonal work was . . . different from what I thought it would be. Dusty loved it. He was so excited to go to new places and try new

things. I loved the joy on his face when he told me about his day
and his plans for the future.

He said that they were our plans, but I didn't know where I fit
into them yet. I didn't feel like I was made for moving around all
the time and not having something tangible to work toward. I was
missing my outcomes, I guess. I didn't really have any goals here.
I worked at a small western wear store in town, which was fine,
but most of the time, I was bored. When I was at work, I wished
I was in the apartment, and when I was in the apartment, I wished
Dusty was there, but he hardly ever was. He left early and often got
home late.

I knew it would get better when the season was over in a few
weeks, but right now, it sucked. And when I was alone, the only
company I had was my thoughts. Did I make a mistake? Did I ruin
my own life by following Dusty?

I read the note again. I miss you. I love you.

I loved him, too. So much. More than I did before we left Meadowlark. Everything about him still felt so right, but almost everything about the life we were living felt . . . wrong. I lashed out at
Dusty all the time—when he left a cabinet open or left his dishes in
the sink or left his work boots by the door. In the moment, I knew
I was overreacting or taking my feelings and frustrations out on
the wrong person, but I couldn't help it. Dusty was patient with
me, but I was filled with shame. I felt like I was trying to sabotage
myself and our relationship.

For the first time in a while, I also thought about my parents.
They knew where I was, but I hadn't spoken to them since a few
weeks after I left. And even then, they didn't act like they were worried about me or wanted me to come home. My mom just reminded
me that my decision meant I was not fulfilling the requirements of

my trust fund. After that, they shut off my phone and froze my bank account—which made sense. It was their money.

I didn't know why I thought they would care more. They never had before.

A long sigh escaped my lips—one of those sighs where you felt your entire body deflate, and you didn't know if you could even hold yourself up anymore.

I made my way to the bathroom and turned on the shower, cranking the handle so that the water was as hot as it could be. When I pushed back the curtain and stepped inside, I sank to the shower floor. I let the hot water rain down on me until it started to turn cold.

The mattress dipped as Dusty climbed into bed with me later that night. He wrapped his arm around my waist and pulled me to his chest. I felt his lips on the back of my neck. I didn't know what time it was—late, probably, but I hadn't been able to fall asleep yet.

I wound my fingers through his. "You still awake, angel?" he whispered in my ear.

"Couldn't sleep," I choked out.

"What's wrong?" he asked immediately, pulling me tighter.

I took a deep breath. "Are you happy, Dusty?"

He stilled behind me. The world had never been more deafeningly silent than it was then. I could almost feel the fissures forming in my heart as I waited for him to respond.

"I love you, Cam," he whispered. "I love you so much."

"That's not what I asked."

"Are you happy?"

"I don't—" A tear slid its way out of the corner of my eye and onto my pillow. "I don't think I am, Dusty." Suddenly, being close

to him, being held by him, felt like too much. I sat up, breaking his hold on me, and got out of the bed.

"What can I do?" he asked.

I didn't look back at him. "I want to go home," I said. "I want to go back to Meadowlark." I didn't know that's what I wanted, but now that I'd said it, I felt like I had a fishing hook in my sternum, and it was pulling me back. I didn't want to be here. I wanted to be with Dusty, but I didn't want to be here.

In Meadowlark, I could at least take University of Wyoming satellite classes. I could at least start working toward something.

"Okay," Dusty said quietly. "I can take you back this weekend, and we can . . . we can figure out the distance thing, all right?"

My brows knitted together as I finally turned toward him. "No," I said, confused. "I want us to go back to Meadowlark."

Dusty ran his hands through his blond hair. I couldn't really see his face in the dark—only what was lit by the moonlight coming in our bedroom window. "Cam . . . I have a job."

"I know. We can go home when the season is over next week."

I heard Dusty sigh. "I . . . I don't want to go home, Cam. This was my plan. I've been waiting for this my whole life—a chance to explore."

It felt like someone had kicked me in the back of my knees.

"Okay," I said, frustration bubbling under my skin. "But my plan was to go to college, and I changed it for you. For us."

"I never asked you to do that," Dusty snapped. He'd never snapped at me like that before. Whenever we fought, he stayed even-keeled. I was the one with the temper.

"But I did," I snapped back. "And I regret it every single day."

"We talked about this before we came here, Cam. I told you that I was worried about you not going to school, that I was *worried about us taking on too much too soon, and you brushed it off."*

"Well." I folded my arms across my chest. "I thought it would be different."

"Whose fault is that? I didn't ask you to come here with me. I didn't ask you to give up on school. I was ready to do the long-distance thing. I was ready for us to move forward that way."

"Okay, well, I'm sorry for loving you, I guess," I said, hating the way it sounded coming out of my mouth.

"Oh my god," Dusty said, standing up from the bed now. "Are you kidding me? That is such a bullshit thing to say, and you know it."

It was a bullshit thing to say, but I didn't care. Dusty had just told me he was choosing this shitty apartment in Montana over our relationship.

"I can't do this anymore. I don't want to be here, and I don't think you want me here."

"Of course I want you here, Cam, but I don't want you here if you don't want to be here. I worry about you all day, every day. I hate that you're here by yourself, but you don't do anything to change that. I can't be responsible for both of us. I'm barely learning how to be responsible for me."

"Okay." I shrugged, trying to play off how hurt and confused I felt. "Then I'm done."

In the dark, I could see Dusty go ramrod straight before he sighed. "I don't think we should keep doing this right now," he said. "It's the middle of the night. I'm tired. You're tired. We're both feeling a lot of things."

I scoffed—like that mattered.

"Can we please talk about this tomorrow when I get home?" Dusty pleaded.

"Sure. Whatever."

After that, Dusty grabbed his pillow and went out to the living room. I cried myself to sleep, and the next morning after Dusty went to work, I packed a bag.

Dusty,
I found a bus that goes to Jackson Hole. Good luck with your plans.
Cam

Chapter 32

Cam

I woke up with the weight of Dusty's arm around my waist and his breath on the back of my neck. When I started to move, he pulled me closer to him and nuzzled into the space between my neck and shoulder.

"Good morning," he murmured against my skin. His morning voice was something else.

"Good morning," I said. "What time is it?"

"Not a clue," Dusty said and then pressed his lips right behind my ear. "Don't care." He kissed me again.

I blinked my eyes open, taking in the sight of the other totally made bed. Last night, after I went to the bathroom, Dusty took a shower. I asked him if he wanted me to move to the other bed. He said, "Don't you dare," and then pulled me back into bed with him. I fell asleep in his arms almost immediately.

"Did you sleep okay?" he asked.

"Mm-hmm," I said and then reached for my phone on the nightstand.

"Please don't make me get out of this bed," Dusty muttered. "It feels early."

"Six," I said. "Which I think is sleeping in for you."

"Not when I went to bed like four hours ago, and I'm sharing a bed with you, Ash."

"Shut up, flirt," I said and turned toward him. Half of his face was hidden in a pillow, and his hair was a disaster. He was perfect. His eyes were closed, and a smile tugged at the half of his mouth I could see.

"Make me," he said and pulled me closer.

I brought my hands up and covered my mouth. "I need to brush my teeth," I said.

"What are you talking about? Give me some of that morning breath," Dusty said with a squeeze to my waist, and I jerked.

"Gross." I laughed.

Dusty brought a hand up to my face and smoothed my hair back. I did the same to him. I loved the way he looked in the morning glow—I wanted to remember the way he looked right now forever, tucked safely into the Dusty box.

I watched his eyes scan my face. "What?" I asked softly. He looked like he wanted to say something.

"I wanted to talk." He hesitated. "About something you said last night."

"Okay . . ." I trailed off, waiting for him to continue.

"About the 'no more babies' thing," he said, and suddenly I was wide awake.

"Is that . . . a deal-breaker for you?"

Dusty shook his head immediately. "No, of course not," he said. "I feel the same way about kids that I did when we talked about them when we probably had no business doing so. I could see my life with or without them—the same thing you said." I did say that back then, and it was still true. Now, I just saw my life with one instead of zero or multiple. "When I heard you were pregnant, I wondered if you'd changed your mind."

I shrugged. "Kind of," I said. "It's not a secret that Riley was an accident, and when I told Gus I was pregnant, the first thing he asked me was what I wanted to do—no judgment. He just said that we would do whatever I wanted because it was my body, and neither of us knew how to be a parent. We barely even knew each other at the time.

"And, I don't know, he just cared for me so easily—again, a woman he barely knew—and I just thought that a kid deserved to have him as a dad. Then I met his dad and knew I was right. So, we made the choice to do it together, and I've never once regretted it, but I knew as soon as we agreed that I was only going to do it one time.

"I hated being pregnant—really hated it. I know some women love it, but I wasn't one of them. I hated how my body didn't feel like my own—like it was stuck in a Space Invaders arcade game. Giving birth was the scariest thing I've ever done, and I ended up in therapy after. I had nightmares about it—even though Riley's was relatively easy from what I've read and heard about since then. It was still traumatic for me." Dusty rubbed his hand up and down my arm. "And it was all worth it to have Riley at the end of it, truly, but now that I know what it entails, I don't want to do it again."

"That makes perfect sense to me," Dusty said softly. "I just—I've always wanted to know more about . . . Riley's beginning, I guess."

I rubbed my thumb over his cheek. I couldn't keep my

hands off him. I didn't want to. "I'm sorry if it hurt you," I whispered. "Finding out I was pregnant."

Dusty brought his hand over mine, so he could move it to kiss my palm. "Don't ever apologize to me for that," he said. "If we hadn't ended, you wouldn't have her, and that would be a damn shame. Plus, we were apart for so long at that point. It did kind of suck when I thought you and Gus were together." Dusty smiled.

"Right," I said. "I forgot that he was your hero growing up."

"Okay, that's a little much," Dusty said. "I thought he and Brooks were cool—that's all."

"Sure," I said with a light laugh. "That's all. So you're okay with the no more babies thing?"

"Yes," he said without any hesitation. "Like I said, I've always been able to see my life with or without them, but even though I've tried, I've never been able to see my life without you."

"Dusty . . ." He was being so direct again, just like when we were dancing last night. I loved it, but at the same time, it overwhelmed me.

"I know," he said. "I'm not supposed to say things like that, but, Ash, you're fucking insane if you think I'm ever going to let you go again."

Chapter 33

Cam

Riley and Ada weren't at the Big House when I went to pick her up after Dusty and I got home that morning, but Amos was sitting at the kitchen table with the paper and a smoothie.

"Howdy," he said as I walked in.

"Hi," I said back with a smile. I shrugged my jacket off and took the seat next to him. "How's your Saturday?"

"Good," he said. "How was your Friday night?" There was a light in his green eyes. They looked just like my daughter's.

"Who wants to know?" I asked.

"An old man," he said. "Who lives in a quiet house, all by himself . . ." Amos trailed off, and I rolled my eyes.

"A big, quiet house that he built himself on the most beautiful piece of land in the state. Woe is you," I said, and Amos chuckled. "What do you want to know?"

"I heard Dusty went with you," he said.

I looked at the dark brown wood of the table. "You heard right," I said quietly.

"And?"

"And it was nice."

"A ringing endorsement coming from you." When I looked up, Amos was giving me a pointed look. "I've been hearing a lot about you and Dusty lately."

"That's because this family loves to talk," I said with a laugh.

"Exactly," Amos said. "And as much as you all love to talk, I love to listen. So"—Amos clapped his hands together—"talk."

I looked at Amos, this father figure whom I loved and respected so dearly. He was looking at me like I wished my dad would—with care and hope and interest. He really wanted to know.

So I talked.

"Dusty and I have got this convoluted history. I guess sometimes it feels like the sun and other times feels like a storm cloud . . ."

Amos nodded as if he completely understood. "And where does the gala fit into that?"

"Well, I knew I was going to have to see my parents, and he makes me feel brave. He's always been my friend before anything else, and that's what we've been trying to be again—friends."

"So last night felt like the sun?"

I took a deep breath. "Actually," I said, "it felt bigger than both of those things."

"Ah," Amos said with a knowing smile. I wasn't sure what he knew, though, because I felt like I didn't know a damn thing.

"What does that mean?" I asked.

"History is just one part of that analogy, Cam. Sure, you've got the sun and the storm clouds, but what about the dirt under your feet? The rain on your skin? Fresh air in your lungs?"

The fresh air in my lungs.

"So if everything about you and Dusty is starting to feel bigger, maybe that's because it is. It's not just about your history anymore because you've started to build on and around it. Your history is still part of this picture, but it's less important than where you are now. There's a reason that rearview mirrors are small and windshields are big."

I dropped my head onto my forearms and sighed.

"You're very wise," I mumbled into the table.

I felt one of Amos's weathered hands rub at my shoulder. "That's what they tell me," he said, and then he tapped on my head a few times. I lifted it, so I could look him in the eye. The gleam in his eye was gone. Now, he looked almost somber. "And I know it's different, but if I had a second chance to be with the person who felt like the sun and rain and air and everything, I would take it without another thought."

I put my hand over the one that was on my shoulder. "It is different," I said quietly.

"But it all comes down to the same thing," Amos said. "A mark on your heart and soul that refuses to fade, no matter how much time passes or how much you think you've changed." I thought of my "T" tattoo, Dusty's physical mark on me. But Amos was right; this mark went a lot deeper. Amos continued: "People, and our feelings for them, stick with us for a reason, Cam."

"And what if it goes wrong?"

Amos let out a half laugh. "And what if it doesn't?"

"Touché," I said. "I just don't quite know how to reconcile

our past with a possible future, I guess. I haven't really dealt with that."

"There's always the possibility of things going wrong, Cam. That's what makes love a risk, but there's just as much of a possibility of things going right." Easy for him to say—he wasn't the reason things went wrong in the first place.

"How did you know?" I asked. "That Stella was the one for you?"

Amos looked at me thoughtfully. "I adored her from the start, and I wanted to know everything about her for the rest of forever—who she was then, who she would be later. I just wanted to exist in her orbit.

"I called my brother from a pay phone outside the diner right after I met her and told him I'd found the girl I was going to marry."

"Are you serious?" I said, my voice full of doubt.

"I'm serious." He nodded. "And I can tell you from experience that the most precious thing we have is time. There's never going to be enough of it."

"Are you going to tell me to carpe diem or some shit?"

"Yes," Amos said. "I am. You have time, Cam. Don't waste it. Stop letting your past hold you back." I understood what Amos was saying, I really did. But Dusty and I had history that informed who we were now—even if we didn't want it to. I had pushed it so far down, so I wouldn't have to remember it, or how so much of what went wrong was my fault. I had never talked about it with anyone. But with everything that had happened in the past twenty-four hours, in the past weeks and months, if I was being honest, I could feel it rising to the surface, churning the soil and threatening to burst through to the light.

"Amos—" I said, but the door opened, and I heard Riley's feet running across the hardwood floors, and within a few seconds, I felt her arms around one of mine.

"Hi, Sunshine," I said and pressed a kiss to the side of her head. She gave my arm another squeeze before jumping into Amos's lap. Next to her grandpa, I was chopped liver, and I didn't mind at all.

"Hey," Ada said as she walked into the kitchen. She was wearing a long black wool coat over black jeans and black Doc Martens. She always looked so cool.

"Hey," I said. "Thanks for watching her last night."

"No problem," Ada said. "Can't wait to hear all about it." She raised one of her dark brows suggestively at me, and I rolled my eyes, but I was trying not to smile. I'd never really had this—someone to talk to the morning after, to debrief and giggle.

"Mom, look at my shoes," Riley said. I turned back to her on Amos's lap and looked at her feet, which had little Doc Martens on them.

"Oh my god," I said, looking back at Ada. "I love them."

Ada grinned. "Aren't they perfect? I've decided I'm going to have to get her a pair every time her feet grow."

"Did you say thank you, Sunshine?"

Riley nodded. "A lot of times," she said matter-of-factly.

"What are y'all up to today?" Amos asked.

"Well," Ada said, "Riley thinks that Cam's plates are boring, and I've got nothing to do, so I was thinking we could hit the antique store?" She looked over at me.

"First of all," I said lifting a finger, "my plates are not boring. Second of all: What do you think, Sunshine? Does that sound fun?"

Riley nodded eagerly.

"All right, let's do it."

The antiques store in Meadowlark was surprisingly well stocked for a small town—probably because it was the only one in the county; the next closest one was nearly two hours away in Sweetwater Peak.

Being in the glassware section did make me a little nervous. Riley was tornado-esque, so I kept a close eye on her as we perused and made sure that she didn't pick things up without help from Ada or me.

"So how did things go last night?" Ada asked as she pushed a small cart next to me.

"Good," I said, trying to play it cool.

"How good?"

"There is a child present, Ada Hart."

Ada giggled. "That good, huh?"

I blew out a puff of air. "Yeah. That good."

"I knew it," Ada muttered. "You don't have a neck tattoo and a nose piercing and not be good. And don't even get me started on his little cropped T-shirts."

"Oh my god," I said. "You and Emmy need a spray bottle. You're both feral cats."

"Because we have eyes," Ada said. "He's a beautiful man—not as beautiful as Wes, obviously, but beautiful. That's just a fact. His face is like perfectly proportioned and almost too symmetrical. I'm an interior designer—I notice those things."

"He does have a nice face," I said. "Among other things."

"Oh, fuck, yeah," Ada said quietly, making sure Riley didn't hear probably. Riley and the F-word had a complicated history, thanks to Gus. We were working on it. "That's what I'm talking about."

A laugh escaped me. "You're ridiculous," I said as I picked up a pair of chicken-shaped salt and pepper shakers—trying to will the blush off my cheeks. "Last night was good," I said with a shrug. It was universes beyond good, but it felt too vast to even put into words.

"Okay . . . so what happens now?" Ada asked.

"I . . . really don't know." I sighed as I set the salt and pepper shakers down. It was true, but I saw Ada clock the hesitation in my answer.

"Cam." Ada nodded. "If you don't start talking about you and Dusty soon, everything about the two of you that you keep just below the surface is going to bubble over."

Damn. Ada was perceptive, and she had me pegged, but I tried to play it off. "Oh yeah? What exactly do you think I'm keeping below the surface?" I asked.

"You tell me," she said. "I'll make it easier by starting with what I already know." I nodded for her to keep going and then looked around for Riley. She was occupied with a bunch of throw pillows.

"You and Dusty dated in high school," Ada said. "No one can give me a straight answer on when or how or where it ended, which is odd, considering everyone knows everything about everyone in this town."

I looked down at my feet. Ada was already treading dangerously toward the exact thing I didn't want to talk about.

"And I've been watching the two of you—"

"Creepy," I butted in.

"Concerned," Ada argued. "There always seems to be this weird tension on the surface whenever you two are together.

But then, it's easy to see the familiarity. Like at Christmas. The two of you looked like you'd rather be sitting anywhere else than next to each other, but then two seconds later, you're gazing into each other's eyes and smiling like there's nowhere else you'd rather be."

"There was no gazing," I said with an eye roll.

"There was gazing. And longing—especially from him."

I scoffed. "Since when did you become such a hopeless romantic?"

"Since Wes, duh." Ada shrugged.

"I don't know, Ada," I said quietly. "We were each other's first everything. That familiarity is always going to be there." After last night, I believed it even more now.

"So was last night just two old flames, stuck with only one bed, giving in to that familiar feeling, or was it something more?"

"Have you been reading Teddy's romance novels, too, now?"

Ada just looked at me, waiting.

I sighed. There wasn't any reason for me to lie. It was time to let this out. "More."

"That's what I thought," she said. She looked smug. "So why don't you seem happier? You had a great night and great sex with a great guy, who seems very all in on you, at least from the outside, but it feels like . . . you're fighting it so hard."

She was right, of course. And I was so tired of fighting. I took a deep breath. "I'm scared," I said.

"Of Dusty?"

I shook my head. "Of what happens if it doesn't work out again." *Because it's my fault it didn't work out the first time.*

"Cam . . ." Ada said quietly. "Please . . . I know you haven't wanted to talk about it. But . . . what exactly happened between you guys?"

I hesitated for a second, trying to find the words. "We had sort of a . . . traumatic ending, I guess."

Ada nodded. She understood those. "I mean, from what I know about Dusty, he seemed to bounce around a lot. Did he just disappear one day?"

"No," I said quietly and swallowed hard. "I did."

Ada's eyes widened, and she waited for me to keep going.

"Dusty and I were more, even back then. I thought we were going to be together forever. So when he went to guide school in Montana, I went with him."

"You ran away together?"

"Yeah," I said.

"That doesn't . . . sound like you," Ada said.

"It isn't like me," I said. "But with Dusty, I was . . . I don't know . . . a bolder version of myself. Carefree." He is still the only person who has ever gotten me out of my head—the only person who made me want to live outside of it.

"So when I think about him or when I'm near him, I think of that girl—that ferocious and courageous girl who decided to set her own expectations and who wanted her own life." It was hard to swallow. "And when I think of her, I think about how disappointed she would be in the woman I became—the woman who came crawling back to a life she didn't want." I thought back to what it was like coming back to Meadowlark. When I got home, my mother was barely surprised to see me, and my dad looked at me with disgust. I'll never forget what he said: "If you do anything like that again, you're out. You're done."

I remember wanting to break down and cry. I remember

wanting them to comfort me and tell me everything was going to be okay and that they were happy I was home, but they didn't. But I still felt . . . indebted to them somehow? They gave me a second chance to do what they thought was the right thing, and I'd never known my parents to give second chances, so I became so focused on not screwing it up that I barely even noticed that I was losing parts of myself that I'd come to love because Dusty loved them first.

I'm still ashamed of how easy it was for me to fall back into their expectations—how relieved I was when I realized how easy my life could be as long as I sacrificed myself and real happiness.

"And honestly, I can't handle that. It breaks my heart. I mourn that girl constantly, and when Dusty is around, the grief is almost . . . overwhelming. Because it becomes so obvious she's too far gone and that she can't come back."

"Oh," Ada said softly.

I gave her a half laugh. "That's probably more than you were asking for."

"No," Ada said. "More than I was expecting, but it's exactly what I asked for." She was quiet for a second after that, and I dragged my finger over some old coffee mugs. "I don't think you need to be scared of Dusty," she said. "And I still think you're ferocious and courageous and all of those other things." I shrugged. "You are. You really are. I mean, Cam, look at the life you're building right now."

"What do you mean?" I asked.

"You took the bull by the horns after the wedding, and I know you didn't really have a choice, but it's still impressive. You found your dream home for you and your daughter, and you created a new life for the two of you, all on your own."

"I mean, I had a little help."

"We all need a little help to get where we're going, you know. What matters is that the end result is yours. And I think that if things had gone differently in your past, with Dusty, with your parents, with Graham, you wouldn't have ended up here. You were so young. You had a lot of discovering to do . . . and maybe you still do. But you deserve everything you have and everything you want—including Dusty. I get you saying you're scared of him and what could happen, but it seems to me like you're just scared that all of this is too good to be true, but it isn't. It's real and it's happening, and I think you should just . . . let it."

Ada's words made me feel . . . lighter. I'd spent years building a wall, brick by brick, inside my head and my heart, trying to block out everything having to do with Dusty. It wasn't until recently that I realized how heavy those bricks were.

Chapter 34

Dusty

GREER: Any update on Alaska? Interested?
DUSTY: Honestly, thanks, but I'm happy where I am.
GREER: What about who you're with?
DUSTY: That, too.
GREER: Happy for you, T. Love you.
DUSTY: Love you.

I opened Cam's back door without thinking about it—
maybe I should've knocked, but I was excited to see her.

Riley was going to be at Gus's, and we were going to have a
date tonight.

Cam turned to me when she heard the door open. "Hey," I
said. Her eyes were wide, even though she was expecting me.
I didn't waste any time in setting the grocery bag and bottle of
red wine on the counter, walking toward her, and pulling her
mouth to mine.

She seemed . . . tense for a minute before she melted into
me. I savored the feeling of her arms wrapping around my
neck and her fingers knotting in my hair.

I didn't know how long we stayed like that, but suddenly there was a deep "ahem," from the direction of the hallway. Cam jumped back immediately, and I saw Gus standing in the kitchen. Oh, shit. He and Riley must not have left yet.

"Hey, man," I said. I felt like a teenager who had just gotten caught making out with his girlfriend in his car—which had happened to me. With Cam. The memory of it made a laugh bubble out of me.

Gus definitely wasn't as scary as Cam's mom, but damn, the look he was shooting me could cut glass. I tried to care, but I just . . . didn't. All I cared about was Cam.

Both Cam and Gus looked at me. Cam burst into laughter a few seconds after me. She slapped her hand over her mouth and kept laughing. "I'm sorry," she said. "This was not supposed to happen."

"The kissing or me walking in on you guys?"

"You walking in," I said. "The kissing was definitely supposed to happen." Cam gave me a warning look, but I just winked at her.

Gus folded his arms across his chest, like he was about to start lecturing someone. Well, me.

Riley appeared behind him before he could with a bubbly "Ready!" She had changed her clothes and was holding her cleats.

"Let's roll, Sunshine," Gus said, smiling down at her, then he looked back at Cam. "I wanted to talk to you about some of these forms I need to fill out to register part of Rebel Blue as a nonprofit. Can I send them to you?"

"Of course," she said. "So the horse sanctuary is happening?"

"Depends on him," Gus said, nodding toward me. I didn't

like the way he said that—like he was waiting for me to tell him I couldn't commit and was out. Fuck that. I was in this— all of this. Cam looked up at me. There was a question in her eyes.

"It's happening," I said, trying hard not to let my frustration show. "I told you, I'm here for the long haul."

I felt Cam relax beside me. Did she think I was going to leave? The thought made it hard to swallow. I didn't know what else I could do to convince her that I was in this with her.

"I hope so," Gus said. His voice wasn't as harsh, but there was still an edge there. Protective motherfucker. "Go tell your mom bye," he said to Riley.

Riley ran over to Cam, who lifted her into her arms and gave her a squeeze. "I love you, Sunshine. I'll see you tomorrow morning."

"Love you," Riley said and then kissed her palm and pressed it to Cam's cheek. When she set her down, instead of going back to Gus, she threw her little arms around my waist. I looked at Cam—the shock probably evident in my face. I didn't know what to do, so I gave her back a pat.

"Are you coming to my soccer game on Saturday?" Riley asked hopefully.

"Oh, um," I stammered and looked over at Cam again. *Could I go? I'd like to. Would that be okay?* Cam nodded.

I always wondered what it would be like for me to know Riley, and now I did. She was amazing—just like her mom.

Riley beamed up at me before running back to her dad and heading out the front door.

"You don't have to come if you don't want to," Cam said when the door closed. She was giving me a way out now that Riley was gone, but I didn't want it.

I wrapped both of my arms around her waist and looked down at her. "I want to," I said as earnestly as I could. "There's nowhere else I'd rather be."

Cam laid her head on my chest, and I took the chance to breathe her in.

Chapter 35

Cam

"Thank you for dinner," I said a little while later. Dusty and I were sitting on the bar stools at my kitchen counter.

He smiled at me. "I've been waiting for us to have something like this for a long time."

"Falafel?" I asked, confused.

"No, weirdo." Dusty reached over and flicked my nose. I smiled at him. "Time." He kissed me then. Softly. "I didn't know if we'd ever get it, but I hoped for it. I hoped for you."

I felt so many things at once, but not all of it was good. "I'm sorry," I said quietly. "That I was the reason our time got cut short last time."

Dusty lifted his hand, and I felt his fingers curl around the back of my neck. "I need you to know that I don't blame you, angel—for leaving me in Montana. I don't blame you at all."

I squeezed my eyes shut for a second. Thinking about that hurt. "You don't?"

"Not at all. I mean, I was heartbroken for a long time, but

with every year that passed, I realized that even if you'd stayed, that didn't mean we would've made it. Maybe things would've gotten so bad we couldn't fix them. I knew you weren't happy. I knew that the life I longed for then wasn't the life you saw for yourself."

"I saw a life with you," I said. "And . . . I think that was kind of the problem. I didn't really see me or what I wanted. I just saw you, and then I realized I was living your life instead of mine or even ours," I said honestly. I didn't leave Dusty because I didn't love him or want to be with him. I left him because I wanted something for myself, too. I didn't know that then, but I knew that now. The problem, I realized once I got home, was I didn't know how to go for it, so I ended up living the life my parents wanted instead.

"I think . . . I think that you choosing to leave—even being brave enough to—is what makes right now possible," Dusty said as his thumb moved back and forth along my cheek.

"How do you mean?"

"We were young, Cam. And that doesn't mean our relationship wasn't real or substantial or all of the things that we know were true." He paused for a second. "We were in love, and as much as I wanted that to be enough then, I don't think it was.

"There's all of these things we can't control that push on us—timing, dreams, stress, hopes—and it makes sense to me that two eighteen-year-olds couldn't handle that heat. We went in two separate directions, but roads that go in opposite directions come back together all the time."

"Is that what we're doing now?" I asked. "Coming back together?"

"I hope so," he said. "That's what I want. Do you?"

"You've always been so . . . forthcoming," I said with a small laugh. "It used to make me nervous. I felt like I wasn't worthy of someone so . . . sure about me."

"And now?"

"It still makes me nervous," I said honestly. "But it also makes me feel more secure in where we've been and where we're at and . . . where we're going."

"And where are we going, angel?"

"Forward? How does that sound—" Dusty kissed me before I could finish. I let everything around us fall away. It was just me and him and all the things we felt for each other. Three words got stuck in the back of my throat, and even though I didn't say them, I think Dusty knew.

Chapter 36

Dusty

C am and I went to Riley's soccer game together on Saturday morning. I didn't want to not show up the first time Riley asked me to do something—even if that something was at the Meadowlark Rec Center on a Saturday morning.

When Cam and I walked in, my first thought was that I had no idea there were this many seven-year-olds in this town.

The place was packed.

I wanted to grab Cam's hand as we walked in, but I didn't. I let my hand brush hers, though, and she didn't pull away, so I did that a couple more times before I saw Gus, Teddy, and Riley sitting on the bleachers. My mom and Hank were there, too.

Gus was putting—well, trying to put—Riley's curly hair into a ponytail. She looked fucking adorable in her purple soccer uniform. She told me last year her uniform was pink, but this year it was purple because she was on the seven-year-olds team.

A grin stretched across Teddy's face when she saw me, and she immediately looked at our hands.

"I like this view," Teddy called as Cam and I got closer. When I glanced at Cam, she was blushing.

My mom looked up then. A wide grin stretched across her face. She stood when we got closer. "Good morning, you two," she said.

"Hey, Mom," I said.

When she hugged me, she whispered in my ear. "Do you have something to tell me, Dusty?"

"We can talk about it later," I whispered back. When I pulled out of her hug, my mom gave me a look that said there was no way we were not talking about it later.

"Hi, sweetie," she said to Cam, and Cam hugged her, too.

"Cam," Gus said. "Can you help me with this?"

Cam laughed. "Riley's curls: eight thousand. Gus Ryder: zero." Cam took the seat behind Riley and kissed her on the cheek. "Your dad never gets better at this, does he?"

Riley shook her head, but she didn't verbally respond. She was bouncing on the balls of her feet—getting her head in the game, I was sure. Cam used to do the same thing before a soccer game. Go quiet and keep her eye on the prize.

"I am getting better at managing them, though," Gus said. "Me and wash day are best friends now."

Cam laughed. "It only took seven years."

"Okay, to be fair, she didn't have that much hair for like four of them." He slid next to Teddy on the bleachers and gave her a quick peck on the mouth before he looked at me. "Hey, Dusty. You came." He sounded disappointed.

"Riley asked me to," I said, and I looked over at her. "I can't wait to see you play, kid." That got a smile out of her, and I felt like I'd won the lottery. "You know," I said, "I used to watch your mom play."

Riley perked up as Cam pulled her hair back. "Really?" she asked, and I sat on the bleacher bench in front of her, so we were eye to eye.

"Yeah," I said. "I bet you're just as good as her," I said. "Maybe even better." Riley looked bashful.

"All right, Sunshine," Cam said. "You're good to go. Go warm up." Riley stood up and gave each of us a high-five before she ran out onto the court with the other purple jerseys.

"So," Teddy said, looking between Cam and me as I sat down beside her, "anything new and noteworthy to report, you two?"

"Theodora," Gus said in warning.

"What?" she asked.

"I'd also like to know," my mom chimed in, and I gave her a look.

Cam was stiff next to me, not ready to take on Teddy's teasing. "I got bucked off a horse this week," I said. "Little asshole got spooked, and I went flying."

"It's true," Gus said. "I saw it."

Teddy pouted. "You guys are no fun," but when I looked at Cam, she mouthed "Thank you" just as somebody blew a whistle.

"Looks like the game is starting," Gus said.

I don't know if you've ever seen seven-year-olds play soccer, but it's equal parts adorable, confusing, and frustrating as hell. There are like two kids who kind of know what they're doing, and then the rest of them are just there for the vibes.

Riley actually had possession of the ball a decent amount. At one point, she got fouled, so she got to throw it in. Truly, I didn't know anything about soccer. Cam tried to educate me when she used to play, but every time she started talking about it and trying to explain the rules, we just started making out . . .

But at least I knew when to cheer.

While the game was going on, all of us chatted. Well, Teddy chatted, mostly. She tried (and failed) to convince me to get a cat she saw on the animal shelter's website.

"You know I'm allergic to cats, Ted," I said.

She rolled her eyes. "I don't know why you can't just grow up and pop a Benadryl like an adult."

"I can't take care of a cat if I'm unconscious," I said. Benadryl took me *out*. I heard Cam giggle next to me, and she pressed the side of her leg against mine for a second.

"How are you liking the house, Cam? Settling in okay?" my mom asked.

"Yeah," she said. "I can't think about the fact that I might have to leave it in a year. It feels like mine."

"And Riley? Does she like it?"

"Loves it," Cam said. "I'm going to have to keep an eye on her when it gets warmer. She's itching to start climbing trees, and I don't want any broken bones on my hands."

Riley's age group played a shortened version of a game, with each half only being fifteen minutes. At halftime, Riley congregated with her team around a cooler with juice boxes and clementines. When she looked over at all of us, we waved.

I didn't miss all the glances that came our way from the rest of the town. I didn't care. I loved being here with Cam and being here for Riley.

Near the end of the game, Riley got her hands (feet?) on the ball, and I stood so I could see. She dribbled it between her feet like a pro.

She was able to break away from the little amoeba that was following the ball and started heading toward the goal.

"Oh, shit, she's going," I said louder than I intended. Gus, who was next to me, stood, too.

"That's my girl!" Gus yelled. "Go, Sunshine, GO!" There was one player who was gaining some ground on her, but Riley was gearing up to try for the goal. I watched her take a big step and swing her right leg back before letting it rip.

The ball went straight into the goal.

"Let's fucking go!" I yelled and heard Gus's victory cry next to me. Without thinking we grabbed each other's hands and did one of those sports bro hugs. I don't know what came over me. I heard Cam and Teddy laugh.

"Are they okay, do we think?" Teddy asked, but Cam never got a chance to answer because I pulled her close to me and kissed her temple. I heard my mom squeal behind me.

"Terrance Tucker!" she yelled. "Have you been keeping this from me?!"

I went still when I heard my full name and looked down at Cam, ready to apologize for not thinking, but she was smiling. She laced her fingers through the hand of the arm that was hanging over her shoulder—keeping me there. When our eyes met, she shrugged.

"Wait a second," Teddy chimed in. "Your real name is *Terrance*?"

Oh my fucking god.

Cam burst into laughter next to me, and my mom joined in—hugging both of us over and over again.

I didn't have a chance to bask in the moment because Riley came tearing toward us.

She went directly to Gus, and then to Cam. Her parents

were both beaming. Cam shrugged out of my arms to hug her daughter, and my mom took another chance to hug me.

"Don't screw this up, Dusty," she said in my ear. "Not everyone gets a second chance at their first love." I was about to tell her that I didn't have any intention of that, but then Riley called my name.

She was blushing under everyone's attention. Teddy gave her a squeeze, and when it was my turn, Riley threw her arms around my neck. She held out her wrist to show me that she was wearing her bracelet—I didn't notice it when we got here.

"Do you think it's good luck?" she asked me.

I grinned. "Yeah, kid. I do."

Chapter 37

Cam

Eight Years Ago

Ash,

Every time I write one of these notes, I feel so stupid. What's the point of writing to you when you're never going to read it? I don't know. But I think it helps. I don't think it makes me miss you less, and I don't know if it makes me feel closer to you, but for some reason, it does make me feel closer to home. And today, I just wish I could be home.

My dad died. He went peacefully in his sleep. My mom is heartbroken. I'm heartbroken. I feel guilty. I haven't seen him in over a year. I canceled my last visit. I told my parents I would fly them and Greer out to the next place I landed, but I never got around to it.

I wish we were in a different place—where I could call you on the phone, and you'd answer. I wish I could talk to you about him. About me. About all of it.

My dad loved you, you know. He'd keep me updated on

*you. He told me you grocery shopped on Thursdays, so
every Thursday, he made sure the Pink Lady apples were
stocked. I think he wanted me to know that you were
okay—that you had people taking care of you and that he
would always be one of them.*

*I haven't written this down in a while because when I
write it down, I remember how real it is. But I miss you.
I miss you all the time. I don't even know what it feels like
not to miss you.*

I miss my dad, too.

Dusty

I didn't even know why I was at the Devil's Boot—especially on a night like tonight. It was busy. People were packed in here like sardines. Five minutes ago I saw Teddy Andersen try to pick a fight with a guy who looked like he was closely related to the Jolly Green Giant.

But I wanted a drink. I wanted to be surrounded by people. I liked people watching. It made me feel less alone, and today, I felt alone.

Today was the first day that I existed in a world without Renny Tucker, which was enough to make me want to lie on the floor and not get up. It wasn't like Renny and I talked all the time—especially since things between Dusty and me ended. But I liked knowing that the Tucker family was still here. Some piece of Dusty was still here.

I'd only been back here a few months. After four years at college, a gap year spent abroad, and the internship my father secured for me before I took the LSAT, everything about this place felt the same.

It was comforting, actually.

And while I looked around the Devil's Boot, my mind did the same thing it had done for the last seven years: wandered back to Dusty. I didn't normally let it stay there for very long, but tonight, I did.

Because even though we hadn't actually spoken in years, my chest ached for him tonight. I wished I could call him. I wished I could offer him something—comfort, someone to talk to, anything.

I pulled out my phone and scrolled through it until I found Dusty's contact. I felt my heartbeat in my ears as my thumb hovered over it. A text wouldn't hurt, right? It was normal for me to send my condolences. After all, I loved his dad, too. I tapped the message icon and typed out a few lines before I deleted them. I did this at least ten times until I settled on something simple—surface level but still kind.

CAM: *Hey. It's Cam. I'm sorry about your dad. Thinking of you.*

My thumb hovered over the send arrow. I took a deep breath, but before I could bring it down and commit, someone bumped into me, and my phone fell to the middle of the bar.

"Oh, shit," a man's voice said. "I'm so sorry. It's crazy in here tonight."

When I looked up, I was met with striking green eyes and a frown. Gus Ryder. He looked flustered, keyed up, kind of, and he was breathing heavily like he had run from somewhere.

"It's okay," I said, reaching across the bar for my phone. When I picked it up and saw the message was still unsent on the screen, I felt my courage from a few seconds ago evaporate. "You probably just saved me from doing something stupid."

I saw Gus glance down at my phone. Could he read the name on the screen?

"I wish I could stop myself from doing stupid things," he said with a humorless laugh.

"Rough night?" I asked, interested. I didn't know Gus very well, though I had been friendly with Wes in school. But I knew he didn't tend to get his feathers ruffled.

He dragged a large hand down his face. "Weird night," he said. "You're Cam Ashwood, right?"

I nodded.

"Gus Ryder." He held his hand out for me to shake. I took it.

"I know," I said. "So, what stupid thing did you do tonight?" Gus let out a long sigh, and I laughed a little. "That bad, huh?"

"That bad." He nodded.

"Do you, um, want to talk about it?" I asked. I didn't know why—I barely knew this guy. He just looked like he needed a friend, and Gus's best friend, Luke Brooks, seemed to be occupied. I could see him by the jukebox. He had his arms around two older men, and all of them were singing along to "Family Tradition" by Hank Williams Jr. very loudly and very poorly.

"Maybe after I get you a refill?" Gus looked at my almost empty vodka soda. One of the corners of his mouth tilted up just a little, and it occurred to me that most people would probably find him handsome. I guess I did, too. I just had a thing for blonds.

"Sure," I said, maintaining eye contact with him. Were we . . . flirting? Gus waved down the bartender and asked for a beer and turned to me.

"Vodka soda," I said.

"On my tab," Gus said. "And kick Brooks off of it while you're at it." The bartender gave Gus a nod.

After that, Gus and I fell into easy conversation. From what I knew about him, Gus wasn't really a talker, but our conversation was easy. He talked about Rebel Blue. I talked about prepping for the LSAT and going to law school. Both of us laughed when one of the bar patrons did the worm in the middle of the floor without a shirt.

And, a couple hours later, when Gus asked me if I wanted to head somewhere else, I said yes without thinking twice about it.

The next morning, my phone buzzed, and when I saw the name on the screen, my heart took off like a rocket. Dusty Tucker. It was a response to the text I typed out last night. I didn't know when I had sent it. Maybe in Gus's truck? Maybe later?

DUSTY: *Thank you. It means a lot.*

Chapter 38

Cam

When I heard a knock on my front door, I found Gus standing in the porch light.

"Riley realized she didn't have her blanket in her bag for her sleepover with the soccer team."

"Oh, shoot. It's in the laundry. It should be almost dry." She probably could've survived without it if she was just staying at Gus's, but when she went to sleepovers, she liked to have a piece of home with her.

"Do you want to come in while I grab it?"

"Sure," he said. "How's your night going?"

"I was just getting some work done." When I shut the door behind him, I noticed his truck was still running. "Is Teddy out there? Does she want to come in?"

"She's okay," Gus said. "Speaking of work, I actually wanted to talk to you about something." Gus and I walked back toward the kitchen, and he sat at the table with me.

"I swear I'm almost done with the nonprofit forms," I said.

"And I'll file them for you, so you don't have to worry about it. Do you want some water or anything?"

Gus shook his head. "I'm not worried about it," he said. "But thank you."

"Oh. Then what's up?"

"Rebel Blue is big, you know. We've got a lot going on—normal cattle ranch shit, Baby Blue, and getting the sanctuary off the ground." I nodded. "My dad has gotten really good at the legal part of things for the cattle ranch during his lifetime. He knows what to look for in contracts and can decipher most things. Me? Not so much."

"You know I'm always happy to look at things for you."

"I know. And I was wondering if you would want to do that in a more official capacity."

I tilted my head in confusion. "You want me to be your lawyer?" I asked.

"I want you to be Rebel Blue's lawyer," he said. "I trust you, Cam. I don't have the same knowledge and experience as my dad, and someday, it's going to fall to me. I want to set Rebel Blue up for success before that happens."

"And your dad?"

"He's all for it." Gus smiled a little. "He loves it when I delegate."

"This is, um . . . wow." I shook my head. This seemed too good to be true.

"I don't know what you make at your firm, and I don't know if I can match it, but I'll come as close as I can."

"I'd do it for free," I said honestly. "Maybe I could do both?" My phone buzzed on the table, and I looked down. Dusty was on his way home.

Gus looked down, too, and I watched him clock the name on the screen.

"Just think about it. I know you could and would. But I want your full time and full attention, and I don't think you should be trying to do two jobs. I know what happens when you spread yourself too thin. Especially when you seem to have a lot going on." He tilted his chin toward my phone. "So the two of you are in it, then?"

I sighed. "Honestly, Gus, I don't know if either of us have ever been out."

"And you're happy?"

"Yeah," I said honestly. I tried to pinpoint it—the moment that my old feelings for Dusty became new, or the moment that I stopped pushing him away and started pulling him closer, but I really couldn't. For the second time in my life, I fell into Dusty—I let him sweep me away, and I had no regrets about it.

"When the wedding didn't work out, I felt like my life had been turned upside down—like all of the pieces of it that I'd picked out so carefully were just shaken up and thrown in the air, left to fall where they may. But now . . . I think they were all falling together.

"I have this beautiful house to raise our daughter in. I have our family. I have a life that's mine, and I have somebody who . . . cares about me. Deeply."

"Cares about you deeply?" Gus asked. His smile was poking through. "I'm not sure, but I think there's a word for that."

"I know," I said. "And we're there." *Permanent.*

"You deserve that—to be happy—and you deserve a partner, Cam. A real one. Someone who can support you and get you gas and help you with Riley, and can love her the same way we do.

"I didn't realize how much I needed and wanted something like that until Teddy, and I just . . . I'm really happy for you if you've found it, too. I know I can be a bit of an ass, but I guess what I'm saying is that you have my approval—even though you don't need it. I just know how much it meant to me when you gave me yours."

"Gus . . ." My voice was a little shaky. "That was a hell of a speech."

Gus laughed. "Yeah, I practiced it a few times. Teddy gave me some notes."

"I'm sure she did."

"But, really. Cam, Dusty is a good man. He's a hard worker. He's loyal and kind, and he's been looking at you the same way for fifteen years—like he would do anything for you. I know that if he got the chance, he would extend that to our daughter, too." Gus reached out and grabbed my hand. "I can't even imagine what he felt when he found out you were pregnant. It probably almost killed him, but he shows up for our daughter anyway." Tears pricked at the back of my eyes. "He was ready to throw down for her at the soccer game."

I laughed at that. "Yeah, you two made proper fools out of yourselves." But then I took a deep breath. "This means a lot to me, Gus. Thank you," I said. Who knew that when I got knocked up, I would get a damn good friend out of it, too?

"Dusty Tucker is a good man," Gus said again. "And you're one of the best people I've ever known. It sounds silly now, but I'm grateful for the night that brought us together because getting to spend my life parenting Riley alongside you and

Teddy . . . and Dusty . . . is going to be one of my greatest ac-complishments."

I threw my arms around Gus's neck, and he wrapped an arm around me. "Did Teddy help you with that part, too?"

Gus laughed. "That part was all me. And it's all true."

I squeezed him a little tighter before pulling back. The buzzer to the dryer went off.

"I'll get it," Gus said as he stood from the table. "Let me know about the job, okay?"

"I will," I said. "Thank you."

Chapter 39

Dusty

When I got home later that night, I sat in my car for a second after I cut the engine. I did this every night when I got home—took a second to be still.

I loved nighttime. I think I loved mornings more—probably because I had to learn to love them because of my job, but still, I loved the night. I think I loved them both because those were the times when the world was quiet. I liked the quiet. I liked the stillness. I liked the weird sense of calm and stability they evoked in me. No matter where you were in the world, there were always going to be mornings, and there were always going to be nights.

So I sat in my truck with my eyes closed in the dark. I thought about this morning at the soccer game—about how much I loved being there with Cam, and how she didn't shy away when confronted with telling people about us.

Something slammed on the hood of my car, and I startled. I think I yelped. When I looked up, Teddy Andersen was grinning outside my driver's-side window. So much for quiet.

"What the hell is wrong with you?" I said loudly, so she

could hear me through the glass. She tossed her head back in laughter before yanking the door open.

"Scoot over," she said. "It's cold as shit out here."

I moved across the bench seat, and Teddy climbed in the cab.

"What are you doing here?" I asked.

"Riley has a team sleepover tonight, but she forgot her blanket. We came here to get it, so we could drop it off to her."

"That doesn't explain why you're sitting in my car," I said.

Teddy shrugged. "I wanted to talk to you."

"About?"

"Everything," she said. "We haven't really had a chance to debrief lately."

"What are we debriefing?"

"Well, you and Cam is the obvious topic of conversation," she said. "But after this morning, I wanted to talk to you about Riley. You showed up for her today."

"She asked me to come." I shrugged.

"And you nearly blew everyone's eardrums with how loud you were cheering for her."

"I think that was your fiancé," I said.

"It was both of you," Teddy said. "Anyway, I wanted to see how you were feeling about it all. If you're with Cam, you've gotta love them both," she said.

"I do," I said without thinking.

I thought about Riley a lot. Just like her mom, she was so easy for me to love.

She was funny and smart and tenacious. I found myself wondering about her more often these days—curious about what she was learning in school or how her day was or if she felt off-kilter in her saddle that wasn't quite sized right.

I thought about the life that Cam had built for Riley—not the life that she'd built with the help of Gus and his family, but the parts of Riley's life that Cam had built on her own. When Riley was at Gus's, she had a seemingly never-ending group of people who wanted to see her and jumped at the chance to take care of her. When she was with Cam, it was just the two of them. Both of those dynamics were special, but I wondered if Cam ever felt pressure to be . . . more. I would, if it was me.

Even though it was impossible for Cam to be more than she already was.

"Good," Teddy said. "Because it's a special thing—to be part of this little unit Cam and Gus have created. Riley has no shortage of people who love her, but it's different being the other half of one of her parents. It can be a lot, but it's worth it."

"Of course it is," I said and then paused for a second. "Do you ever . . . worry about it? About how you fit into Riley's life? I want to be there for her—I want to be part of it all, but I don't want to overstep or anything."

"All the time," Teddy said. "But we have the easy way out. We get to take our cues from Cam and Gus. It's their partnership that makes Riley's life so special."

I nodded. "Any advice?"

Teddy thought about that for a second. "Don't put pressure on yourself to 'fit' into their lives. The Ryders—and I'm including Cam in that family tree—are experts at making room for people exactly as they are."

"You're very wise, Theodora," I said after I let her words sink in.

"I know, Terrance." She grinned.

I rubbed my hand down my face. "I can't believe my mom blew my secret."

"That's why she's my favorite Tucker," Teddy said. A car horn honked, and she opened my driver's-side door. "That's my cue. I'll see you later."

"Thank you, Teddy. You're a good friend."

"I know," she said, and then she was gone. I sat in my truck a little longer, thinking about Cam and Riley and families and futures and love—all of it.

I'd never fallen out of love with Cam—not in all the time we were apart. Cam taught me what it was like to love and be loved. I took that with me around the world. I built upon it and every type of love I'd felt was compared to it, and nothing had ever come close—it was always her. It was always going to be her.

When I got out of my truck, I saw the soft, warm glow that was coming from Cam's kitchen.

I started walking toward it—like a moth to a flame. I paused when I saw Cam through her kitchen window. She had papers spread all over the kitchen counter and the cap of a highlighter in her mouth. Her laptop and iPad were set up near her, too. Working. Always working. Always worrying.

I walked a few more steps to her back door and tapped on it with my knuckles. She had music playing, so I couldn't hear it when she got up from the table, but a few seconds later, her back door cracked open.

"Hey," she said. "Everything okay?"

I nodded. "It is now. Can I come in?"

Her eyes widened for a second. "Um," she said. "Yeah, but I feel like I should warn you that I'm not wearing any pants."

I barked out a laugh. "Wasn't Gus just in here?"

"Whipped them off as soon as he left," she said.

"I think I can handle it," I said.

She pointed a pink highlighter at me. "No funny business."

"Me?" I said with faux shock. "Never."

Cam opened the door a little wider, making room for me to step in, and sure enough, her bare legs were on display from her feet all the way up to her thighs until they disappeared under an oversize Blink-182 T-shirt.

"How was the rest of your day?" she asked as she shut the door and made her way back to her seat and all of her papers. I sat in the seat next to her and draped my arm over the back of her chair.

"It was good," I said. "Ran into Teddy outside. She pulled the full name out on me."

Cam's eyes gleamed. "Well, Terrance," she said. Her tone was amused. "I think it's safe to say you'll never live that down now."

I reached over and flicked her nose. "Little shit," I said. "You wouldn't be happy if Teddy Andersen had her hands on ammunition about you, either."

"Fair," Cam said. "But I don't think your name is that much ammunition if I'm being honest."

"Should I start going by Terrance then?"

Cam laughed. "I don't think so—Dusty is definitely hotter." I raised an eyebrow at her and watched a blush color her cheeks. Fuck, I loved it when she blushed.

"How do you feel after Riley's soccer game this morning? And everyone knowing . . . about us?"

Cam bit her bottom lip and nodded. "I'm glad."

Pride rushed through me. "Really?" I asked. "There are no take-backs in this town."

"I know," Cam said. "I'm not worried about it. Are you?"

I shook my head. "Not even a little bit. This feels—we feel . . ."

"Permanent?" Cam said with a smile.

"Permanent," I agreed.

Cam leaned over to me and pressed her lips against mine. "I'm happy you're here," she said. "That we're here, together." I felt her words like the sun on my face.

"Me too," I said and then kissed her again. Longer. Slower, this time. I pulled Cam closer to me until she moved off of her chair and into my lap with her arms around my neck—all without taking her mouth off mine.

When she pulled away, I sighed, and she laughed a little. "You're a good kisser," she said. "I like kissing you."

"Then why are we stopping?" I asked and tried to bring her mouth to mine again, but she smiled and pushed at my chest, so I stopped.

"I just need to say this one thing, before I start kissing you again and the world stops and the likelihood that clothes end up on the floor gets higher." I gave her an amused smirk. "I don't want us to waste any more time. We've already spent years apart, growing up and becoming our own people. I think the fact that we still fit together is kind of a miracle, and I don't want to miss another moment."

"No more missing," I said with a grin. "You got it."

This time, when she brought her mouth back down on mine, neither of us pulled away. Her hands roamed up and down my torso. They held my face and grabbed at my shirt—like no matter where they were, it wasn't enough.

Cam kissed her way down the column of my throat until she found my tattoo, then she bit down hard and sucked. My head fell back on a groan. "Trying to leave a mark, angel?"

"Yeah," she said against my skin. "That was the whole point of this tattoo, remember? A mark that doesn't fade?" She sucked at it again.

"Fuck," I breathed. "I love you being territorial."

Cam's lips moved up the column of my neck again before she lifted her head and said, "Show me."

I gripped her waist hard as I stood up, and I set her down for half a second only so I could pick her up again in a way that would allow her to wrap her legs around me. My hold on her was firm as I walked us toward the couch.

"I like this," she said against my mouth. "I don't get picked up very often—tall girl problems."

"That's the last time you're ever going to say that," I said. "I'll pick you up all you want—toss you around a bit, too."

When we got to the front of the couch, I held Cam close as I lay down, so she would end up on top of me. "Smooth," she said against my mouth. "That was very smooth." I smiled.

I let my hands roam all over her body—very aware now that she wasn't wearing any pants and that I was getting uncomfortably hard in mine. God, her skin was so fucking soft. And she smelled so good. It was like everything about her was specifically designed to lure me in and make me want her.

And I wanted her so fucking bad.

Cam sat up, and I went with her, helping her pull her T-shirt over her head. She wasn't wearing a bra underneath it. "Fuck," I groaned. "You've just been bare under there the whole time?"

I kissed my way down her chest and drew one of her nipples into my mouth.

She inhaled sharply. "It's not my fault you didn't notice I wasn't wearing a bra." Her voice was shaky. I loved it.

"I was focused on you," I said. "Like a goddamn gentle-man." I switched to her other nipple and felt my cock jerk when she tugged on my hair.

"Is this you being a gentleman?" she asked.

"Not anymore," I said as I pushed her back and covered her body with mine. "I want to do distinctly ungentlemanly things to you."

"Like what?" Cam breathed.

I kissed her hard and pushed my tongue into her mouth, wanting to taste every corner of her. When I pulled back, I slipped one of my fingers into her mouth and let her suck on it before I dragged it down her neck, chest, and abdomen until I got to her black panties. I brushed my knuckle over the top of them. "In a little while, I'm going to bend you over this couch and fuck you from behind, but right now"—I moved her underwear to one side, and slid a finger inside of her— "I want to feel how fucking soaked you are for me."

Cam's back arched, and her eyes rolled back as I pushed my finger in and out of her. Fuck, the noises. "Needy girl," I said softly, and Cam nodded desperately.

"More, please," she gasped.

"More what, angel? Another finger? Or do you want my tongue?"

"Either. Both," she said. "I want it all."

I kissed her again and pulled her panties down her legs, but I didn't throw them across the room. I sat back on my knees and brought the finger that was inside of Cam up to my mouth. Just a little taste. "You're in charge here. Show me what you want me to do," I said as I licked her off my finger. "Show me how you touch yourself when you're thinking of me."

Cam looked up at me with hooded lids, but she did what I

said. My mouth watered as I watched her drag her fingers down her abdomen before they slipped inside of her. I moaned at the sight of it. I unbuttoned my jeans and pushed them and my briefs down enough that I could pull my dick out. While I watched her, I wrapped her underwear around my dick and gave myself a few hard strokes.

Both of us were breathing heavily, and I could hear my heartbeat in my ears. "Oh my god," Cam said. As she watched me use her panties to stroke my length, her fingers sped up on her clit and her hips jerked.

Before she could get much further, I grabbed her wrist and pulled her hand away. She let out a frustrated moan. "Dusty," she moaned, but she didn't look at me—her eyes were still on my dick, and they were heated as hell.

"You don't get to come unless it's on me," I said.

"Then get inside of me," she said. "I'm ready. I want you."

I stopped what I was doing and crawled my way up her body, and leaned down like I was going to kiss her. When she closed her eyes to meet me halfway, I slid her panties into her mouth instead. Her eyes opened immediately. "Remember what I said about rushing me?"

Cam's eyelids went heavy as she nodded, and I slid my finger back inside of her, and she moaned around her panties. "Then don't rush me. I like taking my time with you, angel. I like watching your eyes get heavy and your chest heave. I like watching goosebumps rise on your skin." I brought my thumb to her clit and pressed down. Cam jerked underneath me.

I started working her with my hand—fast, like she was doing to herself, and putting pressure on her clit. Her hips bucked, and muffled cries came from her mouth. "God, you're so needy," I said. "You're going to come already, aren't you? I can feel your pussy tightening around my fingers." I brought my other hand to the bottom of her abdomen and pushed down. Cam's entire body snapped, and her eyes went wide. I felt her pussy constrict. "Atta girl," I said. "Come all over my fingers." Her body jerked over and over again as she rode the wave of her orgasm, and I took in the view.

God, she was stunning.

When her body went boneless, I reached up and took her panties out of her mouth and tossed them across the room before I brought my mouth down hard on hers. She immediately opened for me, and our tongues tangled together.

"You did so good, baby," I said.

"God," Cam moaned. "I can't handle it when you talk to me like that."

"Like what?" I asked. I was grinning against her mouth.

"You know," she said. "You know exactly what you're doing." I got up onto my knees and brought Cam with me.

"Remember what I said about bending you over the couch?" I asked, and Cam nodded. "I want to do that now, if that's okay with you."

She laughed, and the sound was like fresh air in my lungs. "I'd like that," she said, and then she grabbed one of my hands and kissed my palm. "I like these—the tattoos." The hand she was holding had a rose on the back of it.

"You know where they look best?" I asked, and Cam tilted her head and nodded. I brought my hand up to her neck. "Right here." I felt her swallow under my touch. I squeezed and hauled her mouth to mine. "I'm about to jump over the back of this couch," I said. "And it's not going to be smooth or sexy."

"We'll see," Cam said with a grin. I kissed her one more

time before I put a hand on the back of the couch and pushed myself over—the same way I would hop a fence. "Hmmmm, I'd give it a seven out of ten," she said.

"Brat," I said as I wrapped my arms around her waist and pulled her over the back of the couch to join me. She wobbled when her feet hit the ground. "Feeling a little unsteady, angel?"

She gave me a playful slap on the arm. "Maybe if you didn't feel the need to show off all the time, I'd be able to stand."

"Don't worry," I said. "I've got you." I kissed her then, and she brought one of her hands to my aching cock. I gasped when she wrapped her hand around it and stroked me hard. "Fuck," I gritted out. I clutched her face in my hands and licked the side of her mouth as she did it a few more times.

"I want this inside of me," she said. "I want to feel you stretch me and fuck me from behind." Cam bit my bottom lip. "Please."

I brought my hands down to her waist and flipped her around. The front of her body fell over the couch as she gasped. I dropped to my knees behind her and licked up her center. "I just need a taste of your perfect cunt first," I said.

Cam moaned as my tongue went between her legs. "I think you like being on your knees for me," she said breathily.

"You're wrong, angel, I fucking *love* being on my knees for you," I said as I stood. I sunk my teeth into one of her ass cheeks on the way. I felt her shocked gasp rocket through her body. "Are you ready for me?"

"Yes, god, Dusty, please."

I gripped one side of her ass and started to ease my cock into her. "I'll go slow," I whispered in her ear. "It's going to feel deep like this, so I need you to tell me if it gets too intense, okay?"

Her body went rigid as I got farther inside of her. "Relax, angel. I've got you," I crooned and kissed her neck. "I've got you. You can take it, can't you?"

"Yes," Cam moaned.

"That's my girl," I said. "My perfect fucking girl." I looked down at where our bodies joined and cursed under my breath. I was the luckiest man alive—by a long shot.

My breath went ragged as I seated myself fully inside her. "Fuck, you feel so good." I started to move my hips, and I couldn't help the moan that came out of me.

"Louder," Cam said.

"You want to hear what you do to me, angel?" I said as my strokes got a little harder.

"Yes," Cam moaned. "I like it when you're loud."

"Fuck, baby," I moaned.

Cam backed her ass into me in time with my thrusts, and the strangled noise that came out of my throat was barely human. "That's right—fuck me back, I know you can."

After that, we devolved into moans and movements and sounds. Both of our gasps got quicker and higher as we raced toward the edge, ready to fall over at any moment.

I had enough consciousness to reach around to Cam's clit and put some pressure there—didn't want to leave my girl hanging.

"Yes, yes, yes," Cam chanted, and I felt the base of my spine tense. Cam tightened around my dick, and my vision started to go black at the sides.

"Fuck, angel, I'm going to come," I ground out. Her body

went rigid under my hands. She gripped me so fucking tight, and I almost didn't remember to pull out, but I came to at the last minute and liquid spilled all over her back.

"Shit," I breathed. "Holy shit."

Cam's body heaved. "How does it get better every single time?" she asked.

"Because it's us," I said. I leaned down and kissed her shoulder.

After we got cleaned up, I pulled Cam down on the couch with me and held her closer. "Dusty . . ." She trailed off.

"Talk to me, angel," I whispered with my lips in her hair.

"Will you stay over tonight?" she asked. "I want to wake up with you. I don't want to say goodbye."

"Me neither," I said.

Chapter 40

Cam

When I woke up the next morning, Dusty's arm was draped over my waist, so I slid out from under it as carefully as I could before getting out of bed. I didn't want to wake him. Yeah, we did get some sleep together, but only after we *slept* together one more time and took a shower before going to bed.

I moved Dusty's blond hair away from his face as he slept. In the quiet of the morning, everything I felt about Dusty almost overwhelmed me. I couldn't believe we did it—that we made it back to each other, that we made it back to each other ready—better, even.

I walked out to the kitchen and turned the coffee maker on. I looked around the house that had quickly become a home over the past few months. Even though it wasn't *technically* mine, it felt like it was. I couldn't imagine letting it go. Maybe I could buy it from whoever Anne left it to—maybe if they knew that someone was building a life here, they would let them stay.

Because I really wanted to live here. The truth of it in my gut was clear, after so many years of being unable to hear my own instincts. And another thing was clear, too: I wanted to work at Rebel Blue. I wanted to have my own piece of it like the rest of the people in my life did. I didn't want to stay in a job just because it offered security. Because the truth was, Rebel Blue had always offered me the most security, in all the ways that actually mattered. I wanted to give back to the place that had given so much to me. It had given me a family.

Once I had a cup of coffee, I pulled out my phone and checked the time. It was just after seven, which meant Gus would definitely be awake.

"Hello?" He picked up on the first ring.

"I'll do it," I said. "I'll take the job."

"Are you sure?" Gus asked.

"I'm sure," I said. "I'll call my firm tomorrow and put in my notice, and once I finish out my caseload, I'm all yours."

"Fuck yeah," Gus said. "Thank you, Cam."

"Thank you," I said. "I really needed this."

"I'll tell my dad, and we'll make things official as soon as we can. Do you want to come to the Big House for breakfast and celebrate?"

"I've got some things to do here, but I'll talk to you later, okay?"

"Okay, bye."

After Gus hung up the phone, I couldn't stop grinning. When did my life get so . . . good?

I didn't know how much time had passed when I heard my bedroom door open and Dusty's bare feet against the hardwood floors as he made his way out to the kitchen. He was just in his briefs, his hair was a disaster, and he was rubbing the sleep out of one of his eyes.

Beautiful.

Every time I saw more of him, I tried to catalog his tattoos and make note of my favorites—the dagger in the middle of his chest, the bee on his thigh, and the scorpion on his ribs. And, of course, the "A."

"Morning," he said when he saw me. A grin stretched across his face. "It broke my heart when you weren't there when I woke up, you know."

He walked behind me and draped his arms over my shoulders and pulled my back to his chest. "You were out cold, and I didn't want to wake you, and I had to call Gus."

I felt Dusty stiffen just slightly. "Is Riley okay?"

I nodded. "She's fine. Probably still asleep—she hates mornings—I had to call him about a job." I smiled.

Dusty kissed the side of my neck. "What kind of job?"

"A job at Rebel Blue. For me," I said.

Dusty lifted his head and looked at me, confused. I took a deep breath and started to explain. "Last night, Gus asked me to be Rebel Blue's lawyer—full-time—not just looking over stuff when they need it, but actually working for them.

"Gus only talked about a couple of things, but I know there's a million things I could do there. All the little things that slip through the cracks, like the liability waivers for guests at Baby Blue. The sanctuary is going to need someone's full attention when it comes to the back-end stuff, and I think I'd be really good at it."

"You would be," Dusty said.

"And you'd be okay with that? We'd probably work together a lot."

Dusty's lips stretched into a smile. "I can't imagine anything better, angel," he said with another kiss to my neck. "So did you accept?"

I turned around on my stool so I could wrap my arms around Dusty's waist. I liked him here in the morning—liked seeing what he looked like when he woke up. "I did," I said and laid my head on his chest—right over the top of the dagger. "And I'm going to talk to Anne about the house—see if there's any way I can buy it from her buyer or stay longer. This place just . . . means so much. It's finally something that feels like . . . my own. And I want to find a way to hold on to it."

"Oh." Dusty sounded surprised.

"Yeah, oh." I looked up at him, and he looked like he was about to say something, but then he yawned. "Need some coffee?" I asked.

He let out a puff of air. "Yeah, I had this woman wringing me dry all night."

I kissed his chest. "Sounds like you need to work on your stamina—build up that endurance."

"Is that so?"

"Yeah," I said. "Especially because she'd really like to do it again tonight, or you know . . . now." I licked up his chest and heard him inhale sharply.

"Now is good," he said. "Now is really good."

A little over an hour later, Dusty and I were at the grocery store. Neither of us really wanted to leave the other. I had things to do, so Dusty just decided to tag along.

"You buy name-brand cereal?" he asked as I pulled a box of Frosted Mini-Wheats off the shelf. "Fancy as hell."

"I think they taste different," I said with a shrug.

"That's because you've got that sophisticated palate, Ash." We went through every aisle in the grocery store, even though I didn't need to—I had a list—but I liked doing it. I liked every moment of us rediscovering each other—hearing all about his favorite snacks and preferred foods or whether or not he got the ick from eggs every once in a while.

When I grabbed a plastic container of pickles from the refrigerated section, Dusty did a dramatic gag. "Still not a fan?"

"No, pickles are rank, Ash."

"More for me." I shrugged and put them in the cart.

"Cam?" A woman's voice came from in front of us—her hair was darker than it used to be and cut short. She was wearing black jeans, black boots, and a white knit sweater.

"Chloe?" I said. My old high school teammate and Anne's granddaughter. That was ironic. "Oh my god, hi."

She walked toward me and pulled me into a hug, which was unexpected. I was awkward about it, but I hoped she didn't notice. "How are you?" I asked when she pulled back.

"Good," she said. "Hi, Dusty," she said, shifting her gaze to the man next to me, who seemed kind of . . . nervous.

"Hey, Chloe," he said. "Good to see you."

"What are you in town for?" I asked.

"Just a pit stop on my way to New York to see my mom. How are you liking the house?" Chloe asked me, but it looked like she was talking to both of us.

"It's perfect, really. It's such a great house, as you well know."

Chloe smiled warmly. "I love seeing you two together still," she said. "I always knew you'd make it. How long have you been married? Like five years now?"

My eyes widened. "Sorry?" I choked out.

"Oh." Chloe motioned between the two of us. "Sorry, I just assumed that you guys were married when Dusty bought the house."

"Bought the . . . house?"

I looked over at Dusty, who was looking at his boots.

"Oh, sorry, one sec." Chloe pulled out her phone. "It's my mom. I've gotta go. I'll be in town until Monday—maybe we can get coffee or something!"

"Yeah," I said, feeling slightly dazed. My voice felt far away. "Sure." Chloe gave both Dusty and me another quick hug and walked away, unknowingly leaving chaos in her wake.

I turned to Dusty slowly. "You . . . own my house?" There was hurt in my voice.

"Ash . . ." Dusty was looking at me like I'd just kicked him in the stomach. "I was going to tell you."

"When?" I asked. "When you made me fall in love with you again? What if I didn't? Were you going to kick me out?"

"Can I explain, please?" Dusty said. "Let's get your groceries, and we can talk about it at home."

"Whose home?" I asked. "Because apparently you own mine."

"It's not like that. It's never been like that."

"Well, I wouldn't know that, would I?" I spat. "Because you never told me."

"Please," he begged. "I don't want to do this here."

"Fine," I said and then pushed my cart to the front of the store to check out. I walked ahead of him and didn't look at him—not while we were checking out, not while we walked to the car or when he opened my door for me, and not for the entire drive back to my—sorry, his—house.

The silence was tense and heavy, until finally he spoke. "I bought the house five years ago." He sighed.

I folded my arms across my chest. "I got that part."

"Anne's kids wanted her to put it on the market because she couldn't take care of it. They had a buyer lined up who wanted to try and get the permits to tear the house down and develop on it—condos or some shit—and when my mom told me, I knew I didn't want that to happen."

"Why?"

"Because it was your dream house," he said. "Because every time I came home and I passed the turn that took me up the drive or when I parked here for a hike, I thought about you, and I didn't want to lose that. But also because I've watched places like this disappear around the world, and I didn't want that to happen to this house.

"So I called Anne, and told her I would buy it—that I would pay for someone to come and do the maintenance that she couldn't do anymore and that she could live here as long as she wanted."

"And she said yes?" I asked.

"And she said yes. She didn't really want to sell, but her kids and grandkids had moved all over the country, and they couldn't help her, so selling was the compromise. Me buying the house worked for her, and it worked for me. When I decided to come home, I knew I'd have the cabin to go to, and I would get a chance to do a lot of the maintenance myself."

"Why did you rent it to me when Anne moved into the assisted living facility, instead of moving into it yourself?"

"I couldn't imagine living in it without you," he said softly, rubbing his neck—rubbing the "A." "I don't know, Cam. I just wanted you to have it, I guess. I wanted you to have something that was your own."

"But this isn't mine." I gestured around the house. "I just went from being trapped in one situation with a man to another."

"That's not . . ." Dusty's nostrils flared. "That's not fair, Cam. I wasn't trying to trick you or trap you, I was trying to help without being weird and invasive. I didn't know we were going to rekindle things. I mean, I hoped that we could maybe try, but that wasn't the point of me renting you the house."

"Were you ever going to tell me?"

"Of course I was." He ran a hand through his loose blond hair. "I just didn't know when or how. I was going to do it earlier, but then we started picking things up, and I just wanted us to be stable—whether that was as friends or more."

"So when I asked you how you ended up in the cabin, you didn't think that was a good time to bring it up?"

"No," Dusty said. "I really didn't."

I felt overwhelmed. I felt mad and sad and frustrated, and I didn't want him here. I didn't want to be around him. I needed space.

"I need you to go," I said calmly.

"Cam . . ." Dusty tried to reach for me.

"You should go. Just leave. That's what you do, isn't it?"

"Please don't say that, Ash. I came back . . . for you."

That's when I delivered the landing blow. "Yes, you did. But you should have stayed gone."

Chapter 41

Cam

When I got in my car, I banged on the steering wheel a few times in frustration. God*dammit*. I turned my car on and drove straight for Rebel Blue. I needed to talk to someone. How did things get so messed up?

Yesterday, I thought Dusty and I had a guaranteed future. Today, I wasn't so sure. And it wasn't just about the house. Maybe I was wrong—maybe what I felt for him wasn't something new, built to last. Maybe these were the same feelings of that seventeen-year-old girl, so desperate to be loved, ricocheting back on me, and I couldn't see the reality in front of my face.

The thought made my stomach turn, and I started to question everything.

My thoughts blazed like a wildfire through my brain as I drove until I ended up on Wes and Ada's doorstep.

I probably should've called or texted first, but oh, well. I knocked on the door.

Wes opened it a few seconds later, wearing jeans and a

white T-shirt. His feet were bare, and his dog, Waylon, was at his side—like always.

"Cam?" There was worry in his voice. I could only imagine what I looked like. "What's wrong?" He stepped out onto the porch and put his hands on my shoulders, steadying me.

"Is Ada home?" I asked.

"She had a client meeting—I can call her. Find out when she'll be back?"

"No," I said, deflating a little. "It's, um, it's fine. I'll just talk to her later."

Wes's eyes were brimming with concern. "Do you want to come in? I'm no Ada, but I'm a good placeholder until she gets here."

I chewed on my bottom lip for a second before I nodded. Wes led me inside, and Waylon licked my hands on the way in. Ada and Wes had slowly been remodeling this house on Wes's slab of Rebel Blue. They weren't done yet, but every time I came here, there was something new to explore.

Wes led me toward the couch, and I couldn't help but flop down on it. He sat in the big comfy chair across from me and pulled out his phone. "I'll text Ada and tell her you're here," he said.

"Sorry for barging in," I responded, suddenly self-conscious.

"Don't apologize," Wes said. "What's going on?"

I grabbed one of the pillows off the couch and hugged it over my face. "Dusty," I said into the pillow.

"Sorry," Wes said. "I didn't quite catch that, but I think you might have said Dusty?" I nodded. "Ah, I heard you two were canoodling."

I took the pillow off my face and glared at him. "Canoo-dling, really?"

Wes smiled, dimples on display—my daughter got those, too—and shrugged. "You are, though, aren't you?"

"Maybe," I said. "But also maybe not anymore."

"Ah," Wes said like he understood. "I see. Wanna talk about it?"

I let out a long sigh and nodded. "I don't know. Things were going well—I thought we were going to make it this time. But then today, I got this bomb dropped on me, and I'm not handling it well."

"What kind of bomb?" Wes asked.

"A big, destructive, and out-of-the-blue bomb that is making me wonder if everything was too good to be true."

"Does he have a family in Connecticut or Australia or something?" Wes asked.

I shook my head. "Nothing like that."

"But it's gotta be pretty bad for you to be second-guessing, right? From what I've heard, things seem to be going pretty well."

"What have you heard?" I asked, raising my eyebrows.

Wes shrugged. "Ada says you're happy. Riley wouldn't shut up about him when she slept over a few weeks ago. I don't know—it makes sense to me that you guys found your way back to each other. I always envied you guys' friendship in high school and then you started kissing and shit, and I thought you'd be together forever."

"Wes, you had more friends than anyone I knew."

"But I didn't really have a best friend like you and Dusty or Teddy and Emmy or Brooks and Gus. I wanted that. I always thought you guys were lucky to have it. And now I do have a best friend, and I know I was right to want it."

My heart softened for him. Wes loved Ada so loudly and so much.

"Well," I said, "it's not really going well anymore. I found out this morning that he bought the house I'm living in like five years ago, and he didn't tell me."

Wes blinked slowly. "And this is a bad thing because?"

"Because he lied about it. Because that means it's not really mine, and I truly still don't have anything of my own, and the house that was supposed to be my fresh start actually came with its own baggage."

"Okay . . ." Wes replied slowly. "But you're renting it anyway, so it wouldn't have been yours either way, right?"

I worried my bottom lip. "That's not the point. The point is that he let me believe that Anne owned it this whole time even though he did. Plus, he knew how much I loved the house, so I don't like that he bought it with me in mind."

"Do you know he did?"

"He said that wasn't the only reason but that it was one of them. He said he didn't move in because he didn't want to live there without me."

Wes nodded again, and it looked like he was fighting a smile. "So you're mad because your high school slash current boyfriend bought you a house and let you live in it when you needed a place to go?"

"That's a major oversimplification, Weston," I asserted.

"Sometimes these things *are* simple, Cam." He shrugged. "Obviously, I don't have the whole story from either of you, but, I don't know, this feels like a hiccup, not a relationship altering or ending situation.

"Should he have told you about the house? Definitely. I think it would've been better for him to be up front when he agreed to let you rent it. But if he did tell you, would you have moved in?" I didn't know the answer to that—probably not. I was so afraid of getting close to him then. Wes must've seen the look on my face because he kept talking.

"I get wanting to have something to call your own—I really do, Cam. And I know there's a lot of other stuff wrapped up in that feeling—especially after what you went through. But I've also been the person who's just trying to show the scared and fiercely independent woman how much he loves her. And sometimes"—he smiled—"it doesn't go according to plan and you end up scaring her instead of winning her over."

"I'm not scared," I said. "I'm mad."

"So you can tell me with one hundred percent certainty that the combination of Dusty buying that house because of you, then spending more time with him again, and the potential of a future where you're together and happy doesn't scare you even a little bit? It just makes you mad?"

"You're taking a lot of liberties with this little advice column you've got going on, Wes," I said with an eye roll.

"Cam." His face was thoughtful, his voice earnest. "I love you. You're like another sister to me. When everything happened on your wedding day, I was sad for you, but I also kind of felt . . . relieved. Like I didn't have to pretend that I was okay with you settling for less than you deserved anymore." I swallowed hard. "But the thought of you and Dusty finally finding your way back to each other after all this time and letting this get in the way of that breaks my heart in two.

"I think you need to talk to Dusty about the house thing—

tell him that secrets like that won't fly in the future. Talk about what it means for your relationship right now and in the future, but I don't think you need to use this as an excuse to leave him first."

My head snapped toward him. "What did you say?"

"It's easier to be the one that leaves than be the one that gets left. I think you and Ada think similarly that way, but both of you have the same problem: You wait for the other shoe to drop, even though that's never going to happen. Dusty's putting down roots. You have roots already, and now both of you finally have a chance to let those roots grow together, to get so fucking tangled up in each other that you can't possibly part again, and that's a beautiful thing."

"It's a scary thing," I whispered.

"See? I told you that you were scared."

"How did you know?" Wes held his phone up for me to see. It was the message exchange between him and Ada.

WES: Cam is here. I think it's about Dusty.

ADA: I'm on my way home. Don't let her talk herself out of him because she's scared.

The front door to their house opened then, and Ada stormed in. She was breathing heavily, and her hair was mussed. "Don't you dare fucking give up on you and Dusty, Cam, I swear to god" were the first words out of her mouth.

"Wes did a good job at talking me down." Ada smiled. She walked over to where Wes was sitting on the chair and kissed him on the temple.

"Good," she said. "I knew I could count on him. He knows a thing or two about skittish women."

Wes smiled up at Ada, and my heart ached.

"So what should I do?" I asked.

"I think you already know what you want to do. I think you just need to say it."

"I want to be with Dusty," I said.

"That's our girl," Ada said. "Now go get him."

Chapter 42

Dusty

There was a knock at my door. It couldn't be her, could it?
I let out a sigh and dragged my feet over to my door. It
wasn't her. Cam had a long cooling-off period—who knew
when she'd be ready to talk to me.

God, I didn't know how things went so wrong so fast. We
were having such a good day. I almost told her I loved her over
a container of pickles, for god's sake. Maybe I should've.
Maybe if I'd said it, things would be different.

Maybe she'd be able to see the future that I saw with her.

There were a lot of people I'd be shocked to find at my door
on a Saturday afternoon, but I was never expecting to find
Amos Ryder standing there.

"Uh, hi," I said.

"Hey, Dusty. Want to go for a walk with me?"

I couldn't say no. Could I?

No, I couldn't.

"Uh, sure," I said. "Let me put some shoes on." I grabbed
the pair of boots closer to the door and slid them over my

socks. I stumbled a little bit, nervous about what was about to happen on this little stroll.

I had a leather jacket hanging by the door, so I slid that on, too, before meeting Amos on my stoop.

"Nice day," he said with a smile at me. He had the kindest eyes.

I nodded. It was a nice day. There was still plenty of that winter chill in the air, but it was nice and warm when you stood in the sun. I loved being outside. I was like a sunflower; I always turned to face the sun and bask in it for just a second.

"There's a nice walking trail off the big trailhead," I said. "It's low and there isn't any elevation gain."

"Sounds good," Amos said, and we started walking. The earth crunched under our feet. "I was happy to see that you've taken a couple Saturdays off."

Usually, I worked at Rebel Blue every day. Gus insisted I have some sort of break day, but I normally took that on Wednesdays or Thursdays. Until recently, I didn't mind working the whole weekend if it meant someone else didn't have to. Now, I wanted to be at soccer games or sleeping in with Cam.

"Yeah," I said. "Thanks for letting me."

"I was wondering what might've inspired that change in routine," Amos said next to me. The tone in his voice told me he already knew.

"Are you here to talk to me about Cam?" I asked and then muttered, "Word sure travels fast around here."

Amos chuckled. "I didn't plan on stopping by, but I was visiting with Anne when her granddaughter stopped by, so I heard a very interesting story about home ownership."

"Ah," I said. "I didn't know you and Anne were close."

"I've known her a long time," he said. "She was my babysitter if you can believe that." God, this town was so complicated.

"I actually can," I said. "I don't think there's much you could tell me about the relationships in Meadowlark that I wouldn't believe."

"But you still came back," Amos said.

I shrugged. "Well, that was thanks to Gus." Which was true, but his job offer was just the catalyst. I'd wanted to come home for a long time. I finally wanted a chance to settle into a life. But now I didn't know if the life I had always dreamed about finding when I returned home was just that: a dream.

"Rebel Blue wouldn't run the way it does without you, and you've already put in so much work on the sanctuary. I appreciate you. I'm glad we have you for the long haul."

"Thank you, sir," I said. I didn't know I needed Amos's reassurance about my work, my commitment, until he gave it to me. But with his words, I felt my shoulders relax.

"You're a good man, Dusty. Your dad would be proud of you, you know."

My head filled with memories of my dad, how much I wished he was here. He would know what to do and what to say, but I couldn't say much after that, so we walked in silence for a bit. I listened to the noises in the trees and focused on the cool air filling my lungs.

After a while, when we had made it to the actual walking path, Amos broke the silence. "Cam is like a daughter to me. I love her like one, and I worry about her like one. It killed me to watch her go through what happened on her wedding day, and she's been even heavier on my mind since then."

I nodded. "I know."

"And so when something happens to her, it takes up a lot of space in this old head. I think about it all the time. I wonder what I can do to help without being an overbearing old man." I was about to tell him he wasn't that old, but he kept going. "Usually, I settle on talking—trying to pull out some sage advice that might turn on a lightbulb or open a new door. And most of the time, it works. They find their way, whatever that way might be.

"And Cam is no different. I gave her advice about you last month—told her that it was okay to go after it—go after the future she really wants." I swallowed. I didn't know Amos was invested in this—in us. "I'm hoping I wasn't wrong in saying that."

Okay, ouch.

"No, sir," I said. "I want a future with her. I—I love her. I've loved her forever."

"That's what I thought," Amos said. I could hear a smile in his voice. "Is it okay if I give you a little advice, then?"

"Please," I said honestly. I trusted Amos—I valued his thoughts and opinions, and I knew he did his best to look out for everyone. Cam, my mom, and now me, apparently.

"Be careful how much space you give her," Amos said. "She needs some, but at the end of the day, it's more important for Cam to know that she's loved."

"I understand, sir," I said.

"Something else I've learned? There is a time to let things go, but you also have to know when to hold on to something tightly. There's value in clinging to it and not letting it get away from you. The bravest thing you can do when you love someone is work hard to keep them—to hold on to them with everything you've got—and even when you loosen your grip, you don't let go."

I let his words sink in. I had told Cam that she was right to leave all those years ago, and I still believed that. But this felt different. It felt all sorts of wrong. *Even when you loosen your grip, you don't let go.* How could I show Cam that I wanted to be her anchor, her steady shelter in the storm, but I was never going to drag her down? I just wanted to be her true north, just like she had always been mine, the light that guided me home.

"I know you're a hard worker, Dusty, I see it every day, so what are you going to do to make sure Cam doesn't get away again?"

Chapter 43

Cam

When I woke up the next morning, my bed felt empty without Dusty in it, and he'd only stayed over one night.

Ada and Wes were mostly right. I had a right to be mad at Dusty, but the whole house situation didn't need to be the thing that did us in because I was too stubborn to talk about it.

The orange glow coming in my window told me it was early. I glanced over at the clock next to my bed. Six-thirty. I sighed and rolled out of bed. Half of me hoped that when I went out to my kitchen, Dusty would be there, drinking some coffee and ready to call me out on my bullshit.

But he wasn't.

When I looked out my back window, normally I could see his house, but this morning, it looked like there was something taped there.

What the hell?

I slipped on a pair of shoes and walked out the back door and to the outside of the window. In black Sharpie, in handwriting I would know anywhere, "Ash" was written on the back of the envelope.

I tore it off the window and opened it immediately. I didn't even care that it was cold and that I wasn't wearing anything but my pajamas. The first thing I saw was a note and then a stack of papers that were tri-folded together.

I went for the note first.

> *Ash,*
> *I know I should've told you about the house. I'm sorry*
> *I made you feel like it couldn't be yours because of me.*
> *I hope this makes up for it. The box is for you.*
> *I love you.*
> *Dusty*

I looked down and saw the box from Dusty's coffee table at my feet. I felt tears well up behind my eyes. *I love you.* I focused on those three words until my vision got blurry. Then I picked up the box and brought it back inside. I set it on the kitchen table and sat down. I thought I would have to work up some courage to open it, but I didn't; I dove right in.

When I opened it, I noticed that all the notes had been unfolded and stacked neatly, making it easy for me to flip through them.

> *Ash,*
> *I'm at a ranch in Northern California right now. The*
> *cook asked me what the A tattoo on my neck meant. I told*
> *her it stood for "adulterer," but she didn't get the joke.*
> *Thinking of you,*
> *Dusty*

I smiled, and my hand found the spot on my hip where my tattoo was. I kept it there as I kept reading.

> Ash,
> *"Dashboard Confessional" came on the radio today.*
> *I sang every word.*
> Dusty

The next one I read was written on a postcard from Mexico.

> Ash,
> *I'm at a horse rescue this winter. It's owned and run by women, and they don't take any shit. The owner, Paola, is what I think you'll be like in your sixties—fierce as hell.*
> *I wish you could meet her.*
> Dusty

> Ash,
> *Every once in a while, I have a day where I miss you so much it actually hurts to breathe. Today was one of those days. I hope you're okay.*
> Dusty

> Ash,
> *I went to a farmers market in Calgary this morning. I was this close to sending you a box of the most beautiful heirloom tomatoes I've ever seen. The other shoppers probably thought I was insane because I was just grinning at tomatoes like an idiot.*
> Dusty

Ash,

Today, I saw a woman in the airport with hair like yours. For a second, I thought it was you. Sometimes, missing you doesn't hurt. Today isn't one of those days.

Dusty

Ash,

I'm so mad at you for leaving, but I hope you found your home. I haven't found mine yet.

Dusty

I pulled note after note out of the box. There had to be hundreds in here.

Eventually, I saw the words "change of property ownership," on a paper near the bottom. I tore it out of the box. It also had the address to my house, and "deed," and I thought I was going to fall to the ground. Did he . . . did he just give me this house?

I looked over at Dusty's house, and without thinking, started making my way to it. When I got to his door, I pounded on it harder than I meant to.

He opened the door within a second. He looked shocked to see me. "What the hell is this?" I asked, holding up the stack of papers—the note that was taped to my door included.

"I think the technical term is a love declaration or grand gesture," he said. "And also a deed."

"What the hell is wrong with you?" I asked. "You think you can just give me a house and tell me you love me and all is forgiven?"

"No," he said. "But I thought it could be a good start." He moved to the side of the door, inviting me in, but I didn't move.

He was wearing a leather jacket but shrugged it off and brought it around my shoulders. The action brought us closer together, but I still didn't move.

"Cam," he breathed. "I'm sorry I didn't tell you about the house. I know I should've. I know it was crazy for me to buy it five years ago with you in mind. I know the fact that I've been in love with you since I was seventeen is kind of ridiculous, and I know you're mad at me, and you have every right to be. But, god, you are everything to me. You always have been, you always will be.

"I don't even remember what my life was like before you were in it—I don't even think I want to. It killed me when you left, but I don't know, I just felt like it was the right thing to let you go, but I never let go of hope—hope that we'd find our way back to each other after it all and hope that I'd have the opportunity to never let you go. I feel like I've spent fifteen years preparing for this moment, when I could tell you that, without a doubt, I want to be with you forever. I want to wake up with you every day. And that means that I also want to be part of Riley's life.

"I want to go to Riley's soccer games and carry her to bed when she falls asleep on the couch."

My breath was shaky as I exhaled.

"I've always wanted everything with you, and I'm sorry that I got so many steps ahead, but I promise, I'll give you as much time as you need. The house is yours. No strings. I'll move out of here if you want me to. I want to do this on your terms, Cam."

"This note says you love me," I whispered.

Dusty brought his hands up to my face and forced me to look at him. "I do love you," he said. "I love you madly and deeply. I love you in ways that people don't believe exist in real life. I love you for who you've been and who you are and who you're going to be, Ash."

My throat tightened, and it got even harder for me to speak.

"I—I love you, too," I stammered out as tears started to cascade down my cheeks. "In all the same ways."

Dusty smiled softly. "That feels like cheating," he said. "Like you're just copying off my paper on the love confession thing."

"Well," I said, "it's the only time I ever have, and the only time I ever will, so soak it in."

"Smartass," he said, and then brought his mouth down on mine. We kissed in the light of dawn. A new day in Meadowlark—a new beginning—the promise of bigger things yet to come.

It was a new beginning for us, too.

Epilogue

Dusty

Six Months Later

Cam had set up her office for the day on the picnic table right outside the back door of the Big House. She was on her laptop, totally focused on what she was doing, so she didn't hear or see me walk up to her. A few months ago, Cam left her firm in Jackson Hole and started running the administrative and logistics back end of Rebel Blue Ranch's new horse sanctuary. Her legal background made her a godsend with all the nonprofit forms and requirements. She was great at fielding rescue requests and fundraising for veterinary care. Plus, since I did the actual horse parts of the horse sanctuary—taking care of them once they got here—I got the best co-worker out of the deal.

"Hey," I said with a kiss on top of her head. She jumped a little, surprised.

"Hi," she said, looking up at me with a smile. "What are you doing here already?"

"It's three-thirty, angel. We gotta go."

Her brown eyes widened, and she checked the clock in the corner of her laptop. "Oh my god," she said. "How did that happen?"

"What are you working on?" I nodded toward her laptop.

"There's a bunch of old rodeo horses from Cody that ended up in a kill pen. Amos wants them, so I'm trying to figure out how to get them here."

"Do we need to postpone?" I asked, rubbing the back of her neck with one of my hands. I felt her relax and lean into my touch.

"No," she said, shaking her head. "Give me a few minutes, and I'll meet you at the truck."

I nodded. I leaned down to kiss her. I still couldn't believe I got to do this all the time, after all these years. "You got it, wife." I kissed her again, and I felt her smile against my mouth.

"I love you," I said when I pulled myself away.

"I love you, too."

Cam and I got married at the courthouse last week—just the two of us and Riley. I asked her a million times if she wanted a big wedding, or any sort of wedding at all, and she said no every time. I asked her again last week, and she said that she wanted to get married right then.

I'd been waiting to marry her for fifteen years, so I said hell yeah. Every part of it was simple and intimate and perfect. We hadn't told anyone yet, and luckily, the clerk at the courthouse was new in town, so he probably didn't know about his unofficial duty to keep the ladies at the post office informed of everything inside the court walls.

Emmy and Luke were getting married—finally—next week, so we would tell them after. Or they would probably figure it out after we completed the task we were headed to do today.

When we walked through the front door of the tattoo parlor, Shannon was waiting for us. "You're late," he said, but he was smiling.

Every time I walked in to this place, I was catapulted back to that hot summer day, when two kids who loved each other made a stupid but badass decision together. And lucky for them, it ended up working out. It only took a few years, an unexpected pregnancy, a failed wedding, and traveling to five continents for it to do so.

"We're two minutes late," I said with an eye roll.

"Still late," he said, but then crossed the lobby to hug each of us. "You guys ready?"

"So ready," Cam said, then she looked over at me. "Are you?"

"I've been ready for fifteen years, angel." I leaned over and kissed her temple. Every time I touched her, she leaned into me like there was some sort of magnetic pull between us. It pulled us together through time and space. It brought us here, and it would take us through the rest of our lives.

When Cam's eyes were on me, all I wanted to do was kiss her. So I did.

Shannon cleared his throat. "Y'all are worse now than you were when you were teenagers," he grumbled. "Whoever's first go sit in the chair. I don't have all day."

Cam laughed when I pulled away. Her cheeks were red. I wanted to kiss those, too. "I'll go first," she said, and I raised my eyebrows at her. "What?" she asked. "You went first last time."

Hand in hand, we walked toward Shannon's tattoo booth. Cam took the tattoo chair, and I took the one next to it on her right side, so I could still hold on to her.

Shannon got his stencil ready—a simple black line—and wrapped it around Cam's ring finger. When he pulled off the stencil, I had a hard time swallowing. There it was, the thing that would be the physical manifestation of my promise to Cam.

A reminder that I was lucky enough that my first love also got to be my last.

Shannon turned on his tattoo gun, and Cam squeezed my hand she was holding when it met her skin.

"I've got you, Ash," I said softly.

"Permanent?" she asked.

"Permanent," I agreed. Then she pulled me toward her, so she could kiss the "A" tattoo on my neck, and my heart was filled to the brim with everything I felt for her. Camille Ashwood was the love of my life. I loved her with every part of me.

"I love you," I said. Was I about to cry? From the way my eyes were welling up, I would say yes. "I'll love you until we're dust."

"Until we're dust," Cam said back, and I kissed her again. God, I never wanted to stop kissing her.

"And even after."

Acknowledgments

I'm still not all the way convinced that I know how to write a book, so it feels incredibly strange to be writing the acknowledgments for not only my fourth one but also the end of the series that started this whole thing.

It wouldn't be a Lyla acknowledgment section if I didn't thank my parents first. Mom and Dad, thank you for unconditionally supporting everything I've ever done and for proudly telling anyone who will listen that your favorite (only) daughter writes romance novels (and thank you for never reading them).

On that note, thank you to my brothers for hand-selling multiple copies of my books without ever having read them. You guys are real ones for that. Thank you for being both the first people to humble the hell out of me and also the first to brag about my accomplishments.

I look up at the sky every day and thank whatever it is that's out there that you're my family. My biggest dream is to make you proud.

Stella, my girl, we did it. Thank you for being my constant companion through Rebel Blue Ranch and for what's coming next. You are my greatest comfort.

Thank you to my forever gal, Lexie. Meadowlark and Rebel Blue Ranch would not exist without you. Thank you for being part of every high and low on this journey. I've said it before, and I'll say it again: Your belief in me could move mountains, and for me, it has.

Sydney, thank you for celebrating with me on the good days and holding me together on the bad ones. Sharing this part of my life with you has been one of my greatest joys. Thank you for being all in.

Jess, the world's best agent, thank you for seeing something in these books and in me. There is no one out there who is better suited to champion my stories than you. Thank you for being my fiercest protector. I love you.

Emma, there has not been a day that's passed since you came into my life that I haven't thought to myself how grateful I am for you. You are an absolute powerhouse of an editor. Thank you for handling me and my stories with so much care and compassion. I want to do this with you forever.

Thank you to Hannah and Becs for believing in me when I can't remember how to do it myself.

Thank you to my team at The Dial Press for giving my books the most loving home.

Angie, this series has come a long way from that hotel room in Dublin. Thank you for being here every step of the way.

Thank you to *Captain America: Winter Soldier*. Honestly, thank you to all three movies in the Captain America franchise, and, as always, Reese's Peanut Butter Cups.

The most special thank you, of course, goes to you, dear reader. For those of you who have been here since *Done and Dusted* was a self-published debut from a no-name gal and for those of you who have saddled up along the way. The greatest joy of my life has been sharing this world with you.

Thank you for telling your friends about my books. Thank

you for spending your time creating beautiful things inspired by them. Thank you for loving them loudly. I'm a better author because of you, and Rebel Blue Ranch is a better place because of you. Thank you. For all of it.

Cheers to you and, of course, Rebel Blue.

WILD AND WRANGLED

LYLA SAGE

Dial Delights

*Love Stories
for the
Open-Hearted*

A Wedding

Emmy

I leaned forward in my saddle as Maple made her way up our last steep incline before we made it to my favorite ridgeline at Rebel Blue Ranch. It was early—really early. Normally, you'd have to drag me out of my bed kicking and screaming to be up at this ungodly hour. But not today. Today was different.

Today, I was getting married.

I stayed at my dad's house last night—yes, there was that whole "bride and groom can't see each other before the wedding" bullshit, but also because I wanted to spend time with my dad and have a sleepover with my friends. I wanted to wake up in the house I grew up in one more time before it all changed. Mostly, though, it was because I wanted this—a ride through Rebel Blue Ranch with my best girl.

Today was going to be one of the greatest days of my life. I already knew that. I knew that marrying Luke Brooks was already the best thing to ever happen to me—that I'd spend the day surrounded by the people I loved and who loved me the most.

Right now, though, all I wanted was the ground below me, the blue sky above me, the mountains behind me, and the horizon in my sight line. And I wanted to talk to one person—even though that one person couldn't talk back.

Maple and I broke through the trees to make it to the top of Rebel Blue's North Ridge. The wind whipped my long brown hair behind me and around my face. I gave Maple's sides a small squeeze, urging her forward. I loved it up here—on top of the world. I took it all in as Maple walked toward a wild rosebush about fifty yards ahead.

I could see the Big House in the distance—along with the small cabin that I stayed in when I came home. It was only a few years ago, but it felt like a lifetime. The vast expanse of Rebel Blue never failed to make my heart feel like it was too big for my chest to contain. I could almost feel it pushing on my rib cage—begging to be set free to fly through Rebel Blue.

Maple stopped when we made it to the small hitching post that my dad had put here over two decades ago. I didn't come up here as often as I should, but he visited every single day—without fail.

I took my foot out of its stirrup and swung my leg around, easily dismounting Maple, as natural as taking a breath. I appreciated that ease even more now, because I knew how it felt when that comfort was taken away—when you lost the part of yourself that you thought was so tightly woven into your being that you didn't even know it *could* be taken away.

My boots hit the ground with a familiar crunch, and I wrapped Maple's get-down rope around the hitching post. I gave her a few rubs before I opened one of my saddlebags and pulled out a few wildflowers I'd grabbed on our ride this morning.

I inhaled deeply, basking in what it felt like when the cool morning air hit my lungs.

"Hi, Mom," I whispered as I lowered to my knees and set the flowers at the base of her headstone—a small but beautiful slab of agate engraved with "Stella Rhodes Ryder. Beloved. Forever and always." My mom's ashes were scattered all around Rebel Blue, but some of them were here—at Rebel Blue's highest point, along with some roses.

Unlike my dad, my brothers, Luke, and even Aggie and Dusty, I didn't have any memories of my mom. All I knew about her was what I'd been told or what I could see in pictures. I'd always thought I looked like my dad because I looked so much like Gus, and Gus was a carbon copy of Amos Ryder, but both of them told me I looked like my mom—that I had her messy hair and her eyes; they weren't the same color, but my dad said they were wild and free like hers. He said he saw her in me—in my stubbornness, in my determination, and in my softness, too.

"I'm getting married today," I said to her headstone. I looked down at the gold wedding band—the one my dad used to propose to her—adorning my left ring finger. "To Luke Brooks. You knew his dad, Jimmy. And probably his mom and stepdad, too. He's not like Jimmy or Lydia, though. He's kind and open-hearted and reliable. And he loves me in a way I didn't really think was possible."

The wind stirred around me again. "And he's really handsome, too," I said with a smile. "I wish you were here. We miss you a lot," I said. And I did. Not in the same way as everyone else did, but I missed her in my way. "Dad, especially."

Him, the most.

"He loves Luke," I told her. "He loved him before I did. But he's like that, you know? He loves people in a way I don't understand, but I think you probably do.

"Everyone else is good, too," I said, giving her an update. "I have a sneaking suspicion that Teddy and Gus are keeping a secret from us until after the wedding." Mine and Teddy's periods had been synced up for fifteen years, so I knew when she missed one, and then two. She also touches her stomach a lot. "I'm happy for her and Gus, even though I have to pretend that kid was conceived by immaculate conception. Ada and Wes finished renovating their home—it's beautiful. They put three of your paintings in it.

"Dusty and Cam got married," I said. "They think no one knows, but this is Meadowlark, and they're our family, so of course we know." I smiled to myself, thinking about the black ink around their ring fingers that they thought no one would notice. "We're waiting for them to tell us, though.

"Aggie and Hank are doing well. They're happy, so you can tell Renny that if you see him—that Aggie misses him but that she's happy.

"And Riley," I said. "Riley is everyone's pride and joy, but you already know that."

I looked up at the sky and closed my eyes—letting Rebel Blue wrap around me. Sometimes, when I came up here, I felt like I could feel her—like she was here with me. Today was one of those days.

I don't know how long I stayed that way, but after a while, I heard Maple start to scoot behind me. That meant someone else was here, or they would be soon.

When I looked behind me, I saw my dad's unmistakable black cowboy hat making its way toward me on the back of his

black and white painted horse. I started to stand, but he motioned for me to stay where I was.

Once Cobalt was secure on the hitching post with Maple,
my dad walked over, putting his denim-clad knees on the
ground next to me. His movements were slower than they
used to be, and I had to squeeze my eyes shut for a second and
shake my head a little to get the thoughts of him getting older
out of there.

"Mornin', Spud," my dad said as he snaked an arm around
my shoulders and kissed my temple.

"Morning," I said, and then both of us let the silence fall. I
wondered what he was thinking about, whether it was hard
for him to be here with her or if it was one of those things that
he'd done so many times it had become easy. Both me and my
brothers had asked him if he ever thought he'd try again, find
someone later in life that he could spend the years with. We
were worried he was lonely.

"This is what I'm meant for," he had said. "This life. With
the three of you. This family is my happily ever after. I've
never wanted anything else. I miss your mom every day, and I
wish she was still here, but that doesn't mean I don't love what
my life has become—that I haven't found happiness and joy
and love, that I'm not fulfilled and content."

"Hey, Stel," my dad's gravelly voice whispered next to me,
bringing me back to the present. I watched one of his weathered hands reach out and press into the ground in front of
him. He picked up some of the dirt with his hands and let it
fall through his fingertips. "Our baby is getting married today."

That's when it happened—the lump in my throat rose and
I couldn't swallow it down.

"She'd be so proud of you, Spud," my dad said. "So proud of the woman you've become."

"You think so?" I choked out.

"Know so," my dad said. I could hear the smile in his voice. "She would've loved today. She loved weddings. At Renny and Aggie's, she danced until she dropped—lucky me—right into my arms."

I thought about the picture of my parents that my dad kept on his nightstand—his hands around her waist, his lips on her temple. Her eyes on the camera and his on her. In my head, I could see them smiling and laughing and dancing the night away.

"I'm sorry she's not here," I said.

"Me too, Spud, me too." He sighed. It was silent for a few beats before my dad said, "I'm surprised you're up this early—of your own free will anyway."

"I wanted to talk to her," I said. "And I couldn't sleep. Too many things rattling around in my head, I guess."

"Good things?" my dad asked.

"The best things," I said truthfully. All night, I thought about Luke and me. I thought about our lives up to this point—how we had gotten here and how unexpected and perfect it was. I thought about what our lives would be like fifty years from now. "I can't wait to marry him, Dad."

My dad chuckled. "That's a good sign. I'm glad I don't have to figure out how to smuggle you out of here."

I laughed. "You'd do that?"

"I'd do anything for you, Clementine," he said. I looked over at him, his green eyes earnest and kind and thoughtful. "I love you, Spud." I leaned my head on his shoulder like I'd done a million times before, but this time was special, and I was happy I had it. He hummed a tune—"Oh My Darlin' Clementine"—as we sat together. I memorized what this moment felt like, so I could tuck it away close to my heart after it was over.

There was more rustling behind us. "I couldn't keep them away," my dad said. "I hope that's okay."

I turned to see my brothers—Gus on Scout and Wes on Ziggy—getting closer to us.

It was more than okay.

"What's the verdict?" Wes called from atop his horse. "Are we runaway bride-ing it?"

A laugh bubbled out of me, and I shook my head. "This bride is staying firmly in place."

"Are you sure?" Gus asked. "We all know I can take Brooks in a fight if it comes to that."

I rolled my eyes as both of them dismounted. "That wasn't a fair fight," I said. "He didn't even try to hit you back."

"Still counts," Gus said.

Wes crouched down next to me. "Hey, Mom," he said softly. "Miss you."

Gus didn't say anything—he just kissed his fingertips before pressing them to the top of our mother's headstone.

"I love you guys," I blurted out, and tears pricked at the back of my eyes. "Like really really love you." Thinking back, I can't believe there was a time when I wanted to be away from Rebel Blue and Meadowlark. From my family. That thought felt crazy to me now.

Wes ruffled my hair. "We love you, too, weirdo."

"What do you say, Clementine?" Gus reached his hand down to help me up, and I took it. "Should we get you to this wedding?"

I nodded with a grin.

"Before we do," my dad said, "you know, this ridge runs pretty flat for a while. It's nice and soft, too." I knew where he was going with this, and my grin got wider. Wes and Gus got it, too, and after all of us pressed our hands into my mom's headstone one more time, we got on our horses.

My dad led the way on Cobalt, Gus and Wes followed behind him, and I brought up the rear. That wouldn't last very long, though. Maple and I would have no issues kicking all three of these men's asses. Cobalt kicked up into a trot, so the rest of us did, too, and then to a lope.

This was one of the best feelings in the world—flying along a trail at Rebel Blue on the back of a horse. There was a time when I didn't know if I'd ever do this again, but here I was—steering Maple to the side of the line and pushing her into a gallop to pass by everyone else.

I leaned forward in my saddle and let Maple work. The four beats of her hooves hitting the ground happened in time with my heartbeat. I let out an uninhibited laugh as I passed Wes, whose dimples and megawatt smile nearly blinded me, then Gus, whose competitive edge was on full display, until I was next to my dad and Cobalt.

He looked so young and free when he was on a horse. He wasn't looking at me but up at the sky—at my mom, probably, as we rode.

Maple and I pulled ahead of my dad and Cobalt, and I heard him let out a wild "yeehaw."

No matter how often we did this, I couldn't believe this was my life. This was my life, and it was *good*.

And today, it would get even better.

★

"This is my best work," Teddy said as she looked me up and down with a smile.

"You say that every time." I laughed.

"And I mean it every time," she said. "I just keep getting better, I guess." My best friend adjusted a piece of hair that she'd artfully left out of the half-up/half-down situation that I requested.

"Okay, then let me look," I said.

Teddy grinned and grabbed my shoulders to spin me around. My mouth opened slightly when I took in my reflection in the full-body mirror. I hadn't seen the dress since the last time Teddy fitted it. She'd made me the dress of my dreams. It was made out of white silk that skimmed over my body beautifully with a square neck and skinny straps that crossed in the middle of my back. My hair and makeup were simple.

"Oh," I breathed. "I look . . ."

"Stunning," Teddy finished for me. She wrapped her arms around my waist and put her head on my shoulder. Her copper hair was pulled into a low ponytail, and she looked beautiful in her powder blue bridesmaid dress.

"It's incredible, Ted," I said. "You're incredible." Emotions swirled all around my body, and I had to scrunch my nose to stop any tears from falling. Teddy saw and gave me a quick swat on the arm with the back of her hand.

"No," she said. "No, no, no. I swear to God, Clementine. Do not start crying."

I looked up at the ceiling and tried to will the tears back in. "This is your fault," I said.

"Do not blame me for your complete lack of emotional control."

"I'm the bride! I get to do whatever I want!"

"Well, I'm the maid of honor, and I say no crying."

"Maid of honor does not trump bride," I said, my eyes meeting Teddy's in the mirror. As soon as we made eye contact, both of us burst into laughter.

When the laughter died down, Teddy gave me another squeeze. "Well, Clementine Ryder," she said. "I think it's time to get you married."

My dad drove Teddy and me to the trailhead, where there was a side-by-side waiting to take us the rest of the way. Everybody else should already be waiting for us—if all had gone according to plan. I left the logistics up to Cam and Ada, so I had no doubt the plan was going perfectly.

As we drove up the trail, I gave Teddy my ring for her to hold until it was time to exchange them in the ceremony, and my vows, which she folded up and tucked into one of the pockets in her bridesmaid dress.

My dad stopped the side-by-side a few yards back from where the trees opened up into the clearing. I could hear the waterfall running, along with some music playing from somewhere.

"All right, my gal," Teddy said. "Your bouquet is there." Teddy pointed to a small bucket hidden in the trees. It had two wildflower bouquets in it—a small one for her, and a larger one for me. "I'll meet you up there, okay?"

I nodded as Teddy kissed my cheek and hopped out. I

watched her peer through the trees, and when she looked back she said, "Oh, he looks hot," and shot me a wink.

The music changed, and I knew Teddy was walking down the aisle. Cam and Ada had timed it perfectly, with everyone in constant communication all day. I didn't have to think about a thing. All I had to do was put one foot in front of the other and walk toward the rest of my life.

Toward Luke.

"Ready, Spud?" my dad asked. He'd gotten out of the side-by-side and had a hand held out to me. I took it.

"Ready," I said. And I was. I'd been waiting for this day for a long time—maybe since the night I came home and saw Luke at the Devil's Boot. I would've married him the day of my last race if he'd asked, and I would've married him a million times since then. But I was happy that we had a chance to start putting pieces of our life together first—that I got settled in my role at Rebel Blue, that Luke turned the bar around. I'm glad we got to build furniture and take trips and lie on the couch together for a few years before we got here.

But here was where I wanted to be.

The music changed again. This time to a slow instrumental of "Forever and Ever, Amen."

It was time.

I slid my arm through my dad's and took a deep breath. Over the past few months, I'd wondered what I'd feel like in this moment. I thought I might be nervous or anxious, but I'd never felt calmer, or more ready for what came next.

My dad and I started to walk, and when we made it to the point in the trees that opened to the clearing, I gasped.

There were wildflowers and greenery everywhere—lining

the aisle, hanging from the trees somehow. There weren't that many chairs; I didn't want a big wedding, but there, in that clearing, was every person that I'd ever loved. The family my dad found that became mine, the family I was born into, and the family I chose myself. I scanned the faces—Wes, Ada, Hank, and Aggie. Greer was next to them. Luke's mom was here, too. My uncle Boone even came down from his safe haven in Sweetwater Peak. Dusty grinned at me, and he had a hand on Riley's shoulder.

Cam wasn't next to them because she was standing in the center, underneath a wildflower arch, in her spot as our officiant.

My eyes shifted to the man next to her, and my entire world stopped.

There he was. The love of my life. My light in the dark. My safe place. My home. Luke Brooks.

His eyes were on me. They were intense and bright and full of love. He was wearing a white button-down that wasn't buttoned up all the way and dark navy slacks. He was clean-shaven, and his dark hair was tucked behind his ears.

He was beautiful.

Suddenly, I couldn't get to him fast enough. My feet started moving quicker, and my dad chuckled next to me. "Slow down, Clementine," he whispered. "Take it in."

My dad's voice steadied me—like it always did.

When we made it to the front of the aisle, my dad gave Luke a hug, and with a hand on one side of his face, pressed their foreheads together for just a moment before turning back to me and putting my hand in Luke's.

After that, Luke was all I could see. I didn't remember

handing Teddy my bouquet or what Cam said. All I cared about was the man in front of me.

"Emmy and Luke have prepared their own vows," was the sentence that finally penetrated the rosy fog in my brain. Luke pulled one of his hands out of mine and reached into the back pocket of his slacks and pulled out an index card.

But before he started reading the words in front of him, he stopped. "I'm sorry," he said as he looked at me. "You look so beautiful. I just need a quick one." I was confused, until he leaned down and kissed me—just a peck . . . until it wasn't, and then I was bunching my hand in his shirt and holding him to me.

Cam cleared her throat with a laugh. "Three more minutes, you two," she said and everyone else laughed. "Three more minutes, and you can seal the deal."

Luke pulled back from me; it looked like it took a lot of effort. Satisfaction burrowed deep in my chest. This man was *mine*.

"All right," he said, tearing his eyes off mine to look down at his card. "Everyone here knows that I'm not really a big words guy, but I am a big Clementine Ryder guy, so we'll see if I can pull this off." I breathed a laugh.

"Emmy," he said. "When I was thinking about what I wanted to say to you today, I didn't feel like there was anything I could say that would convey how much I love you—how deeply everything I feel for you runs. And, honestly, there isn't, but there is this: I feel like my whole life has been about making the decisions that would lead me to you.

"And I would make every mistake, take every wrong turn, endure every hard day over and over again to end up right here with you. I used to think about how lucky I was to have ended up in the same world, at the same time, as you, and I still do, but now I think about how lucky I am that you *are* my world.

"Because of that, I have some promises that I want to make to you, sugar." Tears threatened to spill out of my eyes now. "I promise to have breakfast with you every morning because we both know that sometimes I can't make it to dinner. I promise to always be your big spoon and to sing loudly with you in the car. I promise to keep you warm. I promise you adventure, and I promise you stability. I promise to look at you the way you look at the sky, and I promise to love you in this lifetime and the next.

"I love you, Clementine Ryder and being your husband will be the honor of my life."

A shaky breath came out of me as Luke reached out to wipe the tears from my face with one of his thumbs.

"That was really good," I said. "Like really good."

Luke smirked at me. "Only the best for you." I stared up into his brown eyes and the way the skin around them crinkled when he smiled.

Something nudged me, and it took me a second to realize that Teddy was trying to hand me my vows. "Oh," I said and then looked at Luke. "One sec," I said to him, and I think I heard a few laughs.

I grabbed the folded-up piece of paper from Teddy and only let go of Luke's hand for as long as it took me to unfold it, and then slid my hand back in his while I held my vows with the other. When I looked down, I read the first few lines and promptly realized that my vows were shit.

So I did what any normal person would do. I dropped the paper.

"Your vows were better than mine, and I do give you full permission to bring that up for the rest of our lives," I said. The way Luke smirked down at me then made me feel like my insides were liquid.

"I love you, Luke Brooks. I love you so much that sometimes it makes me feel crazy. I love you in a way that spans time and universes. I love you enough to not think that your homemade muscle tees are douche-y. I love you so deeply that I feel it in my bones when you breathe and in my lungs when you smile.

"And all I want to do right now is kiss you and start the rest of our lives together." Before I could second-guess it, I threw my arms around his neck and crashed my lips onto his. Teddy cheered behind me.

"Rings, sugar," Luke said against my mouth, and I pulled away just long enough to see Gus and Teddy trade the rings they were holding so I could slide Luke's gold band onto his ring finger, and he could do the same to mine.

And then I kissed him again.

"And by the power vested in me," Cam said. I could hear her smile through the haze of mine and Luke's kiss. "By the great state of Wyoming—the cowboy state—and also the website I got this license from, I pronounce you husband and wife. You can . . . keep kissing the bride."

Cheers erupted from our friends and family, and the music changed again. This time to Cheap Trick's "Caught Up in You."

I wound my fingers through Luke's and pulled away—just a little. "What if I asked you to jump in the spring right now?"

"I'd do anything for you, wife," he said with a kiss to my cheek, forehead, and then my nose.

Wife.

So, I turned. And started to run toward the spring, and Luke ran beside me. "It's going to be cold as shit," he called over the sound of the waterfall as we got closer.

"Good thing you promised to keep me warm," I called back with a laugh.

And then we jumped into the water. Together.

Like we would be forever. And always.

LYLA SAGE lives in the Wild West with her loyal companion, a sweet, old, blind rescue pitbull. She writes romance that feels like her favorite things: sunshine and big blue skies. She is also the author of *Done and Dusted, Swift and Saddled,* and *Lost and Lassoed.* When she's not writing, she's reading.

@authorlylasage

Books Driven by the Heart

Sign up for our newsletter and find more you'll love:

thedialpress.com